THE P

# DOROTHY EDEN

SLEEP IN THE WOODS
SAMANTHA
AFTERNOON FOR LIZARDS
WHISTLE FOR THE CROWS
BIRD IN THE CHIMNEY
LAMB TO THE SLAUGHTER
NEVER CALL IT LOVING
NIGHT OF THE LETTER
WINTERWOOD
SIEGE IN THE SUN
THE DEADLY TRAVELLERS
THE SLEEPING BRIDE
LISTEN TO DANGER

DOROTHY EDEN

# THE PRETTY ONES

**HODDER PAPERBACKS**

FIRST PUBLISHED BY MACDONALD & CO.
(PUBLISHER'S), LTD                    1957
HODDER PAPERBACK EDITION              1965
SECOND IMPRESSION                     1970

Printed and bound in Great Britain for
Hodder Paperbacks Ltd.,
St. Paul's House, Warwick Lane,
London, E.C.4,
by Hazell Watson & Viney Ltd.,
Aylesbury, Bucks

SBN 340 12778 8

# I

It had stopped raining at dusk, and that was when Willie had come panting up to the house with the news. His fair hair was darkened, like sodden corn, with damp, and his red cheeks shone. Never master of a large vocabulary, he had difficulty in explaining even in simple words the awful magnitude of his discovery.

"A skilliton!" he kept saying. "In that field we haven't ploughed since the war." Then he began to sob. "My plough turned up the head, if you please, sir."

Emma thought she would never know why that pitiful and tragic discovery gave her such a feeling of doom. It was as if all the half-felt, half-sensed things that had bothered her since she had come to Courtlands had resolved themselves into that one thing, the discovery of an unknown body buried in a shallow grave in one of the fields. And now her mind was full of horror and pity.

There was nothing she could do except try to keep the news from the children. Dina might shrink into herself and say nothing, but Maggy, little ghoul that she was, would seize on the mystery with glee, and begin to elaborate on it.

If it came to that, Barnaby was not much better. Contrary to displaying horror, his eyes brightened with interest, and he plunged into investigations with the greatest enthusiasm. The body, he said, had been buried too long to require sympathy. Pathologists put the date at anything from two to three years. The grave was at the edge of the field, bordering a little-used road, and it seemed obvious enough that some poor girl had met her fate at the hands, perhaps, of a soldier, for there had recently been a camp not far away. The pathetic remains were those of a female in her late teens or perhaps early twenties. Cause of death was as yet unknown, and this gave Barnaby, who wrote detective novels, plenty of scope for his imagination. He treated the discovery in a purely impersonal and objective manner, and seemed surprised when Emma and Louisa were distressed and horrified.

Rupert, too, was not unduly distressed, his attitude being one of annoyance that someone had had the infernal cheek to try to hide his crime on other people's property. The sooner the mystery was cleared up the better.

Not so Dudley, however. He shared the girls' distress. He kept muttering, "Poor little creature," and his pale, serious eyes were obviously visualising the details of that black night's work. He could not rest. He insisted on being the person whom the police interviewed, although normally his shyness and diffidence would have caused him to give the main rôle to Barnaby or Rupert.

"No stone must be left unturned in an effort to discover her identity and track down this scoundrel," he said. His words sounded melodramatic, like something out of a Victorian novel. But they curiously fitted in with the atmosphere of the falling rain, the leafless trees of the little copse which sheltered the field from the road, and that poor skull turned up to the rain and the low grey sky.

The ploughed field was littered with boulders, large and small, and, when they dried in the brief respite from rain, they were bone-coloured. At first Willie had thought his find was just another boulder. To Emma, the naked field seemed to be littered with skulls.

But that was a fantasy produced by the gloomy evening and that queer sense of impending doom.

She had switched on all the lights in the house, and told Mrs. Faithfull to light enormous fires.

"We're all cold," she said.

"That's right," Dudley approved, rubbing his large, well-kept hands, as if they were chilled. He stood, large and solid, by the fire. "Where's Louisa?" he asked. "Is she frightened, too?"

"Frightened?"

"We all are a little, aren't we?" He spoke honestly, and with a simple dignity. "Oh, not for that child. She's been dead too long. Perhaps of the forces that caused her death."

And the brilliantly lit room, with its relics from several

6

proud generations, seemed suddenly full of mysterious, unseen violence.

"Barnaby isn't afraid," Emma said, resolutely making herself speak normally.

"Oh, Barnaby. Nothing frightens him."

He said no more, for at that minute Louisa appeared. She ran into the room, crying helplessly, "Oh, Mrs. Court, the children have been listening!" and burst into tears.

So that was another thing to be dealt with. Emma had them put to bed, and, as a treat, their tea brought to them. By that time Dina had recovered from her inevitable nausea. It was Maggy who turned large, black, troubled eyes on Emma and said in a still certain voice,

"That was Mummy they found, wasn't it? I know you will all say it wasn't, but Dina and me know different. It was Mummy."

Later still Emma had to repeat this wild, wild fantasy to Barnaby.

"Josephine!" he said. His eyes were almost amused. "But how utterly crazy."

Emma flung herself into his arms.

"Darling, let's go to Spain tomorrow! Let's! We've waited too long. I must get into the sun. I feel like a mole, half blind and full of – of whatever dark things moles dream about."

Barnaby stroked her hair. His hand was gentle.

"My dear, no one would like that better than me. But what about the children?"

Emma had known, almost before she had finished speaking, that her request was impossible. She would not have run away, even had Barnaby let her.

There was nothing to be afraid of, anyway. Soon they would know whose those poor little bones in their *"long unbroken lonely and interminable sleeping"* were. And she would be able to persuade Dina to laugh at Maggy's wicked fantasies.

Yes, there would be nothing significant to this at all, even supposing the police, after so long, were able to discover who had dug that secret grave.

7

# 2

ALTHOUGH it had been a winter of more than usual rain and mist, the sun had been shining the morning Emma woke up to the unaccustomed but movingly sweet knowledge of Barnaby asleep in the bed next to her. Sweet? No that was an inane and foolish word to use in connection with her very new husband. For one thing, he was tall, broad-shouldered, decisive, virile. In a contradictory way he was bone lazy when he chose to be, absent-minded and untidy. He was also possessed of very blue eyes and a broad merry smile, neither of which Emma could resist. He had various faults, among them a determination to get what he wanted as quickly as possible. (This was one reason why Emma was his wife, after having known him only four weeks.)

To Emma his faults were still fascinating and extraordinarily lovable, which was curious, as faults in other people usually irritated her.

His thick blond hair, the colour of dark honey, ruffled untidily as he slept, and all else that was visible of him, his left ear and a portion of his broad bony temple, were also heart-catchingly beautiful. She sat up in her bed and gazed in the blissful knowledge that at last she could look her full without his blue eyes laughing at her or teasing her.

She knew so little about him. She had arrived on his doorstep four weeks before to do an interview with him, for the purposes of an article in a woman's magazine. She had been very nervous because this had been her first interview. Usually she did a much more humble job of sub-editing, but influenza had swept the office and she, at the last moment, was the only possible person to keep the appointment. It could not be postponed because Barnaby Court, a considerable figure in the world of crime stories and detective fiction, was too difficult to tie down to another date. They had got off to a bad start, partly because Barnaby obviously disliked being interviewed by a woman and partly because he guessed her inexperience. He hadn't made any effort to find a chair in his cluttered study, and she had had to move a very large edition of Boswell's *Johnson* on to the floor in order to sit down.

Then he had even more effectively put her out of her stride by flinging questions at her.

"Aren't you going to ask me why I wanted to write, and how many hours a day I work, and do I take my characters from people I meet, and what is my favourite form of murder?"

His blue gaze, boring into her, disconcerted her. Emma was not a meek or a humble person. Lately she had learned, during working hours, to control her quick temper. But there was something about Barnaby Court's attitude that she could not endure. She knew that all that was stubborn and feminine in her was not going to stand being talked down to.

"Or," he continued, biting the stem of his pipe reflectively, "you might prefer to know what I eat for breakfast, and what colour pyjamas I wear and what is my favourite type of woman."

Emma had green eyes. They could express a devastating and glassy coldness when she wished. She thought of frosts and winter ice, and turned her gaze on Barnaby Court.

"What I would suggest you need most," she said with deliberate dislike, "is a wife."

Barnaby took his pipe out of his mouth. He looked at her reflectively. "You think so, eh?"

"She would not only dust the furniture," Emma said, fastidiously moving to the edge of her chair, " – at least one hopes she would – but she might also make you more human."

Then she stood up. The interview would now be at an end. So would her five-minute career as a reporter. It was a pity, because she had had ambitions. She had thought she had had the ability to become a journalist, but now she knew that she had not the temperament. She could not become negative enough in dealing with aggressive and ego-inflated people. For some reason it was pure anathema

9

to her to pretend admiration for this large and confident young man who, after all, was merely the author of half a dozen best-selling mystery novels.

But now Barnaby Court was saying, not merely politely, but with genuine warmth: "You would like another chair less dusty? Wait until I get a duster. Mrs. Clack — yes, that is her name in actual fact — keeps a supply somewhere." He was on his way, presumably to the kitchen, but his voice came back, "Things do get in rather a muddle when she has these spells with her back. I'm afraid I don't notice it as much as I should. But that you will understand when you see Courtlands."

He reappeared, carrying a large feather duster, and promptly proceeded to whisk it about the room, knocking over various objects in its path, as if he were the wielder of a miniature hurricane. Emma was still standing stockstill taking in his last remark.

"And why should I see Courtlands — whatever that is?" she asked at last.

"Courtlands is my country house. Of course you will see it." In his sudden enthusiasm, Barnaby reached up and whisked dust off picture frames and lampshades. All of his antagonism had gone, and he was smiling and gentle. Emma watched him in complete fascination.

"You know, I couldn't agree more with that last remark of yours," he said.

"My — last remark?"

"Yes. The one about my needing a wife. Now, please sit down comfortably and I'll talk to you."

"Thank you," Emma murmured dazedly.

"Not at all. Presently we'll have a sherry. Or you might care for a martini. Tell me, what is your favourite wine?"

Emma looked at him in some astonishment. "Who are we talking about, you or me?"

"You," said Barnaby Court, watching her with his bright, interested eyes.

Emma did get her interview, a far fuller one than she had hoped for. But although she had made copious notes she found herself unable to put them together. This was not altogether due to her inexperience and nervousness. It was also because the man who had given them to her was no longer a public figure, impersonal and remote. Exercising beneath his indolent manner a tremendous vitality, he had got himself into her mind and stayed there. She didn't suppose he would give a single thought to her again.

"Emma," Aunt Deb said, when she came in that night. "Someone has been ringing you every ten minutes for the last hour."

Emma paused, her heart skipping a beat.

"Who is it?"

"My dear, I didn't ask, although I feel now that we are old friends. He has a nice telephone technique. No wasted time, no trivialities. Very satisfying. Tell me, has he fallen in love with you?"

"My dear Aunt Deb, I don't even know who you are talking about."

Aunt Deb, who was little and dumpy, with narrow sloping shoulders, from which expensive shawls were forever slipping, and a round, crumpled, rather vacant face that was entirely deceptive, looked thoughtfully at her tall niece.

"It could be so," she said, speaking as if to herself. "You are not to everyone's taste, to be sure. You have green eyes and a temper. That would be a challenge to some men, of course. And you are not always beautiful. You have moments. My dear, shouldn't you eat more?"

"Eat more?" Emma was used to Aunt Deb's irrelevancies, but at this moment she was not quick enough to interpret them.

"You're too thin. Some men like curves. Your uncle, now, was an example of the kind of man who adored what he called the 'feminine figure'." Aunt Deb carefully straightened the fine lace shawl over her unaccommodating shoulders, and went into a happy dream about the merits of her late husband.

"Aunt Deb, if you think I'm going to cultivate voluptuous curves so that men can enjoy looking at me——"

"Not necessarily voluptuous, dear. You're not that sort. Let us say, a slight plumping out——"

Fortunately the telephone interrupted a fuller exposition of Aunt Deb's theory. Emma had no desire to be plump. She liked her tall, lean figure very well – and besides, none

of her clothes would fit. She thought resolutely of this difficulty in order to calm the foolish beating of her heart until
Aunt Deb spoke into the telephone.

"Yes, she has just come in this minute," she heard Aunt
Deb saying. "I was telling her she ought to eat more. Per-
haps you would have some influence – oh, how charming!
I'll call her."

Aunt Deb put down the receiver, and, as if Emma were
in the farthermost part of the house, called resonantly,
"Emma! Telephone! You are being invited out to dinner.
Your friend shares my views that you should eat. Isn't that
nice!"

When Emma got to the telephone she could only say
"Hullo!" very cautiously. She was aware that Aunt Deb still
lurked, beaming and frankly inquisitive, at the door of the
drawing-room, and this increased her self-consciousness.
Oh, ridiculous Aunt Deb! Could she not have a love affair
without that gentle inquisitive eye observing and blessing it?

Because, when she heard Barnaby Court's deep, slightly
indolent, but compelling voice, she knew that it was very
possible she was going to have a love affair.

It did not occur to her that she might marry him.

It seemed so unlikely that he would want to marry her.
All that Aunt Deb said was true. She was too thin, rather
angular, freckled and quite plain when not glowing with
some enthusiasm or excitement. What she did not realise
was how often she was filled with enthusiasm about a fact, a
person or an idea. Then she had a sudden shining beauty of
which she was totally unaware. It was a thing to watch for.

In addition to mere appearance, she was extremely intelligent, with an honest direct mind, and a tendency to be
outspoken. It was this tendency, she told herself ruefully,
that had acquired her a husband, for it was the first thing
Barnaby had truly noticed about her.

Afterwards he went on to notice other things. Her ankles,
he said, were the most shapely he had yet seen. He would
have married her for them alone. But he also liked green
eyes – in cats and women – and the kind of figure that
looked equally graceful curled up in an armchair or breast-
ing a wind on a mountain top.

The fact remained, however, that he would never have

noticed her, much less have wanted to marry her, if she hadn't lost her temper that day in his nat and made one of her direct scathing remarks. The sensation of being spoken to like that by a very junior reporter who should have been all fawning admiration had been so novel that he had looked at her with interest. Then he had seen the glowing beauty in her face and had experienced a sensation of wonder and great pleasure. He could scarcely bring himself to let her out of his sight, and when she had gone he had wanted to run down the stairs after her. He had limited himself to telephoning her six times a day and taking her out to dinner every night for a week. On the seventh night he asked her to marry him.

"I've only waited this long so that you could get to know me," he explained.

Emma knew every inflection of his voice, and every change of his face. She knew how he danced, and what it felt like to kiss him. She knew his amiable, stubborn and absent-minded nature, his kindnesses and the humour that twinkled constantly in his blue eyes. She also knew his determination to get anything that his heart was set upon.

But of the material side she knew nothing at all. He wrote very successful detective novels, he lived in a London flat and had a country house called Courtlands to which he paid occasional but seemingly reluctant visits. He appeared to have no family except two brothers who lived at Courtlands. His friends he neglected completely while he was working on a book, or, alternatively, courting a woman. Emma did not imagine she was the only woman he had courted, for he was thirty years old, and had something of a connoisseur's taste in feminine ankles.

She knew, for instance, that there was someone called Josephine. One evening Barnaby had said abruptly, "I ought to tell you about Josephine." But they had been dancing and drinking wine, and Emma was still airily in the clouds.

"I don't want to hear about any other woman," she said. "Not now or ever. We have no past. We start from now."

"Hopelessly impractical, my darling. The past will intrude."

"Oh, outwardly, perhaps. But not in our most private

lives. Nothing can touch those." She spoke with magnificent confidence.

"All right," said Barnaby. "Have it your own way. No Josephine tonight. No Maggy or Dina either. No one at all except you. You're entirely right, I believe. I love you very much."

His head was near to hers, his eyes very bright.

Emma floated on her invisible clouds, the only woman whom Barnaby Court's blue eyes had ever smiled, or would ever smile, upon.

Impractical, yes. She knew that. But even in the sober light of morning she still did not want to know about any of Barnaby's previous loves. After all, what did they matter? She was the woman he wanted to marry.

Aunt Deb smiled cosily and gave her considered verdict.

"Love him, but don't trust him," she said. "What are you going to wear to be married in, since you are obviously not going to be allowed time for the usual fuss."

Emma seized on her first remark.

"What do you mean by telling me not to trust Barnaby?"

"He's too clever with his speech," said Aunt Deb. "That tongue of his could talk its way round any situation."

"He's a writer," Emma defended.

"And he's in too much of a hurry," Aunt Deb went on. "Does he expect you to disappear?"

"I wouldn't call that a fault, Aunt Deb." Emma remembered Barnaby's urgency and her heart was soft.

"One more thing that may or may not worry you." Aunt Deb, in her lace shawls, looked as cosy and innocent as a Victorian spinster. "He's too attractive to women. He's bound to have trouble – if he hasn't had it already."

"I may be trouble," said Emma. "But I'm not going to worry about any other kind."

Aunt Deb shrugged her shoulders. "Then we'd better plan your wardrobe. I must say I'd always hoped you'd marry somebody like Barnaby Court."

"Aunt Deb, you deceitful old darling!"

The old lady submitted contentedly to Emma's kiss.

"But don't trust him," she added in her unperturbed voice.

The wedding took place three weeks later. Emma wore

14

spring green and carried a small posy of lily of the valley. It was her only material concession to the festivity of the occasion. The rest of it she carried in her shining happy face.

Barnaby was late. He was, Emma discovered, incurably absent-minded. He hadn't forgotten he was being married, but he had made a mistake about the time. He said his taxi, in its haste, had knocked down three policemen and a clutch of old women on the way!

Emma's ten-minute fantasy that the whole of the last incredible month had existed only in her imagination, in spite of the presence of Aunt Deb and Mark Jenkins, one of Barnaby's publishers, vanished and she was so filled with happiness that she could have cried. One curious facet of Barnaby's character was that he had a phobia about a big wedding, or indeed a wedding of any size at all. He had suggested at once that only Aunt Deb and his brothers Rupert and Dudley should be present. But Rupert was in Scotland becoming engaged to a girl called Jean, and at the last moment Dudley could not come. There had been a garbled message about sheep lambing and the shepherd ill. But Barnaby explained that Dudley was incurably shy, and had become almost a hermit.

"He came to London for the Coronation," Barnaby said. "We can hardly expect him to put our wedding on a level with that."

And anyway, Dudley's presence was not necessary. They were married quite safely without him. The four of them had dinner afterwards at Barnaby's favourite restaurant, with red candles alight, flowers and champagne.

At a suitable time Mark Jenkins whisked Aunt Deb off to drink more champagne at a haunt of his own, and they were alone.

Barnaby said, "Well, darling."

Emma said gaily, "We're married."

"From now on those beautiful green eyes are going to shine only for me?"

"Only for you."

His hand closed over hers. Emma half-closed her eyes. The candle flames dipped. She was carried back suddenly to a night in her childhood when she had slept in an attic room in a farmhouse, and the wonder of the night, exquisitely lonely and silent, with only the frail flame of the candle between her and darkness, had burst upon her. How terribly uncertain everything was, she had thought. You were surrounded with a little glow of light and warmth, but if a clumsy hand knocked it over, if a chill wind blew it out, you were defenceless in the dark. Yet somehow you trusted in that frail light, sure that some day it would blaze brightly and strongly and forever. . . .

"What are you thinking of?" she heard Barnaby's deep lazy voice.

"Of red candles. They're so nicely festive."

"We'll always have red candles."

"No. Just when we're specially happy."

"We'll always be specially happy."

She looked at him, nodding, but knowing that it would not be so. And knowing that he knew it, too.

"Emma," he said suddenly. "I need you."

It was so seldom that the smiling and indolent mask dropped from his face, leaving it curiously care-worn and older, even a darkness in his eyes.

Emma, deeply moved, said, "But of course. I need you, too."

"You know so little about me. I haven't even told you about——"

"Not tonight. Please not tonight."

His eyes began to twinkle.

"My darling, is this magnificent disregard for details going to stay with you all your life?"

"As far as I know," said Emma hopefully.

"You're quite beautiful."

"I'm freckle-faced and I've never quite stopped looking like an awkward schoolgirl."

"That," said Barnaby, "is a matter of opinion. Tonight, when we get home——"

He broke off. Emma was still savouring those curiously beautiful words, "When we get home", when she became aware that a woman was approaching their table with out-stretched hands.

"*Barnaby!* Where *have* you been all these years? It must be at least five years since we saw each other. The last time was in Monte Carlo, wasn't it?" She paused, her quick

inquisitive eyes on Emma. She was gaunt, and wore too m[.]
jewellery, and talked as if she were afraid of silence.

"Felice," said Barnaby lazily, without any particular
warmth. "Are you reminding me of my young and foolish
days? Darling, this is Lady Parker. My wife, Felice."

The woman's gaze swept over Emma with heightened
interest. She said, "Is my memory bad, Barnaby? I thought
you said Josephine was dark and beautiful."

"So she is." Barnaby's voice was light, not particularly
interested. He signalled the waiter for his bill. "We're just
on the point of leaving. Shall we be seeing you in town?
Oh, but of course we won't. We're leaving for Spain tomorrow. My memory is even worse than it used to be. I
forget the most obvious things."

"Could be convenient," Lady Parker drawled. She drifted
away, a look of malice on her haggard face.

The malice of a faded woman for a young, attractive and
healthy one? It could have been. But Emma, who had not
spoken one word during the whole of the prickly little en-
counter, was concerned momentarily with the fear that
Lady Parker's swift movement had blown out the candle
flames. They flickered dangerously. If they went out, she
thought hypnotically, if they went out, then it was darkness
and doom.

"I think I've had too much champagne," she said carefully, aware that Barnaby was watching her with interest.
Even perhaps a little anxiety. "But I don't seem to remember
your telling me that we are going to Spain tomorrow."

"As far as Lady Parker is concerned," Barnaby said, "we
are."

"Oh, yes, of course. Your past. You said it would probably intrude."

"Felice Parker has nothing to do with my past."

"It isn't important to me, darling, but I shouldn't have
particularly admired your taste if she had." Emma suddenly
gave a sigh of relief. "The candles are burning again," she
said.

"They haven't been out."

"Nearly."

Barnaby looked at her quizzically. His face was faintly
amused.

17

"Darling, why don't you ask me who Josephine was?"

"I've told you, I don't want to know about other women you have been in love with. And that's still true. We're in our own room with the lights burning. The others are locked. In darkness, too, I hope. But this is ours."

Barnaby put his hand over hers.

"You'll have to know about Josephine sometime, darling."

"And what did you do to Josephine, the dark and beautiful Josephine?" Emma's voice was light and gay. "Turn her heartlessly off your doorstep into the snow?"

"No," said Barnaby. "It wasn't anything like that. I married her."

# 3

THEY were going to look for a larger flat when they had time. Emma had been very contented indeed to plan her move into Barnaby's present flat. It was small, over-full of books and, although clean, Mrs. Clack had not distressed herself by over-working.

"As long as I can find a chair unoccupied by Boswell's *Johnson* it will be all right," Emma had laughed, and Barnaby had capped that with, "Even more important is to find a bed in a similar condition."

He had rearranged his own room to make space for the extra bed, and Emma had once been allowed, by a disapproving Mrs. Clack, to inspect the arrangements. Mrs. Clack, she was sure, thought the whole thing highly indecent, especially the frilled bed-coverings that Barnaby himself had chosen.

It was true that they did look a little incongruous in the very masculine room. Emma pondered on that as she let Barnaby take off her wrap and throw it over the leather armchair at the window. This room bore no trace of a woman, and it would have seemed that such surroundings, apart perhaps from a young man's adventures outside his home, had always been his.

18

But that was not true.

"You never meant to tell me about Josephine," she accused.

"Liar," Barnaby said good-humouredly. "You would never listen."

"But, Barnaby!" Emma was deeply in earnest. "When you mentioned Josephine it was just as if she was someone you had once been in love with. A fleeting thing. You didn't say she was your wife!"

"Tonight," said Barnaby, taking her in his arms and kissing her, "you are very young."

Emma wriggled free.

"I'm not young at all. I'm old." But she drooped her head miserably. He was right. She was young, too, and gauche. She had thought herself so impervious and sophisticated, but after all she was not. Coming home like this for the first time had been so shining and new a thing. Now, by discovering that it was not new to him, it was spoilt.

"Emma, don't be childish," said Barnaby sharply, "and I'll tell you about Josephine."

Emma flung up her head.

"No," she said fiercely. "No. She doesn't belong in here."

For a moment their eyes met in antagonism. Emma's were the first to drop. She gave her shoulders a small shrug. She put up her arms to unclasp the necklace she was wearing. Then she kicked off her shoes with a casual at-home gesture. Wisdom had come to her. She was married to this man who was not only familiar but a stranger. She had married him in haste and without asking questions because she loved him. That had been reason enough. So she would cling to the remnants of her sophistication, and this first night would be a success.

Then Barnaby took her in his arms again.

"Emma, let's go to Spain tomorrow after all. Let's be impetuous and reckless and crazy. Let's be happy."

"Of course we'll be happy," she said, her heart leaping.

So the night was a success after all. Josephine, who had married Barnaby when he was only twenty-two, even more impulsive than he was now, and much more liable to make mistakes, did not come into the room at all. There was only herself and Barnaby. They belonged, and it was forever. . . .

"Love him but don't trust him," Aunt Deb had said.

"How much more interesting that makes you, my darling," Emma murmured, with all the tolerance and wisdom she had learned since yesterday.

Barnaby Court, married at twenty-two and divorced five years later because his wife, too restless and demanding and selfish, could endure nothing about his life, was hers now, and she was going to be equal to any situation.

Even as that thought went through her head the telephone gave a ping, preliminary to ringing. She grabbed the receiver, hoping that the sound would not have woken her sleeping husband, thinking, with that foolish softness in her heart, that she did not yet know any of his habits or characteristics.

"Hullo," she said softly into the telephone.

"Hullo! Who is speaking?" The voice at the other end was high and autocratic. "Are you one of my father's women?"

Emma moved the receiver away from her ear, as if suddenly it were a wasp. Then, gingerly, she brought it back, and said with dignity, "It would help me if you tell me who that is."

"Oh, this is Maggy. Dina's left me the dirty work again."

"The dirty work?"

"Well, she's the oldest, and she should do these things. But I don't mind breaking bad news."

The voice at the other end suddenly lost its maturity, and broke into a high-pitched childish giggle.

"Bad news?" said Emma. "Look, Maggy, whoever you are, hadn't you better tell me what you want, and then hang up."

"I can't tell you until I know who I am speaking to."

"I," said Emma, with dignity, "am Mrs. Barnaby Court."

There was a very audible gasp. Then the voice, completely childish now, exclaimed, "Gosh! Don't say Daddy's married you!"

And at that moment Barnaby woke up, gave his wide charming smile, and said lazily, "Darling, are you gossiping on the telephone already? Isn't your husband sufficiently interesting to talk to?"

Emma put her hand over the mouthpiece.

"Barnaby!" she whispered agitatedly. "Who are Maggy and Dina? It can't be true! It's some ridiculous joke. They can't be your – your *daughters*!"

Barnaby snatched the telephone from her.

"Hullo!" he said curtly. "Hullo there! Maggy! What the deuce are you doing?"

Then he listened, his brow growing black, his jaw hard.

"Now look here," he said, "this can't happen again. Your mother will be arriving any time, or getting in touch with you. You just wait there like good girls. . . . What's that? Miss Treadgold? Oh, very well, get her to speak to me."

Emma had got quietly out of bed and put on a wrap. Instinct told her that coffee would be needed quickly. Leaving Barnaby to conduct his crisp conversation with some unknown woman she went into the kitchen and plugged in the electric kettle. She was not willing to think at the moment. She hoped vaguely that she would never have to think again.

She clattered cups briskly, and wondered what plane they were going to catch to Madrid. She would pack while Barnaby made the reservations. She had never packed for a man before. . . .

"Emma! Emma, come here, please!"

"Yes, darling. I'm just making coffee."

"Thank God for that! Darling, the most desperate thing has happened. Josephine hasn't collected the children."

Emma returned to the bedroom. She stood in the doorway, one of her dark auburn eyebrows coolly raised.

"What children?" she asked.

"Darling, don't pretend to be dumb!" Barnaby was getting angry, his eyes flashing impatience. "Our children, of course. Whose else?"

Emma was conscious of her legs shaking and her heart beating madly. Her only hope was that Barnaby would not notice. She had to remain cool – cool and calm, not vulnerable.

"Did you say *ours*, Barnaby?"

"Mine and Josephine's. And don't say," he continued loudly, "that I never told you about them. I started to one night and you wouldn't listen, as you know very well, and then somehow they didn't seem anything to do with us. I pay their school fees, of course, but Josephine has always had custody, and I hardly know the little brats."

"Oh – oh, Barnaby!" Emma began, her coolness forgotten.

"It's generally supposed that very young children are best with their mother, and anyway what would I have done with them if I had applied, as I could have done, for custody? Josephine seemed to love them. I saw them now and then, of course."

"How old are they?"

"Eight. They're twins. I believe Maggy exploits Dina because she's an hour or two older. Maggy is slightly difficult."

"Slightly is hardly the word, I would imagine," Emma murmured.

Barnaby looked at her. His face was troubled. He looked both guilty and harassed. Emma went to him swiftly.

"Darling, you've always worried about them, haven't you?"

"Well, maybe I have. They're mine, after all."

"Of course. And they're only eight. And I love you when you do extraordinary things like not telling me you had a wife and two children."

"Darling, this is our life. Started now."

"That's why I love you. But I guess the past has hit us with a bump this morning. What's the problem with the children?"

"Josephine has forgotten their holidays, and nobody seems to have heard from her. She must still be on that crazy South American expedition."

"Has she done this sort of thing before?"

"Actually she has. At Christmas. Before that she had arranged for the children to go to an old aunt of hers while she was in South America. She had picked up some explorer, and they were going up the Amazon. The old aunt died just before Christmas, and since no one had heard from Josephine for some months, I had the children at Courtlands. I got a young woman to be a sort of governess nurse."

"And you haven't heard from Josephine since then?"

"I never did hear from her, except through the children. She moves about the world a good deal. I told you she was chronically restless. She has money of her own, and she does crazy things, like this expedition. The children have been to Nice and Venice and various places."

"After that Courtlands must be dull for them," Emma murmured, thinking of Maggy's precocious voice.

"Nowhere is dull to Maggy. She makes her own entertainment." Barnaby spoke wryly.

"I can imagine," said Emma. She paused and took a long breath. Then she said calmly, "When do we pick them up?"

Barnaby sprang to his feet.

"Emma, this heroism isn't necessary. I'll collect them and find a woman to look after them and take them to Courtlands. Dudley and Rupert will be there, and old Mrs. Faithfull. They'll be perfectly all right. It's only for a few weeks."

"And instead of having two healthy parents, very much alive, they are suddenly orphans." Emma's eyes flashed. "No, you don't. If their mother has fallen down on this job, it's up to us."

"But we decided to fly to Madrid today."

"You can tear up those imaginary tickets. What are we? Child haters?"

Barnaby took her in his arms. His grip was painful.

"My darling! You're a real woman. I knew you would be."

Emma moaned. "And if strength is any indication as to what your sex is – let me go, you idiot, that coffee will be ruined. And we need it!"

Heroism, Emma realised, was the operative word, when she saw Barnaby's two small daughters for the first time. It had been a long drive to the school and she was cold, and suffering a little from anticlimax. Yesterday, red candles and festivity, she thought wryly, today a school for girls drearily situated on the outskirts of an unattractive town, and two thin little girls with white faces and huge sombre black eyes.

In the charge of one of the younger mistresses, who looked bored and impatient to get away, Maggy and Dina both appeared so miserable that again Emma's kindness overcame her and she warmly embraced them. The embrace, however, was plainly not welcome. She felt their bodies stiffening, and the hostility growing in their faces.

"Which is Maggy and which is Dina?" she asked cheerfully. "They're awfully alike, aren't they?"

"This is Dina," said Barnaby, indicating the slightly smaller child. "She isn't quite as tall as Maggy and her hair is curly where Maggy's is straight. Also she has a dimple – when she smiles."

The child's lips, Emma noticed, were pressed hard together, either in an attempt to stop from smiling and showing the dimple, or more likely to prevent tears. The other child was not in any danger of tears. She was scowling ferociously. Probably she resented her sister having soft dark curls where her own hair was straight witch-like stuff, but more likely tears were not part of her make-up. She was tough, Miss Maggy Court, and she intended everyone to know it at once.

Barnaby patted them each affectionately on the shoulder.

"Well, aren't you pleased to see us? This is Emma, my wife. We were married yesterday."

"I'm very happy to meet you," Emma said, with the smile that illumined her face.

Dina made a slight, shy movement, then glanced at her sister's small granite face and was still.

"Maggy!" said Barnaby sharply. "Say how do you do to Emma."

"How do you do," said Maggy, like a parrot. Then, impatiently, "When do we go?"

Barnaby began to frown. Emma took his arm. She squeezed it slightly.

"The children have been waiting a long time," she said.

Barnaby relaxed. "All right. Are these your bags? Then say good-bye to Miss Treadgold." He himself held out his hand to the girl and thanked her for her care of the children. Nothing was said about Josephine's failure to appear. They went off, Emma thought, as if this were the normal procedure – as if it would happen every time the school closed for a vacation. . . .

Miss Treadgold, the young mistress, turned away. Queer, she thought. And him so nice, too. But you couldn't always trust the nice ones, for all that. There was no doubt that

24

the mother was unreliable. She had never put in an appearance yet. Even when the children had come, a year ago,
they had been brought by a nanny, or somebody. It was no
wonder they were difficult, particularly Maggy. Poor little
creatures. Unwanted. It must be hell.

But if the mother had genuinely forgotten all about them,
the father looked kind enough. So did the girl with him,
the new wife. But that, after all, was another complication.
Maggy, little firecracker that she was, would resent that.
And Dina was her faithful slave. One could feel sorry for
that red-headed girl, acquiring a family like that.

"Hi! Mary! You'll have to hurry with your packing if
you're catching that train."

Miss Treadgold quickened her step.

"Just coming," she called. "I've been seeing the Court
twins off."

"Oh, did the mother turn up after all?"

"Not the mother. The father. And the new wife."

"Gosh! She's inherited a handful. What was Barnaby
like?"

"Barnaby?"

"Didn't you know he was Barnaby Court, the mystery
writer? I adore his books. His victims usually die of some
frightfully obscure poison and of course the bodies are never
discovered until it's far too late to analyse anything. Very
ingenious."

"Do you suppose that explains the mother not turning
up? She's never put in an appearance, you know."

"Mary! What a thought! Barnaby Court, my favourite
mystery writer! But I agree, it is awfully odd about the
first wife. Personally, I'll have to see her to believe that she
exists. . . ."

The weather outdoors had not improved. The sky had
grown darker and there were odd snowflakes, like drifting
feathers. It was nearly sixty miles to Courtlands. The little
girls were put in the back of the car and wrapped in rugs.
Emma, getting in the front, had the feeling that the storm
was now in the car as well as outside. But it was a very
silent storm. The children did not speak unless asked a
direct question, and then the speaker was usually Maggy

who answered as briefly and sullenly as possible. They did not even whisper to themselves. Much less giggle, as normal children would, Emma thought. One could not imagine those little tragic muses ever doing anything so childish as giggling.

They were play-acting, of course. Perhaps they were deeply disappointed and disillusioned that their mother had not come for them. That would be a serious blow for any child. And on top of that had come the knowledge that their father whom perhaps they adored had remarried. It was unreasonable that the stepmother in stories should always be wicked and cruel. There must be thousands of very kind stepmothers, but inevitably there was an in-eradicable prejudice against them in a child's mind. Maggy and Dina would be the last children to be free of this prejudice. Something told Emma that they would be all for prejudices and grievances of any kind.

But again one had to remember their plight, the children of divorced parents, one of whom inexplicably forgot their existence. Which was an unforgivable thing to do.

Josephine, whose dark shadow had crossed Emma's wedding night, now became an even more selfish, shallow and disagreeable person. It might be that the time would come when she would persuade Barnaby to seek custody of the children, and thus see that they had some love and security.

But here Emma gave another apprehensive glance over her shoulder at the small sphinx-like faces. Her courage quailed. She thought of the children she herself might have. Suddenly she wanted to burst into tears.

Barnaby tried to keep some warmth in the car by chatting in a normal voice, pointing out objects of interest, talking of the new book he was planning.

"Varying the lethal method is the difficulty," he said. "There are only so many things an intelligent murderer would do. So the field gets somewhat limited. Never mind, Courtlands in late winter is a most stimulating place for getting plots. I'm warning you."

And suddenly, from the back seat, Maggy's small crisp voice came.

"Will Sylvie be there, Daddy?"

"No, of course she won't." Barnaby's voice was curt.

26

Emma shot him a curious glance. Sylvie? A memory of her early morning telephone conversation stirred. *"Are you another of my father's women?"*

"Then who is going to look after us? Just — her?"

Emma felt the two pairs of black eyes boring into her back. She turned and said pleasantly, "My name is Emma. I'd like you to call me that."

Barnaby said, "You'll be looked after. I'll get someone to take Sylvie's place."

"Someone who won't run away?" Maggy's voice was ever so slightly insolent.

"We'll hope not. Sylvie," Barnaby explained to Emma, "left us rather abruptly. But that is a way I believe young women have nowadays."

"You mean without telling you she was going?" Emma demanded.

"Actually, yes. However, we won't criticise Sylvie. It might be that her task wasn't particularly easy."

"She was a silly," Maggy said contemptuously.

"I liked her." Dina's voice was little more than a whisper.

Maggy gave her a fierce nudge in the ribs. She subsided into silence.

Emma looked at Barnaby. "Darling, we're all rather cold and tired. I think we should stop for tea."

They found a roadside place a little farther on, and Emma, shivering still from the cold wind that had struck her as she had got out of the car, took the children in to wash. At about this time, she thought, she and Barnaby should have been driving from the airport into Madrid. Instead, here she was in a cold, draughty cloakroom, with two strange sullen children who resented her even more than she resented them. Were the candles really out, those lovely gay warm candles that had burnt last night?

She sat at the speckled and dim little mirror trying to improve her face. It looked back at her, as white as the children's, strained, plain. How could Barnaby go on loving that face?

Maggy ran water noisily in the basin. She wasn't dirty, but she suddenly decided perversely to scrub herself very thoroughly. Dina, however, lurked behind Emma, fidgeting.

27

A strand of her dark hair was in her eyes. She looked very little and miserable.

"What is it, Dina?" Emma asked. "Something you want?"

Dina shook her head vigorously. Maggy ran the water again, deliberately making as much noise as possible. Under cover of the hissing Dina suddenly whispered loudly, "Is Mummy really dead?"

"Dead!" echoed Emma. "But of course not. Wherever did you get that idea?"

"Maggy says she is."

"But how would Maggy know if you didn't? You silly child——"

"Because she didn't come last holidays either," Dina said rapidly. "And Maggy says Daddy wouldn't have married another woman if Mummy was alive."

Maggy's face, dripping, emerged from the basin.

"If Mummy's dead, Daddy might at least have taken us to the funeral. It's not as if we're babies. We know people die, even mothers and fathers."

"But, Maggy darling, your mother isn't dead. She's in South America. Didn't you know?" Suddenly it seemed so unlikely that a delicate, spoiled person like Josephine should set out on an expedition up the Amazon. The story sounded very thin, even to her ears. "Of course your father would have told you if anything had happened to your mother," she finished lamely. "Whatever makes you think he wouldn't?"

"Because sometimes he tells lies," Maggy said starkly. She looked at Emma, her face rubbed red from the cold water, her eyes wide and accusing. "You must know that," she said.

# 4

DUDLEY and Rupert, Barnaby had said, knew they were coming, but Emma would be wise not to expect too much. Courtlands was not a country mansion. It was merely a large farmhouse, once prosperous, but now in a state of decay mostly because Dudley, who managed the farm (Rupert had political ambitions and was away a good deal), was something of a recluse, and had forgotten, or despised, the softer ways of life. One of his curious phobias was his dislike of servants. He wouldn't, he said, have the place cluttered up with people just to look after himself, one solitary country gentleman.

So the large house was run by old Mrs. Faithfull, his housekeeper, who had originally been his nurse, and the wife of the farmhand who lived in the cottage.

"We can't expect them to look after all of us," Emma said.

But Barnaby intended to get a girl to look after the children. That was the most Dudley would allow. Even the girl he would object to. He was almost pathologically shy.

"Then it isn't fair for us to burst upon him like this," Emma protested.

"Courtlands is mine as well," Barnaby said mildly. "We inherited it in equal shares. Dudley has it all the time except for these emergencies. Fair enough, don't you think? And what would we do with the children in a London flat?"

What indeed? Emma wondered. But she had a moment's intense longing to escape from the darkening countryside, the leafless trees, scarcely budding in the tardy spring, the long empty fields, black in the dusk. She thought of Spain and sunshine and wine and music. She thought of Barnaby's flat, left only this morning but already so far away, as if it had existed only in a dream. She even thought wistfully of her room in Aunt Deb's house, vacated, she had thought, permanently, but now the only piece of normality there seemed left in the world. She felt the inimical sleepless eyes in the back of the car giving her prickles down her spine. Uncontrollably she shivered.

Barnaby's hand reached for hers.

"Cold?" he asked.

But the word he really meant was "sorry". Was she sorry she had become involved in this dreary journey? Did she regret her marriage that already had brought such unexpected complications? Was she letting herself worry about the extraordinary things Maggy said?

Emma said firmly, "Not a bit."

29

Barnaby relaxed. He said gaily, "Well, here we are. These are the gates to Courtlands. In a moment you will see the house."

But it was too dark to see the house as anything but a vast shadow among its surrounding trees. A gravelled sweep of drive led to the front door. In only two windows lights shone. One was a large downstairs one, obviously the drawing-room, and the other a thin slit under the eaves. Apart from not having a welcoming glow of light, the house was as any other, lonely perhaps, but solid and unpretentious.

Emma got out of the car and helped Barney to lift out the children, who, although still wide awake, were stiff and awkward in their movements. As they stood on the steps, thin-legged and silent, Dina suddenly surreptitiously slipped her hand into her sister's. The action got under Emma's guard. Sure already that the hostile little creatures could demand no sympathy from her, she was irritated with herself for being moved.

Maggy and Dina were complete with each other. They required neither mother nor father.

Barnaby rapped on the door, explaining that the bell had been out of action the last time he had been down and he didn't imagine that Dudley would have had it mended.

In a few moments the door opened. Within the oblong of light stood a large person, not quite middle-aged, but with grey hair that gave him dignity, and a round ruddy smiling face that took it away. He was dressed in shabby tweeds that made his figure look very rotund. He held out a welcoming hand to Barnaby and said in a rich deep voice.

"I say, old fellow, you've come on a wretchedly cold night." His eyes, a paler blue than Barnaby's, and shyly evasive, slid over the others. Suddenly and unexpectedly he gave a loud bark of laughter. "What a lot of women, eh!"

"Emma, this is my brother, Dudley," Barnaby said.

Emma held out her hand. "I'm so sorry you couldn't come to our wedding."

Dudley waved a large vague hand. "Farm duties, you know. I have a great many animals. In fact, I must go and attend to things now." He was already turning away, scarcely vouchsafing Emma a look. But the children suddenly leapt forward. "Uncle Dudley! Didn't you see us?"

"Of course I saw you." He good-humouredly allowed himself to be stopped as Maggy and Dina dragged on either arm. He was not so shy with children, Emma noticed. His voice gained authority, and he said in disgust, "You know I don't recognise you in those singularly unattractive school clothes. Go and put on trousers."

Maggy gave a wild whoop and sprinted for the stairs, followed by Dina. The house was suddenly full of the clatter of their feet. Dudley, ignoring it, as if he were the still centre of the whirlpool, said over his shoulder in his slow voice, "You've rather upset Mrs. Faithfull by this invasion, Barnaby. You'd better explain to – er – your wife that there might be a little coolness for a day or two."

Then he continued his way down the hall.

For the first time Emma found herself identifying herself with Josephine. Had she wondered, too, what sort of a family she had married herself into? And been frightened?

But Josephine had produced Maggy and Dina, a by no means insignificant part of the family. And somehow she didn't think Josephine was the kind of person to be frightened. Neither was she herself that kind of person.

She tucked her arm into Barnaby's and said serenely,

"Do show me the house, darling. So far I'm enchanted with the doorstep."

Barnaby laughed and suddenly swung her into his arms and carried her inside. He put her down and sketched her a bow. Emma curtsied. "My lord," she murmured. Suddenly she realised that from the shadows at the far end of the hall Dudley had turned his head to watch. She had an impression of acute embarrassment on his face. Then he vanished.

Emma realised that she was standing looking into the cold blind eyes of a marble bust. She looked curiously at the high arrogant nose and square chin that bore more than a fleeting resemblance to Barnaby.

"Great-grandfather Court," Barnaby explained. "Grandfather stands on the other side, but at the moment he is away being cleaned."

"Why?" Emma asked simply, for now that Dudley and the children had disappeared she had time to notice the peeling walls, the damp ceilings, the worn rugs, the dust. In the drawing-room, to the right, a fire was smouldering in a large marble fireplace. It had not begun to take the chill off the room.

The room itself was furnished haphazardly, with relics from several generations. Emma noticed the Empire couch, with its threadbare brocade, the chairs looked like Chippendale, but the two very masculine leather armchairs by the fire were definitely Victorian. The walls were covered with old prints of battles and parades, spotted with damp, the Dresden candlesticks on the mantelpiece were grimy, the lampshades over lamps made from Staffordshire figures tilted crookedly and were discoloured with dust.

Emma looked from the struggling fire to Great-grandfather Court's chilly marble nose sticking insolently in the doorway.

"The other rooms are more – cosy?" she suggested tentatively.

Barnaby laughed gently and tweaked her ear.

"I told you we can still go to Spain tomorrow, when I've found a governess."

"The last governess didn't stay," Emma said, without surprise. The ceiling suddenly shook as the children began some mad game upstairs. Maggy seemed to be pursuing Dina, for Dina was shrieking, and Maggy's confident voice shouted derisively, "Cowardy-custard! Cowardy-custard!"

"Who do they take after?" she asked politely.

Barnaby grinned. "Me, I should think. Their mother was not – hoydenish. Let's take our things upstairs, and then I'll see if there's any supper. And I promise you," he said over his shoulder, "the governess I get tomorrow will not be the running-away kind. I'll see to that."

Emma followed him meekly. Her feet were frozen, and it seemed, in this house, they would stay that way. But she tweaked Great-grandfather Court's nose as she passed. So much for him and his lordly dominance of the entrance. Presently, if she had her way, he would be removed to one of the attics.

Barnaby took her upstairs, and along a long passage to the room at the extreme end. He opened the door and switched on a light. Draperies at the long windows whirled in the draught. The room was dominated by the bed. In the centre of a faded, rose-coloured, circular carpet it stood, massive and important, its four dark mahogany posts reaching almost to the ceiling.

There were other things in the room of course: the old-fashioned dressing-table with ornate carving, the enormous wardrobe, the couch at the windows, the dim and badly-painted portraits, the framed sampler with its stark message, "Count the hours." Emma drew back the long velvet curtains and tried to look out of the windows. But all she could see were wind-tossed elms and the diamond shine of raindrops on the panes.

Barnaby had put a match to the fire that was laid, but instantly it began to smoke. Great clouds billowed into the room. He swore softly, and Emma, choking and coughing, began to laugh. If she hadn't laughed she would have cried.

"Darling, this is absolutely delicious. I'm going to write a ghost story. I can't think how, coming from a place like this, you have never written ghost stories. But I can quite see how, too, your mind turns to murder. Did your Great-grandmother Court do that sampler? Count the hours. . . . So appropriate, I should think, poor thing. Waking up to find that cold marble face on the pillow beside her. Darling, never never let yourself be done in marble."

The smoke had cleared a little, and Barnaby was watching her. Tentatively she sat on the edge of the bed.

"Is is a feather mattress?"

"I'm afraid it is. If you don't like it we'll move into another room. But this——"

"I know. This is the family bed. It's the thing to do, of course. Except that one shares it with so many other people, somehow——"

"Emma," said Barnaby very quietly, "Josephine was never here."

"Not – in the family bed?"

"No. She never lived here. She didn't like the country. We lived in London and on the Continent. She was quite cosmopolitan. She also was fairly wealthy and went her own way. There was the fact, too, that Dudley would have been quite miserable with her. And this, after all, is his home." Barnaby paused. He said, "With you it is different."

Emma drew a deep breath. Then she said, "I *adore* feather beds."

33

Barnaby put his arms around her.

"Darling, I love you," he said. "I love you very much."

And suddenly, for all its chilly strangeness, its lack of welcome, its air of lost prosperity, and also its curiously inimical quality, the house was her home.

# 5

BARNABY had gone downstairs to see about a meal. Emma lingered in the bedroom, standing by the now warmly blazing fire, listening to the wind against the windows and dreaming idly of the previous occupants of this room. It was a strange beginning to her married life, but perhaps she was going to like it after all. In London, or in Spain, or in any other impersonal place, she would have discovered none of Barnaby's background. She would have remained a little in awe of him as a successful writer and a man of the world, and never perhaps known him completely at all. Now, as well as the man she had married, she was going to catch glimpses of the child and the youth. It would be of absorbing interest, as well as a matter of tenderness and amusement.

Now she knew about the wreck of Barnaby's first marriage and his thwarted love for the children that he could no longer regard as his own, she felt doubly tender towards him. She even, extraordinarily enough, felt tender towards Maggy and Dina, whose ferocious exteriors no doubt arose from their lack of security. In four weeks, she promised herself, she would tame them and turn them into naturally affectionate children. That was, if Josephine did not appear....

Josephine, Maggy said, was dead....

But Maggy was a wicked little exhibitionist. She told shameless lies to shock people and to get attention. Whatever reason would Barnaby have for concealing the death of his former wife? The suggestion was quite absurd. But

it was also unlikely that Josephine should be lost somewhere in South America. . . .

A sudden burst of noise broke into her thoughts. Footsteps
flew down the passage. It was the children, shrieking with
excitement, while above their high-pitched screams came a
deep "Ha ha ha!" and heavy lumbering footsteps that followed the flying children.

Emma threw open her door. She saw Maggy and Dina,
dressed in jeans and shirts, scampering down the stairs,
pursued by Dudley, red-faced and pop-eyed. He stopped
abruptly on seeing Emma, and laughed shyly, looking like
an overgrown and embarrassed schoolboy.

"Turned 'em into boys," he said, indicating the children.

Emma remembered Dudley's exclamation when he had
met them — "What a lot of women!" She realised now that
he had been alarmed. Poor Dudley! This invasion could
not be at all to his taste.

"Don't you like women?" she asked lightly.

Dudley sucked in his rather full lips. He was breathing
heavily from his exertion. His eyes flickered over her and
slipped away.

"I'm not my brothers," he said. Then he gave his short
loud laugh and turned away to pursue the children.

But Emma was not going to allow him to escape like that.

"What do you mean?" she demanded. "You can't say
things like that without explaining them."

Dudley paused. "I didn't mean anything, really." He
lifted his face and gave Emma a wide abashed smile. In
spite of his greying hair and slight corpulence he was more
like a schoolboy than ever. "Well, the thing answers itself,
doesn't it? I'm a bachelor and likely to remain one. There's
Rupert engaged and Barnaby with two wives already."

Emma's forthrightness demanded the next question.

"And don't you like his wives?"

"Don't know you. Do I? The other one, Josephine — she
was easy on the eye."

Suddenly Josephine's dark, beautiful, unknown face
seemed to float in the air.

"How long is it since you saw Josephine, Dudley?"

"Oh, let me see, not since that summer she was here —
must be more than two years ago."

Emma, standing in the chilly draughty passage, was seeing the house as it would be in the summer, the windows open to the warm air and the sound of bees, the sunlight lying in golden squares on the floor, the scent of June flowers in the air. There would be the late dusk, and midges, and moths fluttering, and drying hay and the sound of owls. Perhaps nightingales. She must ask Barnaby if nightingales sang in the woods here. Then they would come down in the summer, too, and listen to them in the warm dark night. Just as Josephine, who Barnaby said had never been there, had listened to them. . . . Josephine who Maggy said was dead. . . .

"Emma! Come down, darling. Supper's ready."

That was Barnaby calling from downstairs. As Emma went down she saw him standing in the hall looking up at her, smiling. His hair was mussed, as usual, his eyes sparkling, his face full of warmth. Dust, muddle, cold, inconvenience, she realised that they passed him by. He set his eyes on his objective and went towards it, obstacles unnoticed, other days' and years' happenings forgotten.

She was momentarily his objective. Was it momentarily? To ignore that small treacherous thought Emma ran down the stairs gaily. Later she would ask him those troubling things about Josephine. Had he just been absent-minded again? Or was somebody lying?

"A cold meal, I'm afraid," he said. "Mrs. Faithfull has left the food and retired, exhausted, apparently. Tomorrow we'll get straight. I'll ring the employment agency first thing in the morning and see who they have found for us."

"I can put the children to bed," Emma said.

"They can do that for themselves, noisy brats."

Supper was laid on the large, circular mahogany table in the dining-room. Dudley did not join them. He had made another of his silent disappearances. Emma sat facing an enormous sideboard over which hung a print of the Battle of Talavera. As in the drawing-room, here, too, the element of horses and battle prevailed.

Horses, it seemed, had sat down to the table, too. Maggy was prodding at Dina and whispering, "Giddap! Giddap!" Dina whimpered. She was very tired and very close to tears. Maggy's black eyes glowed with an indestructible energy.

"That's enough of that," Barnaby said sternly. "Eat your supper."

"If we were in Venice," said Maggy pertly, "we wouldn't be having cold pie for supper."

"You're not in Venice. You're at Courtlands. If you don't behave you'll go right back to school."

Dina could no longer control her tears. She pressed her hands over her face and they ran through her fingers.

"She wants Mummy," Maggy observed contemptuously. "I've told her it's no use wanting her, ever again."

Barnaby's brows went up.

"Oh? And why not?"

"Because she just won't be coming, that's all," Maggy said, with sudden weary philosophy.

Barnaby gave a wry smile. Emma watched him in an agony of interest. What would he say now – this her husband whom she thought she had known, but did not know at all.

"I shouldn't be too alarmed about that," he observed. "We'll hear from her any day. Maybe even tomorrow. You may go to Venice after all – not that I approve of this junketing about at your age. But eat your supper, anyway, and keep your strength up."

His lazy words, which told nothing really, were somehow immensely reassuring to Emma as well as to the children.

The not too palatable cold supper proceeded, and if Emma's thoughts lingered on vanished red candles and gaiety, she sensibly told herself that a little food could do nothing but improve the situation. The extraordinary day, which the children had dominated since the very moment of waking, was almost over. As soon as the children were in bed she could talk to Barnaby again. And he would reassure her as he had already reassured her once this evening – with lies?

The children did put themselves to bed. When Emma went up they were tucked in separate beds in a high-ceilinged room furnished with the same heavy furniture as was in all the rooms in Courtlands, and with traces of rose-buds on the faded wallpaper.

They hadn't had a bath, Maggy said. Dina was too tired. This was true enough, and Emma made no comment on that particular subject. She noticed that Maggy's thin wrists were sticking out of pyjama sleeves, grown much too short, and she thought suddenly of what it must be like to have a mother who forgot one's existence, so that to keep one's pride one had to say she was dead.

"Maggy," she said, "how long is it since you heard from your mother?"

"Oh, years and years."

"It is not!" Dina said fiercely. "We got parcels last birthday."

"Those were from daddy. I told you they were all the time. Mummy wouldn't send us books and soap. She would send us gold bangles and French perfume and humming-birds."

"Oh, come, not for little girls!" Emma protested.

"She would so! She would so!"

"Then she must be rather extravagant, and not very wise."

Those words probably summed up Josephine, Emma reflected. Jewellery, an aura of expensive perfume, exotic clothes, a dark delicate beauty that concealed a forgetful, selfish and pampered little soul.

Emma sighed. She felt very plain, very unsophisticated, very dull and readable. Did Barnaby prefer, for a change, an uncomplicated woman? But how soon would he tire of her?

Maggy's dark unwinking eyes were watching her. Emma was sorry she had started the conversation. She said briskly, "Never mind about those things now. Lie down and let me tuck you up."

"Mrs. Faithfull has tucked us up."

"Oh!" said Emma inadequately. Mrs. Faithfull would no doubt at some time appear, like a mouse from the wainscoting, but she was obviously not a particularly friendly mouse. Perhaps that was understandable. This invasion into her private little world of old-fashioned furniture, marble statues, long-ago battles and dust could not be welcome.

Emma debated kissing the children goodnight, and deciding against it was just leaving when a muffled sob came from Dina's bed. The child was completely covered by

38

blankets. She was curled up in a small ball of misery, trembling and crying.

Was she upset by the talk about Josephine? Or was she just worn out and perplexed and unhappy?

Emma sat on the edge of the bed, turning down the blankets and exposing the little tear-stained face. Her heart turned over in pity. What was her postponed trip to Spain compared to the enormous disappointment a child could suffer over a lost holiday?

"Darling, what is it? Why are you crying? Are you unhappy?"

Dina snuffled like a puppy. Maggy's clear contemptuous voice came with the explanation: "She isn't unhappy, she's frightened."

"Frightened?"

"She's always frightened in the night here. Someone walks about. We"— Maggy's voice quavered slightly — "we don't know who it is."

Dina gave another stifled sob. Maggy went on firmly:

"Of course whatever it is wouldn't *hurt* you, we know. But we don't like it particularly. Sylvie didn't, either."

"Sylvie?"

"The governess for our last holidays. Daddy told you about her. She ran away. Everybody said why did she run away, but we knew, didn't we, Dina?"

Dina nodded reluctant assent.

"And why did she run away?" Emma asked calmly.

"Because she was frightened in the night. Even though Daddy looked after her and kissed her. She still ran away."

"She cried, too," Dina ventured.

"Yes, one day she cried and we asked her what was the matter and she said nothing, she was just being silly."

Emma said very firmly, "And I think you are two silly little girls, imagining things. Nobody walks about in the night, and nothing is going to hurt you. So lie down and go to sleep. I'll leave the light on in the passage. If anything does frighten you, you only have to call out, you know."

When Emma went downstairs again there was no one about. The supper dishes had been removed from the table. Barnaby was presumably washing up.

39

She went down the passage in the direction of the kitchen, and presently found herself in a large, old-fashioned room, hung with copper pots and pans, dim from lack of polishing, and littered with dishes.

Mrs. Faithfull was presumably getting past her work, or else was indifferent to dust and muddle. Emma herself, though no martinet for order, did not like dirty dishes. Several years in Aunt Deb's orderly household had made her appreciate good housekeeping. She tut-tutted as she saw Spode and Minton dishes stacked carelessly, having been used as mixing bowls. Half an hour would clear up this muddle. And if by any chance she and Barnaby ever made their home here . . .

"Who are you?" came a high, sharp voice.

Emma turned swiftly. The little woman, brown-skinned, miniature, as wrinkled as a walnut, stood accusingly in the doorway. Her nose and chin were sharp, her mouth tight. But her eyes were soft and wandering, not quite focused, dim and disturbing.

"You must be Mrs. Faithfull," Emma said. "I'm Mrs. Court."

"You can't be. Mrs. Court is dead."

"Jo——" Emma bit off the word. "You mean old Mrs. Court?"

"Both of them. They both died."

Death, death, death! Emma tried to smile, to be patient and gentle with an old woman whose wits were no longer what they should be.

"I'm Mrs. Barnaby Court," she explained. "We've come with the children."

"Oh, the new one." The old lady came closer to peer at her. Emma realised now that the dim eyes were partly blind. "Well," she said, "Barnaby didn't choose so well this time. You're not very pretty, are you?"

"No," said Emma regretfully.

"Strange," Mrs. Faithfull murmured. "He always chose the pretty ones."

"I don't like that plural much, Mrs. Faithfull."

"No." The old lady was not wandering, she suddenly nodded her head wisely. "I expect you don't." But Emma's lack of dazzling prettiness seemed to have reduced her hostility, for she added quite kindly, "You mustn't be in the kitchen, madam. Angelina does the dishes when she comes in the morning. Don't worry about them. Red hair, eh? That's a new one."

Emma looked questioning. Mrs. Faithfull suddenly opened her tight little mouth and gave a dry cackle of laughter.

"Oh, things get lively when Mr. Barnaby's home. We shall have more governesses, eh? Well, well, I tell Mr. Dudley and Mr. Rupert it makes a change, at least."

Yes, it made a change, Emma thought, as she crouched over the dying fire in the bedroom. Tomorrow she would ring Aunt Deb and tell her that instead of going to Spain, or even spending a quiet honeymoon in London, she had arrived literally in the bosom of Barnaby's family, a family that yesterday, as far as she was concerned, had not existed.

Aunt Deb had been quite right when she had told Emma not to trust Barnaby. And she had thought he had told her his life story at that interview he had given her. Certainly she had guessed he would like women. Why shouldn't he? She was glad he did. It meant he had a warm heart, and it was a challenge to her to hold him. Anyway, she was not interested in his past. Even the pretty vanished Sylvie was in his past now, and no concern of hers. . . .

"Talking to yourself?" came Barnaby's voice from the door. "That's Mrs. Faithfull's privilege."

"Oh, does she do that as well?"

"As well as what?"

"Criticising your wife."

Barnaby was amused. "Are you not to her taste, my love?"

"I'm not decorative enough. She thinks you're slipping."

"I disagree. What else did she say to you?"

Was there some anxiety in his manner? Emma said calmly, "That you liked pretty girls."

"So I do, bless them." Barnaby grinned with uninhibited amusement. "That's not to say I'd want to marry all of them."

"No," Emma murmured, thinking of Sylvie who had cried and then run away, even though Barnaby had kissed her.

"Mrs. Faithfull compares me unfavourably with Dudley

who is quite immune to pretty girls, or to any women at all. Except herself, and she hardly counts, as you will agree."

"Barnaby, why did you tell me Josephine had never been here? Dudley says she has been."

"She has? Then I didn't know about it."

"Barnaby, don't be absurd! How could your wife——" Emma's indignant words faltered. The pain, she discovered with surprise, of calling another woman Barnaby's wife was too much for her. " – be here without your knowing?" she finished lamely.

"She may have come down after we had separated. She told me nothing about it. She'd always refused to come before. She hated the country. Yes, I believe the children were here while we were arranging about the divorce."

"What an unnatural marriage!" Emma exclaimed.

"Very unnatural. I told you that."

"Poor darling, you must have been hurt."

"Not at the end. We didn't love each other any more. It was all a mistake on a grand scale. The children have been the sufferers, poor little scraps."

"Let's find them an awfully charming governess," Emma said warmly. "Children adore pretty faces."

Barnaby's brows went up. "So you trust me after all?"

"Not an inch. I fully expect you to break my heart."

His hands curved round her cheeks.

"I have this face now. Why did you shiver?"

"I don't know. The wind's howling."

"It does, at this time of year. The bed's very warm."

Emma looked towards the great bed. A log slipped on the fire. Shadows leaped. She thought, all at once, of Great-grandfather Court's long icy nose.

"The children say they are frightened in the night."

"Are they? I know the house creaks. Did you leave them a light?"

"Yes, and I told them to call. I suppose it's nerves. Why did that girl Sylvie leave?"

Barnaby stooped to mend the fire.

"Heaven knows. Probably found it too lonely. All I complained about was that she gave no notice. One at least expects that."

"The children said she was frightened."

42

Barnaby straightened himself slowly. He looked angry, all at once.

"Then why didn't she tell someone? If anything happened——"

"What would be likely to happen?" It seemed as if the words were forced from Emma.

"I haven't the foggiest notion, unless it was an old house creaking at night, in the wind. Women get neurotic. Look at Mrs. Faithfull, she's talked to herself for as long as I can remember. Look at——"

"You were going to say?"

"Forget it."

"Josephine," Emma said dreamily, and again the dark delicate face seemed to float in the air. "Barnaby, why does Maggy say Josephine is dead?"

"Dead!" Now she had his startled attention.

"She's been saying it off and on all day. She's got Dina into a state, and I suspect is in quite a state herself."

"It's pure nonsense," Barnaby said angrily. "Maggy's a romancer. Because her mother hasn't turned up it pleases her to be dramatic."

"But why hasn't she turned up?"

"My dear girl, if I could get in touch with her, I would. But telegraph boys or even postmen are not familiar sights on the Amazon."

"What about letters to the children?"

"Josephine is no letter writer, even if she were in reach of a post office. The telephone is her medium, and one doesn't telephone children from the ends of the earth."

"I think that's unforgivable!" Emma exclaimed indignantly.

"Granted. You don't know Josephine. She doesn't mean to be unkind. She's purely selfish. She's got a new boy friend and she's on a new adventure. She's either lost count of time or the whole party is temporarily lost."

"Then Maggy really is just making that up about her being dead to cover hurt feelings."

"Of course. I should have thought you'd have guessed that."

"Poor lamb," Emma murmured.

"My darling, if you can soften Maggy you're a miracle worker."

43

Emma shook her head wryly. "I expect Maggy is really the reason Sylvie left."

"I should think so."

"Then for goodness' sake prepare the new girl. To be forewarned——"

Barnaby held out his arms.

"All the ghosts gone, darling?"

"How did you know there were – ghosts?"

He buried his face in her hair, and the wind outside stopped howling.

"Why do we spend so much time in talk? . . ."

# 6

MISS JAMES looked doubtfully at the girl sitting on the opposite side of her desk. It was true that Mr. Court had said, "Don't send another of those attractive blondes. They're not reliable," but this girl was rather going to the other extreme. Mousey was not the word to describe her. No, she was more like a thin little terrier, eager, and inclined to shiver. A terrier who had not been too well treated, but who, with a constant blind trust, still looked for a hoped-for caress that may well prove to be a kick.

"Would you be prepared to go into the country, Miss Pinner?" she asked. Louisa Pinner. That was another thing. Anyone else with a surname like that would have dropped the "a" off Louisa. But not this girl. She kept her baptismal name either religiously or without question.

"Oh, yes, I'd love the country," the girl replied eagerly. "I'm awfully tired of being in London, actually. One never feels one can breathe deeply or expand."

Expand was a thing she could do with, Miss James thought, looking at the meagre chest. Well, one thing, Mr. Barnaby Court would not be able to complain that this girl was too attractive.

### Attractive to whom?

It was too bad of Sylvie Lester to have gone off like that, without any explanation. Miss James became very angry when her girls let her down, and they were promptly struck off her books. But it was exasperating that she was never going to know what had happened to make Sylvie, a formerly reliable person, behave like that. There had been only one cryptic message from her, and that during the first week of her employment when she had made an inquiry about her salary. She had put a postscript at the bottom of her letter, "Wolves down here!" and that was all.

Remembering that probably highly imaginative piece of information, Miss James again looked doubtfully at Louisa Pinner. But was there any need to worry? The most wolfish wolf, whether he lived at Courtlands, or in the surrounding district, would not be likely to raise even a half-hearted whistle at the sight of Louisa. She was definitely not wolf-material.

"The position is to look after eight-year-old twins, girls, during their school holidays," Miss James explained. "You will not be required to give them lessons, but to keep them occupied, plan excursions, see to their clothes and meals, and generally keep them out of trouble."

"It sounds heavenly!" cried Louisa, clasping her thin hands. Although so nondescript in appearance, it seemed that she was given to superlatives. "It's really just what I want. I *adore* children, especially little girls. And twins! How enchanting."

"I warn you not to be too enthusiastic," Miss James said. "According to their father, the Court twins are quite a handful."

"Mean old man!" said Louisa playfully. "I suppose he just hasn't time for them. What does he do?"

"Writes detective novels."

"Oh, how exciting! Oh, I shall look forward to this job, Miss James. Is it only for a month?"

"A month may be long enough. It's only fair of me to tell you that the last girl didn't stay."

"Oh, I suppose she was one of the flighty kind. Didn't like the country in winter. I promise you I shan't do anything like that."

45

Miss James found Miss Pinner's small bright brown eyes, sharp face and eagerly pointed nose obscurely irritating. Even if Barnaby Court agreed that she had sent an earnest and reliable woman to care for his children, what were the children going to think of her?

"There's one thing, Miss James," the girl went on in her breathless way. "Do you think they would let me take Humble down?"

"Humble?"

"My little dog. She's very small and no trouble at all, and I thought, since it was a large country estate, there would be plenty of room. She'd never be noticed. . . ." Her voice trailed away, perhaps because of the expression of exasperated doubt on Miss James's face. Indeed, Miss James was in doubt, not about the dog, but about the dog's mistress. Was she really sending the right person? She liked to please Mr. Court. She had always found his secretaries for him, and until the Sylvie Lester episode he had been entirely satisfied with her choice. But this girl. . . . However, there it was. He had asked for someone not too attractive (had the fact that he had just acquired a brand-new wife anything to do with that?), and really she had no one else on her books who was willing to go into the country for a month before the winter was over.

"Courtlands isn't a large country estate, Miss Pinner. It's a farm with an old farmhouse. I have never seen it myself, but I gather there isn't very much help, and you mustn't expect luxury."

"Oh, I didn't expect *luxury*, Miss James. I only wondered whether——"

"As for your dog, I think you'd be wise to go alone to start with. Then, if nobody minds you having the dog you can send for him." Miss James was rarely in this state of indecision, and it worried her. For no particular reason at all, she wished that she could see Sylvie Lester.

"Humble's a she, Miss James. She's terribly good, really. Never any trouble. But I quite see what you mean. I ought to see how the land lies. And my landlady will look after Humble in the meantime. So it will be quite all right. When do I go to Courtlands?"

"Today, if you can. Let's see, we could decide on a train,

46

and I'll telephone them to have you met. Will that be all right?"

"Perfectly, Miss James. I'm so thrilled, really. Country air, and the little girls, and — who else did you say?"

"Mr. Barnaby Court and his wife, and his two brothers."

"And the brothers' wives?" Miss Pinner's question ended on an anticipatory note. Her small pointed face seemed to quiver.

"Mr. Dudley and Mr. Rupert Court are not married," Miss James said shortly.

"O-oh! Oh, indeed."

"Rupert has just become engaged, and Dudley is supposed to be a recluse, so don't get any ideas there."

"But how interesting," murmured Miss Louisa Pinner.


# 7

RUPERT arrived home in the morning. He was thin and dark with a luxuriant moustache and an air of heartiness that no doubt his political aspirations had fostered. His eyes had the same merry look as Barnaby's, but there the similarity between the brothers ended.

He shook Emma enthusiastically by the hand.

"Sorry I couldn't get to the wedding." His eyes moved over her with deliberate admiration. "One must hand it to old Barnaby," he said.

"Aren't congratulations in order for you, too?" Barnaby inquired.

Rupert sighed and shrugged and laughed.

"Yes, the straight and narrow for me now, old boy. But I mustn't complain. Jean's a deuced nice girl, and her old man can lend more than a helping hand. We're not in a hurry, of course. I'll try to get my seat in the House first. But it's the straight and narrow for me, I fear. I hear you've got the children again. What are we going to do for a Sylvie this time?"

"I've got that under control."

"Well, that's fine. Not that I'm here much, but old Dudley likes his peace. Get someone who won't run away this time. What did you do to Sylvie, by the way, to make her skip? I was disappointed in her. But she was sweetly pretty, as our mother would have said. Wait until you see my bonny Scotch lassie. Well, so long, Emma, I've chores to do. See you at lunch."

It was an exhausting morning. Maggy and Dina could not have been more exasperating. First they insisted on wearing the disreputable jeans that Dudley encouraged them in, and then charged about the house alternately shrieking and giggling.

Barnaby had retired early to his small study on the ground floor, saying briefly that he had work he must do. Dudley, looking very large and comfortable in extremely shabby tweeds, had gone swiftly and rather furtively through the hall and outdoors, obviously hoping not to be seen. Rupert had also disappeared. So the house was left to the women.

To the children's noise was added the deep rich chuckle of Angelina, the large, good-natured daily, who slopped about in carpet slippers and beamed unceasingly.

"It's like Christmas again," Emma heard her confiding to Mrs. Faithfull. "I must say I like the house full of life, even if it means extra. As long as my feet stand up to it. Is she really his wife?"

There was a murmur of protest from Mrs. Faithfull, and Angelina went on unabashed, "I was only thinking of that pretty piece at Christmas, Sylvie what's-her-name. Her minding the children! That was rich. I must say it was a bit hard on Mr. Dudley, him not being partial to women. But perhaps they'll draw him out these holidays. I always say he's only shy, really. Oh, I say, Mrs. Faithfull, you've gone and broke the sauce boat. And it's one of them fancy chinas, too. Never mind, dear, it ain't your fault, you can't see what's under your nose, can you?" Again came the rich chuckle. "Fancy women, fancy china, they're all treated careless in this house. It's only your age and my size that protects us, eh? Otherwise we'd be packing and off in a huff, too!" Angelina evidently thought this statement the height of brilliance, for her laughter came pealing forth.

"Barnaby, I promised you your past was your past," Emma whispered to herself. Anyway that was only servants' gossip which she shouldn't be listening to. Angelina was a romancer, in another field to Maggy's, but in the same way. Everything had to be dramatised. . . . Anyway, what did it matter if last Christmas Barnaby did flirt with a pretty girl called Sylvie. . . .

A month, Emma thought, of rain, of looking at pictures of old battles, of coping with the children's quarrels and listening to servants' gossip, of trying not to embarrass Dudley by being either too obtrusive or too conspicuously feminine, and of being tolerant of Rupert's heartiness. . . .

Really, it was the craziest honeymoon.

Poor Barnaby. . . . Poor Emma. . . .

But then, just before lunch, when the men had re-appeared, the telephone rang and it was the employment agency in London. Barnaby, who spoke for a few minutes, put his hand over the mouthpiece and turned.

"It's Miss James. She's sending a young woman by this afternoon's train." He looked pleased. "I told you it would be all right when someone came, didn't I?"

There was a clatter as Dudley dropped his pipe. He stooped to pick it up. His face was red.

"I say, old chap, not another – I mean, that young woman——"

"Oh, this isn't another Sylvie. I gave Miss James explicit directions." He spoke into the telephone. "What does she look like, Miss James? Yes . . . yes. . . . Oh, splendid. That really is clever of you. Louisa – what? – Pinner. Right. We'll have her met at the station. Yes, I assure you, she sounds exactly the kind of person we want. Thank you very much indeed. Good-bye."

Barnaby replaced the receiver. He was grinning. He had the mischievous guileless look that Emma both loved and distrusted.

"This will ease your mind, Dudley. Miss Louisa Pinner, aged twenty-eight, is plain and sensible. She adores the country and children. She is looking forward to long walks in the rain, and she likes nothing better than draughty rooms and smoky fires. Her favourite music is the har-monium——"

49

"Barnaby!" But Emma was laughing helplessly.

"I don't see what this has to do with me," said Dudley stiffly. "The woman is no concern of mine."

"Except that she'll be living in the same house." Barnaby was serious now. "That can be awkward if she behaves badly. But I'm sure she won't. Miss James tells me she lavishes all her affections on her dog."

"I tell you again, it's none of my business," Dudley muttered, and went out of the room.

"Poor old Dudley. Sylvie really was naughty. An eligible bachelor seems to be an irresistible challenge to some women."

"You mean she pursued Dudley!"

"He spent three weeks evading her. Then she left, in a huff, or a temper, or from boredom. Why, what did you think, my sweet?"

"Something quite different," Emma murmured, and allowed Barnaby to kiss her. But a thought nagged at her. "Darling, you were an eligible bachelor at Christmas, too."

"And even more elusive than Dudley."

"I would have to see that to believe it." Emma allowed Barnaby to kiss her again, and murmured, "Funny!"

"What?"

"How the world steadies when you kiss me."

"Has it been rocking?"

"A little."

"Poor darling. Don't worry. Miss Louisa Pinner is the answer to our problem. In a few days, when she's settled in, we can be off to Spain."

"And leave Dudley undefended?"

"That old turtle. Let him go into his safe, solitary shell."

"But why does he love his shell so much?"

"Heaven knows. He was just made that way."

"Then I'm going to encourage Miss L. Pinner to draw him out."

Barnaby's eyebrows went up.

"You horrible little schemer."

"Why not? One must do something on wet days."

"I can think of better things."

"But can Dudley? Poor dear, I think secretly he's very lonely. Louisa and I will work on him."

"Don't neglect your husband."

"Oh, you! You can find another Sylvie. And if you don't want me to hear tales about her you'll have to muzzle Angelina!"

The children had thought the telephone might have been their mother ringing at last. That had been Dina's idea, actually, but it was obvious that Maggy was also hiding hopefulness behind her scepticism. They came bursting into the dining-room, faces grubby, hair untidy, demanding belligerently, "When is she coming for us? Today?"

"Miss Pinner is coming today," Barnaby said.

"Not Mummy? It wasn't Mummy!" Dina's face had puckered into incipient tears, but Maggy's eyes sparkled, and her voice was full of childish menace.

"Who wasn't Mummy?" Barnaby asked patiently. "Oh, you thought the telephone—— Oh, I'm sorry, little ones, but that was just your new governess. A very nice person called Miss Pinner."

"We don't want to hear her foul name," said Maggy, legs astride, eyes snapping.

"Maggy!"

"We don't, do we, Dina? We're going to be more awful to her than we were to Sylvie. We're going to pinch her, and put things in her bed and poison her tea and probably murder her."

Dina, round-eyed at her sister's scandalous behaviour, had forgotten her tears.

"Maggy, go to your room!" It was the first time Emma had seen Barnaby as angry as that, with brows drawn into a straight line, and pinched nostrils.

Maggy threw back her head impudently and did a little skip.

"We'll do the candle game. Dina, you know. The one Angelina told us about. And when the pin falls out Miss *Pin*ner will die!" Maggy, not sure whether to laugh at her inadvertent pun, or to put the emphasis on melodrama, did another little skip, and she stared at her father unflinchingly.

Barnaby took her by the shoulders and steered her to the door.

"Out!" he said. "Upstairs! No lunch! I'm sorry, but your behaviour is abominable."

Maggy, a taut little figure full of blazing hate, flung back, "I don't care! I couldn't eat, anyway. Food would choke me!" and flew upstairs. Dina made a timid movement to follow her.

"Not you," said Barnaby. "You can come and eat with us like a civilised being. And stop crying."

"Barnaby," Emma said, taking his arm. "After all, the children did think their mother — I mean, it must have been a great disappointment to them."

"And why should they think their mother would telephone here when she neglected them at school? They're just playing up."

Barnaby's eyes were stony. Emma suddenly thought, "He's disappointed, too. He had been secretly hoping Josephine would arrive." And she had a feeling of utter forlornness.

But at least that discounted the theory that Josephine was dead, and Barnaby had known. Josephine, somewhere, even on her so-unlikely South American expedition, was very much alive, waiting till the whim took her to crook her little finger lazily, smile in sweet invitation, and have all her family tumbling over themselves to get to her side.

The incipient arrival of Miss Louisa Pinner was temporarily forgotten. Lunch was a miserable affair, with Dina dropping tears into her soup, Barnaby eating in utter silence, his brows still a bleak straight line, Rupert absorbed in the political page of the newspaper, and Dudley, head bent over his plate, stealing occasional surreptitious glances at Emma as if he were determined to accustom himself to the sight of her.

The crisis of Dina suddenly announcing that she felt sick was almost welcome. Emma whisked her upstairs to the bathroom. Maggy, whose ears were undoubtedly much too sharp, appeared instantly and said, "You don't need to fuss. She never is sick. She only feels like it." And Emma, looking at Dina's white, tear-streaked face, wondered whether perhaps her more childish weapons were not even more effective than Maggy's lashing impudence.

"I think you're both over-excited," she said calmly. "As your father suggests, an hour's rest on your beds would be a very good thing. Then you can put some more respectable clothes on and we'll all go to the station to meet Miss Pinner."

Louisa, Emma reflected wryly, two hours later, was not going to get a very gay welcome. One hoped that, on sight of Maggy's and Dina's sullen faces, she would not turn tail and catch the next train back to London. For, although Barnaby had recovered from his brief anger, and was doing his best to coax smiles from his difficult daughters, they were refusing to respond.

Emma, torn between pity and perplexity, decided that she almost wished it were Josephine, smiling and gay, who was to get off the train. With furs and jewels and perhaps a cage containing humming-birds in one hand. A touch of exotic colour in the bleak little station.

It would be nice to see the children looking happy and not so silent and depressed and pathetically adult. Although certainly the repression was better than the wild tantrums. Emma did not feel herself capable of banishing either state, and neither, she was afraid, would Louisa Pinner.

But it seemed that question was not to arise. For the train came in and nobody at all got off. Miss Pinner had failed to arrive.

Maggy changed swiftly from sulkiness to jubilation.

"I expect she got frightened," she announced in a more friendly and conversational way than Emma had yet heard her speak.

"Why should she get frightened?" Barnaby demanded. He was annoyed again, his jaw hardening. "What's come over people nowadays? You can't rely on any of them."

"I expect she has just missed her train," Emma said soothingly.

"With a name like that? Oh, no, the Miss Pinners of this world would catch trains with at least half an hour to spare. Clock watchers. Fidgeters. You'll see."

"Poor Miss Pinner
Will miss her dinner . . ."

Maggy chanted, and burst into irrepressible giggles.
Barnaby sighed.

53

"Now we'll have this all the way home. Well, at least Dudley can relax."

Emma turned to smile at the two frantically giggling children.

"I think we all can. None of us seemed frightfully sold on Miss Pinner." She thought of the feeling of obscure dread that illogically the impending arrival of the nondescript young woman had given her, and resolutely shook it off. "Let's go home and make waffles for tea. Who likes waffles?"

"I adore them above all things," Barnaby answered satisfactorily. Neither of the children spoke, but glancing at them Emma saw that their hostility had definitely lessened. Anyway, it was difficult to be hostile and madly amused at one's own joke at the same time. For Maggy was murmuring variations of her Miss Pinner rhyme and Dina was an appreciative audience.

The house seemed deserted on their return. Dudley, postponing the ordeal of meeting a new woman, had made himself scarce. Rupert was making his daily call at the village pub. Angelina had gone to the cottage, and Mrs. Faithfull, Barnaby said, retired to her room for the greater part of the afternoon. The hall belonged to Great-grandfather Court, with his haughty nose and blank stare, the drawing-room to the Chippendale furniture, the battle scenes, the gilt clock ticking primly, the harmonium in the corner. The scene was Victorian. They were usurpers, Emma thought. They had strayed out of their age. Dudley, in his slow, bumbling, modest and bashful way, belonged. So did Mrs. Faithfull, who, with her small hunched figure, her myopic gaze and her murmuring voice, disturbed the house no more than a mouse. But they did not. Neither had Josephine, nor, at Christmas, the pretty Sylvie. . . .

It was a relief to be in the big kitchen, investigating cupboards, finding equipment and ingredients for making the waffles. Barnaby went away to ring Miss James at the employment agency, but the little girls stayed with Emma. She showed them how to measure and mix ingredients. It grew darker and Dina went to draw the curtains.

"Oh, you've shut out the last of the daylight," Emma said.

Maggy, who had become a great deal more cheerful and human, and who even had a little pink in her cheeks, stirred

54

her mixture absorbedly and said, "Dina doesn't like it getting dark. It scares her."

Dina turned defensively. "Once somebody used to knock at the windows."

"Who?" Emma asked.

"We don't know. Nobody ever knew."

"When was this?" Emma was tolerantly amused. Dina was an exceedingly nervous child, and a quiet old house was no place for her.

"When Sylvie was here she was frightened, too. She said someone was knocking for her and if she went outdoors they would get her."

"Oh, nonsense!" Emma exclaimed. "She was just frightening you. It was very naughty of her."

Maggy delicately scooped up some of the mixture on her little finger and ate it.

"Well, she disappeared, didn't she? So someone must have got her."

Barnaby came in at that moment. He was large, real, very reassuring.

"Couldn't get a reply," he said. "The office is closed, I suppose. So we'll have to weather another night, Miss Pinner-less. I say, this looks good."

"Your daughters are learning to cook," said Emma sedately.

Barnaby put his arm round her waist.

"You take everything in your stride; Boswell occupying most of my study, an inadequate wedding to satisfy my impatience, Josephine turning explorer, those two hobgoblins, this Victorian museum you find yourself in, the mysterious Miss Pinner mysteriously unarrived. . . ."

Emma quietly evaded Barnaby's embrace. She had noticed the dislike beginning to smoulder in Maggy's eyes again. These children were like suspicious wild birds, a step forward, two alarmed steps back. They had temporarily, in the warm kitchen, forgotten Josephine and their enormous disappointment. Now they remembered again.

"Go away and light the fire in the drawing-room," she said calmly. "We'll have tea in there. And find Dudley. He'll surely join us now that we're alone and quite harmless."

Dudley did consent to join them. He even seemed almost at his ease, smiling his wide bashful smile, his plump cheeks catching a glow from the fire, Maggy and Dina sitting on the hearthrug at his feet.

"It's almost like old times," he said.

What old times? Emma wanted to ask. Christmas when Sylvie was there, or earlier still during that brief visit of Josephine's, when Barnaby had said he himself was not there? But it seemed that Dudley was speaking of their childhood.

"Do you remember Mother playing the harmonium?" he said to Barnaby. "I can see her sitting there now, her quiet face, her little figure – she used to wear grey silk – like a little dove...."

Barnaby's expressive eyebrow went up in a private message to Emma. "Old chap's too much alone," he seemed to be saying. "Lives in the past...."

"I remember that she used to make us sing hymns," he said aloud, lazily. "Usually Moody and Sankey ones. They were your choice, if I remember rightly."

Dudley beamed with pleasure. He looked like an overgrown child, flushed and excited.

"*Shall we gather at the river*. That was my favourite. I believe I could play it now. Let's try."

Maggy and Dina scrambled up eagerly.

"Uncle Dudley, you've never played the harmonium for us."

Dudley wagged a large fat forefinger. "If I play, you'll have to sing. Like Mother used to make us do. Every Sunday afternoon."

He lumbered to his feet, and went over to the harmonium. It was wheezy from long disuse. The first notes were barely audible, breathy sighs that seemed to express the feeling of the whole room, reluctantly stirring to life.

Then the sentimental tune, beneath Dudley's firm fingers, creaked forth and in a fruity bass voice he began to sing,

> " 'Shall we gather at the river
> Where bright Angels' feet have trod....'

Come along, you two. Sing up. Don't they teach you these

hymns at school? What nonsense! Part of one's childhood. I'll remember them forever. Come, let's try again."

Rupert came in and gave his loud hearty laugh at the scene, then enthusiastically joined in the singing, throwing back his head, opening his mouth wide.

Emma, in the warm flickering firelight, felt for Barnaby's hand. He held her fingers sleepily. He was stretched in his chair, long and relaxed. His head was silhouetted against the wall, his nose high and arrogant. Great-grandfather Court's nose. . . . But on a warm human face, Barnaby's dearly loved familiar face. . . . Perhaps the honeymoon was turning out well after all. It was the family, belonging, catching the past when a gentle little mother had sung with her three sons, and giving Maggy and Dina a memory for the future. . . .

How strange it all was. . . . Yet somehow right.

And then the rapping came at the window.

It was Dina who screamed. Maggy merely clutched Dudley's arm, her eyes black in her bloodless face. Dudley, too, had suddenly frozen on the piano stool, his head tipped slightly sideways, listening, and Rupert's fingers were absently twisting his moustache as he turned, staring.

The window was black with night. Nobody had remembered to draw the curtains. There was a faint shine of raindrops on the glass. Nothing else.

Barnaby stirred lazily in his chair, the least disturbed of all.

"Who's that?" he said. "Is it Willie wanting something? Go and see, Dudley, old man."

"Willie," said Dudley rather thickly, "would come to the door."

But he got up and began to go towards the window.

"It's Sylvie!" screamed Dina suddenly. "It's Sylvie! Don't let her in!"

And there, sure enough, as if it had materialised out of the black night, a face was pressing against the pane, a pale face with wet strands of hair stuck to thin cheeks, and an open mouth calling something inaudible.

It was, thought Emma, in slow horror, like someone drowned. . . .

She was aware that Barnaby had sprung up and was

standing tense, also that Dudley had halted, and Rupert stared, his eyes narrowed. For one moment it was like a tableau, everyone in the room petrified to stillness.

Then the woman outside rapped on the pane and beckoned, and Maggy and Dina flung themselves at Emma to cling in an extremity of fear.

"Why," said Barnaby, in sudden amusement, "I believe it's our lost and strayed Miss Pinner. We really must get that doorbell fixed. The poor girl has probably been standing there ringing for hours."

He left the room, and the face disappeared from the window. Now there was nothing but a comfortable blank there. But the white imploring face was strangely fixed in Emma's mind. Her obscure dread was stirring again. . . .

She unloosened the little girls' grip on her. It was nice, she thought, that they had instinctively run to her. She could hear Barnaby, in the hall, speaking genially, and a woman's voice, rather high and shrill, answering.

"There," she said soothingly. "It is Miss Pinner, after all. There was no need to be frightened. Dina, let me wipe your tears. Silly girl. You must say how do you do nicely to Miss Pinner. Dudley, where are you going?"

This last she said playfully, for Dudley had been slinking towards the door. For all his size, he could move very silently.

"Have to do some chores," he mumbled vaguely.

"Wait and meet Miss Pinner first. The poor girl. We must welcome her."

The stage was set again when, a few moments later, Barnaby brought Miss Pinner into the room. There was Dudley, large and reluctant, edging away from the light, Rupert staring at her with unabashed curiosity, the two little girls rigid with dislike, and Emma herself smiling a rather fixed smile.

There should have been no need for this stiff and awkward welcome. If only Miss Pinner hadn't given them such an uncanny fright. Yes, uncanny was the word. As if everyone had expected the lost face to belong to another woman. . . .

But Emma's uneasiness vanished in genuine sympathy for Louisa Pinner, who was wet through and tense with nervousness. As Barnaby introduced her to them all in turn she stood beside him, nodding and smiling eagerly, at the same time trying to control her shivering.

"I couldn't make anyone hear the doorbell," she was apologising nervously. "You were all singing. So sweetly, too. I had to rap quite loudly on the window. And then I slipped on something – a paving stone, I think." She indicated ruefully her torn stocking, and gave a nervous giggle. "You must have thought I was playing a game, rapping and disappearing."

"Miss Pinner missed the first train," Barnaby explained. "She had to arrange about her dog and that took longer than she had thought it would."

"I'm so sorry about that," Miss Pinner said in her quick eager voice. "But I couldn't come down to the country without leaving my darling little Humble provided for. I had to wait to see my landlady and she was late coming in."

She had brown eyes that looked larger than they should because of the extreme thinness of her face. Her teeth, also, were too large, making her face all eyes and eager smile. Her wet hat drooped over her forehead, a lock of hair was stuck lankly to one cheek. She was quite unprepossessing, yet she gave one strongly the impression that she was small and delicate and needed to be taken care of.

It was to her credit that her look of eager willingness did not fade as she observed Maggy and Dina, each glowering and looking their most unfriendly.

"And these are the children," she said. "I do hope we'll be great friends."

Emma belatedly remembered her duties as a hostess.

"You'd like to come up to your room and change. You look terribly wet."

"She has walked from the station," Barnaby said. "I told her she should have telephoned."

"Oh, not when it was my fault that I missed the train. Really, I didn't mind a bit. I'm just so excited to be in the country."

Emma exchanged a look with Barnaby. It was both amused and wry. If Barnaby enjoyed flirting with pretty girls, there was going to be no temptation here, but also was this kind of a person going to have any control at all over Maggy and Dina?

Well, perhaps she would improve when dried out and fed. One would have to hope for the best.

# 8

EMMA came down, after showing Louisa her room and sending the children off to have their baths, to find the men idly discussing the new arrival.

"She won't stay," Barnaby was predicting gloomily. "Maggy will run her ragged. Sylvie did manage to keep her in control, more or less, but Miss Pinner—— Lord, what was Miss James thinking of?"

"Anyone who could name their dog Humble!" Rupert said amusedly. "I ask you. Poor little devil, I bet he goes round with his tail between his legs. Emma, what did you think of her?"

Emma, already sorry for the rather pathetic creature whom she had left upstairs unpacking and changing, said carefully, "I'm sure she's awfully well-meaning. With two ordinary children, I mean placid and well-behaved children – I'm sorry, Barnaby, but you must admit Maggy and Dina are neither of those things – she might do very well."

"Well, it's only for a month," said Barnaby. "At least, she must be of some use."

Dudley, who had been seated at the harmonium silently fingering the keys, said suddenly, "Give her a chance. I only hope she's not too nervous, that's all. Sylvie used to shriek her head off sometimes, and she wasn't exactly the nervous kind."

"What at?" Emma was impelled to ask. Maggy had said Sylvie was frightened in the night, Dina had pulled the curtains carefully in the kitchen as if afraid, and then, when Louisa had rapped at the window, had screamed that it was Sylvie. . . .

"Oh, Mrs. Faithfull has a habit of walking about late at night talking to the owls, or something. Or else the house creaks, or a fox gets one of the chickens, or a ewe loses her lamb in the bottom field and bleats all night. Town girls aren't used to country sounds. I wouldn't think your Miss Pinner is used to much at all." Then he added thoughtfully, almost tenderly, "She looked like a wet puppy," and in embarrassment crashed his fingers on the keyboard. "I think she'll be much better than that flibbertigibbet Sylvie. I think she'll be all right."

"What's this! Old Dudley defending a woman!" Rupert gave an astonished laugh.

But Emma suddenly was conscious of affection for the large clumsy man overflowing the piano stool, like a too-fat boy. Louisa, she thought, did not frighten him. She was a little lost and helpless and pathetic, and that appealed to him. Josephine and Sylvie, with their sophistication and good looks, would have driven him nervously into his shell, but in Louisa he had recognised already someone to whom he could feel superior.

Emma was conscious of a mild amusement. She had threatened to Barnaby that she would persuade Louisa to draw Dudley out, but perhaps it would not be necessary. Perhaps, unwittingly, Louisa had begun to do so already.

It was not Dudley, however, who had to cope with the crisis that night when Louisa screamed piercingly because there was a mouse, quite dead and harmless, on her pillow. She had thrown back the coverlet, and there it was, she explained, shakily and apologetically, when Emma rushed to her room.

Looking meagre and childish in a white cotton slip, she hugged her arms across her breasts and tried to laugh.

"I shouldn't have screamed. I know it's only a prank of the children's. And the – the creature is quite dead. But I've always been terrified of mice. I thought for a minute it was alive."

Emma remembered all too clearly Maggy's threat as to the things she would do to the new governess. This trick certainly bore the stamp of Maggy's peculiar sense of humour. But nothing could be done about it just now, for both children, who had put themselves to bed an hour ago, were asleep, and it was a state too precious to disturb.

"I'm so sorry," she said, "I'm afraid the children are rather out of hand. We have to make allowances because they've had a most uncertain life up to now. I should have warned you that odd things might happen for a day or two, until they accept you."

"They did look two little rebels," Louisa admitted.

"I know. But I do hope you won't let them frighten you away." Emma wondered if it were the children, with their unfunny pranks, who had frightened Sylvie away, even though Barnaby had kissed her.

"Oh, no, Mrs. Court." Louisa's pointed face was full of eagerness. "I'm going to love it here. I know I am. Such a lovely old house." She looked round her room, large, Victorian, the walls papered with a pattern of fat faded roses, the bed covered with a white tasselled spread. "Why, in London my room is hardly bigger than that wardrobe. Imagine living in a wardrobe!" Louisa, who had recovered from her shock and was garrulously inclined to talk, giggled and went on, "Not that it doesn't suit me very well. It's cheap enough for me to keep on when I go away on a job, and my landlady is awfully sweet about looking after Humble for me. Humble is the only reason I don't like going away like this, but after all it's only for a month, and one sometimes feels one has to *breathe*."

Louisa inflated her narrow chest, and at the same moment Dudley's deep, diffident voice came from the passage.

"Is there anything wrong? I thought I heard someone call out."

Louisa gave a stifled scream and darted behind the bed, grabbing for her dressing-gown. Really, she was as mid-Victorian as the room, Emma thought, and went to the door to reassure Dudley who lurked a little distance away, large and anxious.

"It's all right. Just the children playing a trick on Miss Pinner. We'll deal with it in the morning."

"I say, really that's too bad! I've spoken to Barnaby before. Those children need discipline. That school they're at can't be any good."

"What they want," Emma said slowly, "is their mother. But now you're here, Dudley, you might like to remove the body."

"The bo——" Dudley's eyes were palely protuberant.

"The offending corpse." Emma gingerly took the dead mouse by its tail and advanced towards Dudley, while Louisa, out of sight, giggled hysterically.

"Oh, I say!" Dudley muttered. "Oh, that's too bad. Little devils." He lumbered off, bearing the corpse, muttering indignantly.

Emma went back into the room. "Now you'll be all right. I hope you sleep well."

"Oh, I shall." A little pink had come into Louisa's cheeks and her face had its look of quivering expectancy. "Isn't Mr. Court— I mean Mr. Dudley Court — awfully sweet. Oh, not that I don't think the other brothers are sweet too, but there's something so kind and almost innocent about Mr. Dudley. Oh, I am being silly, aren't I? But I think he's a perfect darling."

"She's absolutely a period piece," Emma said to Barnaby when she went back to her room. "She'll be crocheting antimacassars tomorrow, or working a sampler. *Count the hours.* I think Miss Pinner is a natural hour counter, and all as far as possible to her own advantage. But, poor little creature, she doesn't seem to have had much up to now, except that horrible dog Humble."

"When you've finished this potted biography of Miss Pinner," said Barnaby, "perhaps you'll tell me why our period piece screamed."

"Oh, there was a dead mouse in her bed. You remember, Maggy threatened to do things like that. Barnaby, I know your children have had a rough time, but all the same they'll have to be taught the things that simply aren't done."

"Now wait a minute," Barnaby said. "Let's analyse this. First, supposing Maggy put the mouse there, where would she get it?"

"I should think this house is full of mice."

"Live ones, my darling. And even Maggy isn't quick enough to catch one of those."

"Haven't you got cats?"

"In the stables, yes."

"Then I expect the children went down there and relieved one of the cats of a trophy. After all, they knew Miss Pinner was coming, and they weren't exactly overjoyed."

"Granted," said Barnaby. "It's possible. Not particularly probable though."

Emma flung up her head.

"Then how do you suggest the mouse got into her bed?"

"Witchcraft, my dear." Barnaby grinned. "As a matter of fact, I'm thinking of doing something on those lines in my new book. Did you know that Angelina is something of an authority on witchcraft? Her husband Willie gets quite uneasy about it at times."

"Angelina!" Emma thought of the plump, slipshod, garrulous Angelina who seemed to have nothing in her untidy mind beyond gossip. "Now if you had said Mrs. Faithfull I shouldn't have been surprised."

"Not Mrs. Faithfull. True, she's a little dim-witted now, but she has always been very prim and severe. Church every Sunday, no hanky-panky. In fact, I think that's why Dudley is such a puritan. He's always been her favourite. Rupert and I rather escaped the treatment."

"Obviously," Emma murmured. "I would hardly think Mrs. Faithfull is responsible for the gleam in your eye."

"Don't you like it?" he asked provocatively.

"Darling, we're getting away from the point. The dead mouse in Miss Pinner's bed."

"Unimportant," said Barnaby, his head coming down to hers.

It was later that night that Barnaby gave her the cameo. It had belonged to his mother, he said. Now it was hers.

Emma looked at the heavy brooch he had put in her hand. It was very old and beautifully designed. For a moment she had the odd moving fancy that she could feel the little palpitating heart of Barnaby's mother beneath it.

"My mother didn't have much jewellery. It was her favourite piece," Barnaby said.

Emma lifted her eyes. "Why didn't Josephine have it?"

"It wasn't Josephine's kind of thing," he answered simply.

No more was said, but Emma was suddenly very happy. Later she was to remember with longing that moment of pure confident happiness. . . .

In the morning Maggy and Dina flatly denied any knowledge of the dead mouse and the joke played on Miss Pinner.

Their eyes were round and innocent, their voices full of indignation.

"Oh, but we didn't. Truly we didn't. We went straight to bed when you told us to. Anyway, how would we catch a mouse? We haven't got claws."

This last sally was from Maggy and produced the inevitable giggles from Dina, who suddenly pretended to be a cat and began pouncing at her sister.

"Oh, please, Mrs. Court!" Miss Pinner begged. "I don't believe they did do it."

Emma turned on her coldly. "And if they didn't, who do you suggest did?"

This flustered Miss Pinner, who twisted her rather bony hands and said uneasily that she hadn't yet met everybody who lived there. "It was probably the cat," she murmured.

"Miaou! Miaou!" began Maggy and Dina in unison, leaping about the room. Miss Pinner was on the verge of tears.

"Please forget the incident, Mrs. Court. I'm sure it won't happen again. I'll keep my door shut, so that if it was the cat it can't get in."

"My husband tells me that the only cats here are stable cats. Never mind. Take the children down to breakfast. I'll speak to the others."

"It was Angelina," said Maggy loudly. "I saw her come out of Miss Pinner's room last night. She carries things in her pockets, you know. Frogs' legs and spiders!"

Miss Pinner gave a stifled gasp. Maggy looked at her with malicious black eyes.

"She tells fortunes and casts spells, too. She cast a spell over Sylvie."

"What did it do?" Miss Pinner asked, fearfully fascinated.

"She lit the death candle. So Sylvie had to go away or she would have died."

"Maggy, this is all nonsense!" Emma said severely. "If you go on making up stories I will have to tell your father."

Maggy gave a little skip.

"I don't care. Mummy will be coming for us today. Or there'll be a letter."

"But I thought you said she was dead," Emma couldn't resist saying.

Dina said, "She isn't dead!" violently. "She *will* come for us today."

Maggy's eyes flickered and her bravado died. Emma caught one flash of intense misery, then it was concealed and the child shrugged and said, "It would only be because she was dead if she didn't come for us. It wouldn't be because she had forgotten us."

"Oh," breathed Miss Pinner. "Poor little——"

Emma motioned her to be silent. She took Maggy's hand. "Come along. Down to breakfast. Who knows what might be in the mail today? But I warn you, if you don't behave with Miss Pinner and with everyone else, there won't be any treats of any kind."

Much as she disliked it, Emma felt she must go into the kitchen and pursue the matter of the unpleasant joke further. There she found Angelina and her husband Willie sitting at the big table having breakfast, while Mrs. Faithfull pottered backwards and forwards with dishes.

Everyone looked up on her entrance. Angelina promptly beamed, her broad face creasing attractively. Willie, who was shaggy-haired and inarticulate, muttered something and bent his head over his porridge. Mrs. Faithfull stood quite still, as if listening rather than seeing, her small, brown face very aware.

"Breakfast is in the dining-room, madam," she said in her thin, high, severe voice. "Is there something you wanted?"

"Just a small matter I'm curious about," Emma said. "Who has a hobby of catching mice?"

Willie lifted his head suspiciously. He had a heavy, rather stupid face, weather-reddened. "I set traps for them," he said. "Have to. The house would be overrun. Catch a couple at least every night. Ain't that so, Mrs. Faithfull?"

Mrs. Faithfull said, "I've told you I don't object so long as you remove them yourself. I detest the creatures." She gave a faint shudder.

Angelina suddenly chuckled. She had a deep, rich chuckle that shook her plump body gently.

"You're not afraid of anything, Mrs. Faithfull. You only pretend to be."

66

"Dead things I'm afraid of," Mrs. Faithfull insisted in a high stubborn voice. "Begging your pardon, madam, why are you asking these questions?"

Emma noticed that Angelina had one hand in a very capacious apron pocket. Maggy said that she carried dead things in her pocket, snails and spiders and such. It couldn't be true. Angelina had a warm, laughing open face that loved life.

But the mystery was explained easily enough now. If mice were caught in traps in the kitchen and pantry it would have been quite simple for Maggy and Dina to remove one during the day and keep it for their unpleasant prank. Obviously they had been lying.

"Oh, nothing serious," she said lightly. "A joke was played on Miss Pinner, the new governess, last night. I just wondered about the mechanics of it, that's all."

A strange thing happened then. Willie looked apprehensively at Angelina.

"Be you up to your tricks?" he demanded. "Last Christmas——"

But Angelina's face had changed from laughter to thunder. She glared angrily at her husband.

"What nonsense are you talking? I did nothing at Christmas but tell the girl's fortune. And a queer one it would have been if she hadn't taken my warning."

"Angelina!" Emma spun round at the sound of Barnaby's voice. It was sterner than she had ever heard it. His brows were drawn in their straight line of anger, his eyes cold. "I don't want any more of that fortune-telling. Do you understand? It's a lot of arrant nonsense, besides being wicked and harmful. Willie, see that your wife obeys me."

Willie humbly nodded his head.

"I will that, sir."

Angelina, scarlet and scowling, flounced away from the table to the sink and began noisily clattering dishes. Mrs. Faithfull nodded twice to herself, like a small wise bird. Barnaby took Emma's arm.

"Come and get your breakfast."

Emma felt herself compelled to explain the reason for her visit to the kitchen.

"I only wanted to get to the bottom of this silly prank last

67

night. Barnaby, if Angelina does tell fortunes I'm sure she doesn't mean any harm."

"Can you imagine the effect of something like that on a silly impressionable creature like Louisa Pinner?"

But surely he doesn't want to protect Louisa, Emma thought. Not the way Dudley does, his pity for someone small and weak making him feel a fine, brave person himself. Then abruptly the answer came to her. Sylvie! Angelina had told Sylvie something that had upset her and made her go away. And Barnaby had been unduly distressed about it.

The past was the past. . . . Emma tucked her arm firmly into Barnaby's and said, "Yes, I agree. Fortune-telling isn't particularly healthy. Darling, what shall we do today?"

Still lost in thought he answered absently, "I have to work. I'm already a week behind in my next instalment. I'll have to get on the telephone and placate Mark somehow this morning."

"You shouldn't have taken time off to marry me!" Barnaby caught the hot flash in Emma's eyes, and his own irritation vanished. He laughed.

"Darling, I adore you when you hate me. But you'll have to go on hating me this morning. I find all you women too distracting."

It had stopped raining and although overcast was fine enough for the children to take a walk. Emma watched them leave, spider-legged creatures in their gumboots and mackintoshes, running ahead of Miss Pinner, who, small and resolute, tramped doggedly behind, a canvas bag over her shoulder in which to gather specimens, for she rather fancied herself as a botanist.

Suddenly, for the first time for two days, Emma felt she could relax. She had an overwhelming impulse to talk to Aunt Deb and decided to do so by means of a long letter. In her bedroom, looking out of the tall windows over the rain-soaked country, it was a relief to put the whole strange story on paper. "Love him, but don't trust him," Aunt Deb had said.

"I do still trust him," Emma wrote defiantly, "even with two children as unmanageable as little wild creatures, an ex-wife who — yes, I am ashamed to admit it — haunts me,

68

rather, and a great-grandfather petrified in marble who watches every step I take. Also the ghost of pretty Sylvie who vanished last Christmas. . . ."

When she went downstairs two hours later Barnaby was talking on the telephone, the children were just coming in from their walk, followed by Louisa and Dudley who seemed to be in earnest conversation, and it was raining again.

"All right, darling, write to me at once. . . ." Barnaby was saying, and Maggy and Dina rushed forward, scarlet-cheeked.

"It *is* Mummy this time! Let us speak to her, please!"

Barnaby put down the receiver and said irritably, "Why do you children think every time the telephone rings it is your mother? I know a great many other people——"

"Whom you call darling," Emma interposed, indignant for the children's disappointment.

Barnaby said slowly and distinctly, "That was Mark's secretary whom, if you care to know, I always call darling. It's a thing I have about secretaries, especially attractive ones."

Rupert, looking up from his newspapers, said approvingly, "Quite right, old boy."

Miss Pinner, coming in, gave a stifled giggle. Dudley, behind her, looked embarrassed. He was carrying her canvas bag, and seemed embarrassed, too, at being observed with that. He put it down as inconspicuously as possible, muttering something about having met the children at the gate.

"Barnaby," said Emma, noticing Dina's quivering lip, "isn't there any possible way of getting in touch with Josephine?"

"I've told you before," Barnaby said impatiently, "if I could get in touch with her I would." Then he relented and smiled at the children, his eyes kind.

"Cheer up, youngsters. Perhaps tomorrow there'll be a letter."

Dina would have nodded meekly and suppressed her tears. But Maggy's violent way of expressing her disappointment swept Dina away, too, and the two went on a long whooping circuit of the hall, scattering rugs and making pictures tremble, then tore up the stairs and began thumping up and down the passages. Miss Pinner, with a cry of distress, flew up the stairs after them.

"Children!" she called in her agitated voice. "Children, stop that at once!"

Maggy gave a derisive snort and slid down the banisters. Then, before anybody could say anything, she was at the top of the stairs and fleeing with Dina again.

"Children!" wailed Miss Pinner. "Maggy! You bad, bad girl! I'll have to punish you severely."

Barnaby, torn between amusement and anger, shrugged his shoulders.

"Good Lord, she's hopeless. A voice crying in the wilderness."

"I told you she was pure period," Emma said, making no attempt to hide her laughter. The earnest little walk, the canvas bag of specimens, the morning of healthy country air, and now this helpless attempt to curb the wild birds she had thought she had already tamed.

"What can one do?" said Barnaby.

"Give her a chance!" That was Dudley's voice, slow and deep with anger. "What do you expect? You – and that flighty wife of yours – have done this to your children, you've let them run wild, taught them no manners, filled them with complexes, and then you expect a nice decent person to instantly be able to cope with them."

For a moment Dudley, unexpectedly full of indignation, glared at his brother, his pale blue eyes protuberant, his cheeks flaming. Then, as if overcome by his surprising behaviour, his eyes dropped, the old bashful diffident look came over his face and he mumbled, "Sorry for that outburst. But it's true, you know."

"It's absolutely true," Barnaby said humbly. "I don't deny any of it, particularly my share."

Dudley patted his back with affection.

"It isn't your fault, old chap, except for choosing the wrong women. But perhaps you've got the right ones now." His glance slid shyly to Emma. "Emma, and – and Louisa. She asked me to call her that." Dudley was blushing in earnest now. "She's got quite a lot to her. I'd give her a chance."

"All right," said Barnaby abruptly. "I'll fix this mêlée."

He bounded upstairs in the direction of the storm centre. Dudley looked apologetically at Emma.

"She's only got that dog, you know. That's all she has in the world. A dog."

# 9

THERE was still the long afternoon stretching ahead. Emma, who had explored the house that morning, and found that the second flight of stairs led to two roomy low-ceilinged attics filled with a miscellany of junk, including children's playthings, an old rocking-horse, a wooden cradle, a collection of faded and worn toys, suggested that Maggy and Dina should go up there to play. It was raining again, a thin depressing drizzle that veiled the fields and trees, and brought a premature dusk. Louisa's eyes were still reddened from the tears of humiliation or unhappiness she had shed, and the children, although subdued by their father's scolding, had a look of smouldering trouble.

The attic suggestion, however, was enthusiastically seized on, and they all clattered up the stairs and began to explore the dim dusty rooms.

"No one else has ever let us come up here," Maggy said. "What will we play, Dina? Oh, there's a horse. Shall we fight battles?"

"No," Dina murmured dreamily. "I want to play with this old cradle. Look, it's made of wood. It rocks. It's even got a lid. Do you suppose there's a baby shut inside?"

"You mean one strangled at birth?" said Maggy dispassionately. "Let's look. Oh, no. There's only clothes. Dina, you be the baby and I'll be the mother and rock you to sleep."

"Oh, yes, let's," said Dina, and her face was round with happiness at last.

Emma beckoned to Louisa.

"This is the first time I've seen them behave like children. They'll be all right for an hour or two. Let's go down and have a rest by the fire. I'm sure you must be tired."

Louisa followed her gratefully, tears gleaming again in her anxious brown eyes.

"Actually I am rather. That scene before lunch – I was *so* ashamed. Mr. Court will think I have no control at all over the children."

"They have to get used to you," Emma said rather lamely.

"Yes, I know that." Louisa was rapidly regaining her eager determination to be a success and indispensable in the household. She followed Emma into the drawing-room, where the fire was burning with a cheerfulness that dispelled the gloom, and sitting down grew garrulous.

"You're all so kind to me that if I can manage the children I'll *adore* being here. Your husband, if you don't mind my saying so, is an absolute darling. Do you know, when I was upset before lunch he patted me on the shoulder and kissed me!" The pink was bright in Louisa's cheeks, her mouth soft with pleasure. "Oh, I know he only meant to *comfort* me, Mrs. Court, but he really has a way with him, hasn't he?"

"He has indeed," Emma murmured, wondering if Sylvie's kisses had been of this nature, also. Barnaby had obviously gone through life thoroughly enjoying his way with women. Perhaps being amused, perhaps even a little derisive, when they instantly fell for him.

"Rupert, too, is so amusing. But Dudley" – Louisa's eyes grew dreamy – "is quite different. Not nearly so handsome or gay, but in his own way so sweet. Do you know, I think some time a woman – you know, a bold scheming type – must have *frightened* him to make him so shy. But then I like shy men. I think there's a great deal more to them, really." Louisa's eyelids flew up in alarm. "Oh, not that I'm criticising your husband, Mrs. Court, but one could hardly call him shy."

"No, one couldn't," Emma agreed, thinking that her part in the conversation was going to be limited to meek admissions of Louisa's rightness. She was rapidly regretting her friendly impulse to make the silly little thing feel at home and happy. One wouldn't have realised she would be quite so naïve and inane. And scheming. . . .

"But Dudley," Louisa went on, " – he asked me to call him that – made it seem that he encountered us by accident this morning although I know really he had intended it. He was *enchanted* by my interest in botany, and told me just where to look for interesting specimens. Not only that, but he wanted to know *all* about me, where I lived and what family I had and so on. When I told him that Daddy died when I was ten and Mummy when I was seventeen he was *so* sympathetic. He said he knew what it was like to lose a loved mother. I say, Mrs. Court, am I boring you?"

"On the contrary, I'm fascinated," Emma said. Her innate kindness made her instantly repent her sarcasm, which, anyway, Louisa had not noticed, and she had said conversationally, "We were singing the hymns Dudley's mother used to sing when you came yesterday. He seems sentimentally attached to them." One could not imagine Barnaby or Rupert with a little dove-like mother who sang *Shall we gather at the river*. But Dudley, yes. Dudley, large and awkward, still, at forty, inclined to blush, and obviously full of repressed emotions. . . . Dudley who had been so distressed to discover that all Louisa Pinner had to love was a dog. . . .

Louisa had clasped her hands.

"Oh, how *moving*!" she said softly. "Oh, I do think——"

"What do you think, Miss Pinner?" Emma asked, as she paused.

The brown eyes, eagerly roving round the room, came back humbly. "I'm going to be so happy here!" Miss Pinner breathed. "And please call me Louisa. Dudley does."

At five o'clock Barnaby left his study and came in, smoothing his ruffled hair, looking tired but relaxed and content.

"That's done," he said. "Victim murdered, clues laid."

Louisa gave a pleasurable scream, and Barnaby said lazily, "It's a satisfying occupation, murdering nasty people." His eyes flickered over them, gleaming faintly. "What are you girls doing?"

Emma wanted to say that she was regretting that Dudley, whom one had thought disliked women, should fall so unexpectedly for this small, colourless, rather sly person whom he thought needed protecting. . . .

"Being very lazy," she said casually. "The children are playing in the attics. They're entranced with that old wooden cradle. Whose was it?"

"Great-grandfather's, I believe," Barnaby answered, and Emma, staring unbelievingly at the haughty marble nose poked round the door, hooted with laughter.

"Oh, no, he was never rocked in a cradle!"

Barnaby ruffled her hair. "Even more sinister things than that have been rocked in cradles. Ah, here's tea."

Mrs. Faithfull, small and silent, had come in with the tea tray. She never spoke, Emma realised, unless it was necessary, so that one scarcely was aware of her hostility, but it was there. One sensed it in the withdrawn little face, the myopic eyes that avoided one's glance. She's waiting, Emma thought, until we all go away and leave her in peace with her adored Dudley. Because obviously he was the person she cherished. One had only to see the secret softening in her nut-like face when he came into the room, her unobtrusive but watchful attention to his requirements.

Dudley, still dressed in his shabby, shapeless tweeds, had followed her into the room, his big gentle face beaming in anticipation of tea, and as he sat down Mrs. Faithfull looked critically at his feet.

"Your boots are wet and muddy," she said in her high, sharp voice. "Take them off. You'll catch cold." But her tone was that in which she might speak to an adored child.

Dudley shrugged in embarrassment. But he obediently followed her out of the room, and presently came back in carpet slippers, for which he apologised.

"Nags at me," he complained. "Don't know how I stand it."

His gaze shyly sought Louisa's, and to his obvious delight she playfully wagged a finger at him.

"I expect you spoil her shamefully. So what can you expect?"

"Ah, tea," said Rupert, coming in rubbing his hands. "I need this. Had quite a session at the pub. Celebration, you know. I must put in a call to Scotland, too. Barnaby, can you recognise me in this rôle?"

"Scarcely. It makes you damned dull. Better give the children a call, Miss Pinner."

74

There was no need to do this, however, for the children were coming. There was a great deal of giggling and scuffling in the hall, and suddenly they appeared. It was a stage entrance, for they were dressed in adult clothes which apparently they had discovered in the attic. Maggy wore a green silk evening dress, elaborately ruffled and extremely decolletté. The skirt trailed behind her as she teetered on high heels, the neckline exposed the greater part of her own homely knitted sweater. On her head was perched a red-velvet toque with a curling osprey feather, and over her arm, with studied negligence, she carried a dirty white ostrich-feather stole. The whole effect was comic, incredibly vulgar, and extremely clever.

Dina was less obtrusively dressed. Her main garment was a quite shabby, dark-red coat of a much later period than Maggy's finery, and although she could not resist the lure of high heels and wore, incongruously, a pair of tarnished silver evening slippers, the navy-blue beret she wore and the shabby handbag she carried were quite cheap and simple.

Both little girls, after a moment of solemnity, had burst into mad giggles.

"We're visitors," Maggy announced.

"We'd like to be asked to tea," Dina said primly. And the gale of laughter swept them again.

"Oh dear!" Miss Pinner exclaimed. Her eyes darted round nervously to see what the effect of this masquerade was on her employers.

Emma jumped up. "Why, of course you shall be asked to tea," she said warmly. "Though really, madam, in this weather, that green silk gown. . . . A little unsuitable, don't you think. Your sister, now, shows much better sense. At least she wears a coat——"

She stopped, aware of the way the men were staring at the children. Not in amusement. No. Barnaby's narrowed gaze was unreadable, Rupert's puzzled, Dudley's showed plain revulsion. It was Dudley who got to his feet and pointed to the door.

"Go and take those disgusting clothes off at once!"

The giggles died. The children looked at Dudley in astonishment. Maggy said, "But we only dressed up. We

75

found all these masses of clothes——" Her mouth grew mutinous. "Miss Pinner said we could."

Louisa made a vague negative gesture. Dudley said, "Miss Pinner said nothing of the kind. She told you to play in the attics, not to wear dirty and disgusting clothes. Go and take them off."

Rupert suddenly gave his hearty peal of laughter, as if he had just had a secret and amusing thought.

Barnaby said quite mildly, "Yes, run along and get tidy for tea. You've had your fun." But his brows were still drawn, in perplexity or some other emotion that Emma could not identify.

Louisa jumped to her feet and agitatedly hustled the indignant children out of the room. Dudley subsided, his face still flushed with whatever emotion had caused his outburst.

"A travesty of decency," he muttered. "Sorry if I was too harsh, Barnaby."

"What I can't understand," said Barnaby, "is where those incredible garments came from. Dina's were harmless enough, but Maggy's! They certainly didn't belong to Mother, and I can't even imagine our grandmother wearing anything quite so vulgar, even if the period tallied. Those things looked more like the twenties to me."

"Rather intriguing, what?" Rupert murmured, caressing his moustache.

Dudley gave an embarrassed laugh. "I've been meaning for years to clean out those attics. Lot of useless junk up there. One never knows where it comes from."

He had recovered from his outburst. Emma realised that he must be a little given to them, which was not surprising, since his shyness must cause him to bottle up a great many emotions. She remembered that even on the children's arrival two days ago he had encouraged them at once to put on jeans and look like boys. Evidently he had a phobia about women's clothing, particularly finery. That was something Louisa would have to cure. Though with her meek, sparrow-like taste she was not likely to offend.

It was a pity, though, that the children's fun had been spoilt. It seemed that there was no middle state for them. Either they were wildly excited or plunged in sulky gloom. Gloom became uppermost during tea, but later, when they went upstairs for their bath, there began another of their periods of noisy intractability.

Emma, fearing more helpless tears from Louisa, which would be really too boring, went up intending to impose some discipline. But in the passage she came upon the little heap of discarded clothes, the flamboyant green silk dress, the faded and dirty toque, almost pathetic in its now limp vulgarity, the inconspicuous, shabby, dark-red coat and beret. On an impulse she picked them up and went on up to the attics with them. Where had the children found them, and were there more of these interesting relics to be discovered?

It was almost dark in the attics and the lights did not work. But there was, curiously enough, a stump of candle on the window ledge, and this Emma lit. The frail flame threw a wavering light over the chests and trunks, the drunkenly upside-down tables and chairs, the dusty pictures and packing cases. One of the trunks, the largest, stood open, and the air was full of the musty smell of old used clothing.

This was where the children had made their rich discovery. Emma stood looking at the tumbled mass of materials, silks and velvets in rainbow colours, wilting feathers, shoes with spindly heels. Period early 1920, she decided, gingerly lifting out a black velvet gown, and studying its design. Then the clothes must have belonged to the boys' mother. But they said she had been a quiet and gentle little person. One imagined her in soft greys and fawns. Not by any stretch of imagination did one see her in these ostentatious and tasteless clothes. Then where——

Emma's thought broke off. She dropped the gown she was holding and stood quite still. She was not alone in the attic. She had not so much heard a sound as sensed a presence. There was a shadow, the almost inaudible sound of breathing. She was being watched.

Or had she imagined it? For when she said lightly, "Is there someone there? Who's hiding?" there was no answer.

She took a step forward to look into the other room. At the same moment the candle went out.

A gust of wind shook the house. The wind had risen and she hadn't noticed. Of course that was why the candle had gone out. The room was full of draughts.

77

And the darkness was somehow full of menace . . .

Without moving from where she stood, Emma turned her head. It was too dark to be sure, but again a shadow seemed to move. She had the overwhelming sensation of being watched. And all at once panic gripped her. She picked her way towards the doorway where dimly the light from the stairs showed. Stumbling against a trunk she bruised her leg. The clatter, in the stillness, seemed appalling. Then she reached the door, the safe, lighted and empty stairway, and she fled. The smell of the blown-out candle was still in her nostrils as she reached the first floor.

To discover who had lurked so secretly in the attic one had to see who was still innocently downstairs. Barnaby would be, she prayed. It was so terribly important that it should not be Barnaby who, for some mysterious reason, had refused to make his presence in the attic known. Dudley and Rupert would be down there, too. Mrs. Faithfull, Angelina, Willie . . . Louisa and the children. . . .

It was Louisa who delayed her by appearing abruptly from the bathroom, flushed and distraught.

"Oh, Mrs. Court, the children! Really – unbelievably naughty——"

She was a little incoherent, and in her now familiar state of incipient tears.

"Maggy!" she gasped. "Talking such nonsense. And water everywhere."

The immediate trouble dispelled Emma's panic. She marched into the bathroom, which was practically awash, and demanded of the two little girls, uproariously sharing the big bath, "What's going on here? Who made all this mess on the floor?"

"Maggy!" said Dina. "She was being a whale."

Maggy turned up her wet impudent face.

"I love you too much . . ." she chanted.

"So I am going away . . ." Dina finished in a sing-song voice.

"What *is* this nonsense?" Emma demanded impatiently.

"It's not nonsense. It's real. I love you too much so I am going away. It's what people say. It's silly, I think."

"*Who* says it? Maggy, who says it?" Emma was ashamed of the urgency of her voice. But for a moment, Josephine and Barnaby – or was it Sylvie and Barnaby – flitted through her mind.

"I don't know," Maggy answered airily. "Just people."

"But how do you know anyone says it?"

Maggy looked at Dina. Dina, inevitably, began to giggle. Then both of them, skinny, spider-limbed, with dripping black hair, dissolved into irrepressible laughter.

Emma looked helplessly at the more helpless Louisa.

"What is this they're talking about?"

"I don't know. They say it's a song they made up. They've been singing it all the evening. Mrs. Court, I don't want to have to call their father——"

"And you won't have to," said Emma firmly. She plucked one squirming body after the other out of the bath, then seized a bath towel and muffled Maggy's protests by vigorously rubbing her head and face. Louisa had sense enough to perform the same service for Dina, and all at once, as one had expected, the fragile balloon of their excitement collapsed and they were trembling and shivering.

"It was *fun* dressing up!" Maggy whimpered. "Why was Daddy cross?"

"Daddy wasn't cross, darling."

"Yes, he was. I saw his eyes."

"I liked the little brown cradle," Dina whispered. "Can we play with it again?"

"Perhaps we'll bring it downstairs," Emma suggested. "And I think you're wrong about Daddy being cross, Maggy. It was Uncle Dudley."

But Maggy shook her damp, rat-tailed head stubbornly.

"No, Daddy," she insisted. "Daddy."

So it was too late, when at last she went downstairs, to see who had not been there while she was in the attic.

Barnaby did not give her any time that night to brood, for he said on a sudden impulse, "Let's go to London tomorrow. I've got some business to attend to. You can shop and call on Aunt Deb. Then we'll do a theatre and have dinner."

"That sounds like heaven."

"I didn't realise this place had got you down that much. You look as if you've been granted a reprieve."

"It isn't that. It's just that I feel I'm sharing my husband

79

with the whole world." She was glad she had hesitated, and not said "other women" or "ghosts" or any of the other words she might have used.

"You're not, you know. Are you thinking of those absurd clothes the children found? Rupert and I suspect" – his eyes twinkled – "that my father must have been hiding a mistress. It's the only way we can account for those extraordinary garments."

"But why leave them here?" Emma asked.

"That's the mystery."

"Dudley knows," Emma said suddenly.

"I believe he might. Perhaps the old boy was a little ostentatious about his affairs and upset Dudley's sense of nicety."

"As naturally it would," Emma said.

Barnaby's eyes glinted with amusement.

"I believe you're a little prudish yourself."

"I am not! I——" Then she realised that he was teasing her, flushed angrily, began to laugh, and was in his arms. There were no more questions to be asked. The world had stopped rocking again. There was nothing but this all at once familiar and intense delight.

There was the question, of course, as to whether Louisa could be left unsupported for an entire day and half the night, but Barnaby said cheerfully that it would be good for her. Knowing she had to cope would make her cope. Anyway, what was his wife, a wet nurse to Louisa Pinner?

Louisa herself promised eagerly that all would be well. Dudley, she said primly, would help her. The children were quite subdued that morning, so perhaps they would remain in that state all day.

Nothing, thought Emma, was more unlikely. But all at once it didn't matter. Today she was Barnaby's wife, and belonged to no one else at all.

They called first at the flat where Mrs. Clack, doing a little desultory dusting, exclaimed in surprise,

"Why, I thought you'd gone to Spain!"

"Not yet," said Emma. "We've been in the country." She wandered into the room where she had first met Barnaby, shifted Boswell's *Johnson*, which had stubbornly climbed back on to the same chair, and sat down. Mrs. Clack, unaware of her departure from the kitchen, was still talking.

"Well, I declare! In all that rain. Gloomy, I calls it. Now bull-fighting would be another thing——"

Barnaby came in and said, "You have that look on your face."

"What look?"

"The one you ensnared me by. I must bring you here more often."

"It must be Boswell's *Johnson* who gives it to me. Is Mrs. Clack going to be here all morning?"

"She's leaving immediately. I've given her the morning off."

"A sort of royal holiday?"

"Something like that. We have a honeymoon to get on with."

Mrs. Clack called shrilly, "I've just dropped everything like you said. Good day." And the door banged.

"Oh," Emma murmured presently. "Do you think we should turn Mr. Johnson's head the other way?"


So that when she visited Aunt Deb she was able to say with emphasis, "But I'm very happy," and then, almost involuntarily, "I'm so happy I'm a little scared."

Aunt Deb watched with bright discerning eyes.

"It was just all those things you told me in your letter. I must admit you've taken them very well. Not every man could get away with saddling his wife with two children of a previous marriage on her honeymoon."

"Not every man is Barnaby."

Aunt Deb snorted. "Oh, you're love-struck. Not that I blame you. The man has a mesmeric power. But I told you not to trust him."

"He didn't tell me about Josephine and the children simply because I wouldn't listen to him. I kept saying 'No past, the present is ours and all we need.' Because I knew a man like Barnaby must have a past, and I really didn't want to hear it. It wasn't to be any part of his and my life – at least, that's what I thought. I suppose I was very naïve, a kind of Mrs. Malaprop. 'Let us not anticipate the past.'"

Aunt Deb gave her cosy, appreciative chuckle. "I think you may handle him, my dear. Keep him in love with you."

"Yes," Emma breathed. "Yes, that's what I must do."

"Well, then, tell me all about everything."

Some time later Aunt Deb gave her considered verdict.

"Of course the mother can't be dead. Maggy is obviously the kind of child who builds herself up by being dramatic. I know South America sounds far-fetched, but if instead Josephine were dead, whatever would be the point in Barnaby concealing the fact from you?"

"What indeed?" Emma murmured, but again a tantalising vision of the delicate-faced girl, perfumed and gay, seemed to hang before her.

"As for this Sylvie, I'd say she was an empty-headed little creature who found she wasn't getting anywhere with any of the men, so walked out in a fit of pique."

Suddenly the children's silly chant last night echoed in Emma's head. *I care for you too much so I am going away. . . .* But when would they have heard those words, and why remember them suddenly yesterday?

"Yes, I expect that's exactly what happened," Emma agreed. Everything was so vague, so half-realised, Mrs. Faithfull's cryptic references to "the pretty ones", the children's chatter about Sylvie's tears. Dudley's suspicion of women which did not extend to the plain prim kind like Louisa Pinner. . . .

"You'll find nothing will happen," Aunt Deb said disappointedly. "Such a pity, such a perfect setting for a melodrama. But do tell me if Josephine, at least, turns up."

Emma wondered why, suddenly, a shiver of apprehension went over her.

The next morning Louisa reported that all had been well the previous day. The children had been a little out of hand, but Dudley had taken a firm line with them, and they had behaved after that. It had been a very pleasant day, she stressed in her eager voice.

But all the time Emma was aware of a suppressed agitation about her, as if something had happened which she was keeping secret. It was not until after breakfast, when the men had gone out and the children were indulging in one of their noisy games in the hall, that Emma discovered what troubled her.

Louisa leant across the table to Emma and began to whisper nervously, "Mrs. Court, a strange woman telephoned yesterday. At first she thought I was you, and she began to ask me to meet her urgently in Canterbury today. But when I explained I wasn't you she said it was you she must see. She said could you meet her in the cathedral at three o'clock this afternoon, and not to tell anyone you were coming."

Emma's heart had begun to beat rapidly. She felt cold. Josephine, she thought. Josephine at last.

She contrived to make her voice sound normal.

"But who was this woman, Louisa? She told you her name, I imagine."

"Just her first name, Mrs. Court. She said she was Sylvie."

# 10

SHE had been married only four days. It was much too soon to be keeping secrets from Barnaby. But Louisa was so emphatic about the mysterious Sylvie's injunctions that one felt, until one had seen her, they had better be obeyed.

Emma was on tenterhooks to see the girl, but was secretly appalled at her guilty feeling of relief to know that Sylvie, at least, was alive and well. She had never imagined anything else. And yet. . . .

Well, at least, she told herself briskly, now she would be able to hear the true story as to why Sylvie had left Courtlands so suddenly, and whether what the children had said about her being frightened was true.

Did this strange rendezvous in a cathedral comprise disloyalty to Barnaby? Emma told herself that it did not, for she intended to tell him all about it afterwards. In the meantime she would do as Sylvie had requested and keep silent.

It was simple enough to announce at breakfast that, having never seen Canterbury Cathedral, she planned to take a bus that afternoon and spend a short time in Canterbury. She knew that Barnaby had planned to work all day, and that he had a rule to let nothing but matters of extreme urgency interfere with his work. Nevertheless, she was relieved when he approved instantly of her plan, and said, "Good idea. Why don't you take Louisa and the children, too? It's time they absorbed some culture."

But Louisa said quickly, "Oh, if you don't mind, Mrs. Court, I had other ideas for the children. A ramble in the woods while the rain holds off, and perhaps tea in the village. I hardly think, Mr. Court, Maggy and Dina are quite old enough to *appreciate* cathedrals."

She finds lying easy, thought Emma, in sudden distaste. She's sly.

"As you like," said Barnaby indifferently.

Rupert, getting up from the table, said, "I'd drive you in, Emma, but I'm expecting a telephone call from Scotland. I'll have to hang around until it comes. Must do one's stuff, eh?"

"Of course," said Emma. "Thank you all the same."

And then Dudley unexpectedly upset the smoothness of her plans by saying, "I happen to be going into Canterbury this afternoon, Emma. I'll take you."

"Oh, that's very kind of you, Dudley. But actually I was looking forward to the bus ride——"

Emma knew that she had spoken too quickly. The quick, embarrassed flush spread over Dudley's face and he dropped his eyes.

"Of course. If you prefer the bus. I'm going, anyway—some farm business to attend to. But if you prefer the bus ride——"

"Might as well have a lift," said Barnaby without looking up.

"Yes, of course." Emma tried to make her voice warm, to make up for having hurt Dudley by her rejection of his offer. "I'd love to come with you, Dudley. If you really have to go."

Louisa, she noticed, looked extremely put out about this turn of events. No doubt she had expected Dudley to accompany her on her ramble in the woods.

But Dudley, bless his innocent heart, was looking delighted at her belated acceptance of his offer, and was saying diffidently, "As a matter of fact, I know a good deal about the cathedral. I'd be glad to show you round it myself if I have time."

It was Louisa's turn, then, to look maliciously pleased, at the same time taking the opportunity to give Emma a meaning frown, and putting her finger to her lips.

Oh, it was all a lot of unnecessary histrionics. Why couldn't this silly Sylvie come and tell everybody frankly whatever it was that had got into her last Christmas? Why make such an issue of it?

"She said not to *tell*!" Louisa whispered frantically, as soon as they were alone.

"I didn't tell, did I?" Emma was cool. "Personally I think it is all a lot of nonsense."

"She didn't seem to think so. She said it was very important. I got the impression that——" Louisa stopped suddenly and looked uncomfortable.

"What impression did you get?"

"I didn't really mean to tell you this, Mrs. Court. But I think it was something about your husband's first wife."

Emma froze.

"If Sylvie knows something about the children's mother, why this perfectly absurd secrecy?"

"That's what I can't understand," Louisa said eagerly. "You'll have to go. Won't you?"

Emma found Louisa's look of avid interest acutely distasteful. She terminated the conversation by simply walking out of the room, and there, in the hall, she almost stumbled over Mrs. Faithfull who was doing some painstaking dusting of Great-grandfather Court with a feather duster.

It occurred to her a moment later that she had never before seen Mrs. Faithfull doing any dusting. That chore had been left to the happy-go-lucky Angelina, who slopped about singing and flicking her duster indifferently at any objects within reach of her haphazard path.

Mrs. Faithfull was muttering to herself, as usual.

"You didn't mind if I let your face get dirty when you were a little boy. Eh? You were a one." She was obviously confusing Great-grandfather's cold marble features with Dudley's plump and very much alive face. Poor dear, she was getting a little odd. Emma lingered, and heard her say,

"You shouldn't be going out with women. You know you don't like it. Nasty deceiving creatures. . . ."

And then Emma knew that the old lady had been listening to the conversation in the drawing-room, perhaps deliberately listening.

"You'll get into trouble like Barnaby. . . ."

Emma, halfway up the stairs, turned and ran down them.

"Mrs. Faithfull, what did you mean by that?"

"By what?" The faded myopic eyes were on her, all expression hidden.

"By what you just said about Barnaby being in trouble?"

"Did I say something about Mr. Barnaby?" Mrs. Faithfull gave the feather duster an airy flick. "Dear, dear, you mustn't pay any attention to my wanderings."

"Mrs. Faithfull, you said quite distinctly that Barnaby had got into trouble through women."

The little sunken mouth twitched slightly. The heavy eyelids drooped in a prim way.

"Not as much as he has escaped, my dear."

"Mrs. Faithfull——" But the old lady had wandered off, tut-tutting to herself, as if Barnaby had been caught in a childish prank, and served him right, indeed. She was crazy. One had to remember that. But she had been shrewd enough to loiter near the drawing-room door to overhear a conversation. . . .

What was it that Sylvie had to tell? Tense with apprehension Emma found herself almost unable to make normal conversation with Dudley as they drove down the long straight road to Canterbury. Dudley, who was by no means an easy conversationalist, was making earnest efforts himself. He looked nicely comical in a tweed cap pulled rakishly over one eye, and a capacious, dirty old raincoat dragged on over his habitual tweeds. He was a nice kind bundly person, like an overgrown small boy, meaning well, but obviously nervous of a great many things. Life, to Dudley, was an alarming business, to be approached carefully, like a bather dipping a cautious toe into cold water. No three brothers could have been less alike.

He gave her sundry pieces of information about the farm, then made a valiant attempt to discuss the international situation. Emma suddenly burst out laughing, whereupon Dudley flushed and looked extremely hurt.

She touched his arm.

"I do think you're sweet! I wasn't laughing at you, but at myself for being so unresponsive. I'm sorry. I was pre-occupied."

"And it wasn't the cathedral you were thinking about," Dudley suggested unexpectedly.

"No-o."

"A lot of people," said Dudley, "think because I don't talk very much I'm a bit slow-witted. But I'm not – well, not more than the next man." Having made this statement, he was plunged in thought for a few moments, his plump chin sunk on his chest. Then he said, "At this stage of your life, I don't suppose you're particularly interested in cathedrals."

It was Emma's turn to flush. But she managed to say calmly, "If you mean that one doesn't go sightseeing almost instantly after one's wedding, you're right. But neither did I know I was going to plunge immediately into family life."

"My brother," said Dudley heavily, "is sometimes a devious person. But you must know that, of course."

"I've only known him for four weeks. And if you think," she added defiantly, "I'm sorry I married him, you're wrong."

Dudley turned his head to give her his wide kindly smile. His eyes were gentle. No wonder, Emma thought, that Louisa liked him. He was a nice protecting kind of person, and a woman liked that.

"You've probably a lot to learn," Dudley said. "But at least you're not another Josephine. Feather-brained. We've had more than one of that kind."

"Dudley, I believe you know much more about women than you'll admit."

He grinned. "I see things. The onlooker, you know. Where would you like me to set you down?"

Emma bit back the question as to what things he saw. Barnaby's past was his past. Hadn't she convinced herself of that yet?

"At the cathedral. Actually, it's true I'm not sightseeing.

87

I have to meet someone. I can't tell you about it. I might later. But everything is all right. Really it is."

Dudley rested his hand on her arm. "Of course it is. I never said it wasn't."

Innuendo, thought Emma. It was there all the time. From Mrs. Faithfull, from Dudley, from that woman they had met in the restaurant who had thought Emma was Josephine, even from Louisa. . . . One had the breathless feeling of a storm about to break, and yet which never was going to break. . . .

The cathedral was cool and quiet. It was just after three as Emma stood within the great doors and scanned the vast pillared space. Sylvie was blonde and pretty. She would not be hard to identify. She would be walking slowly about, waiting.

There were numbers of people strolling about, a couple holding hands, several elderly women, a group gathered round a guide who was talking in a loud, important voice. None of the women seemed particularly blonde, particularly young or particularly pretty. There was someone alone at the far end of the aisle – no, there wasn't. She had strayed only temporarily from the group of tourists, and rejoining them moved on.

Emma walked nervously up the aisle, wondering if she really wanted Sylvie to be here after all. For in a few minutes she would have received some information that might cause her intense anxiety. But how could it? What possibly could the silly Sylvie have to tell her beyond a story of flirtation with Barnaby which had come to nothing. Words better left unsaid. . . .

Now it was ten minutes past three. The colours in the great windows were dimmed by the dull day. Slow footsteps echoed on the stone floors. A boy's voice cried shrilly, "This way! This is where the bloodstains are." The tattered and mouldering standards hung motionless. The great organ was silent.

Twenty minutes past three. A verger approached and Emma went up to him.

"I don't suppose you would have noticed a young girl waiting here at three o'clock. I was supposed to meet her. I was a few minutes late."

"Lots of people come in here, miss," the old man said politely.

"Yes, I know. This girl is fair, pretty. I don't know what she would be wearing. You didn't notice anyone who seemed to be looking for someone?"

"Well, now, a few moments ago I saw someone who would fit that description going down to the crypt. She had fair hair – but she wasn't waiting for anybody."

"Oh, I wonder if that's where she meant me to meet her. Thank you very much. I'll go down."

Her own footsteps hurrying down the aisle, down the worn stone steps to the crypt. . . . The sudden forest of pillars, gloomy, shadowy, the hushed quiet. . . . Someone had once told her this crypt was haunted. . . .

An overcoated man moved from behind a pillar. He made his way up the steps. For a moment Emma thought she was alone down there. The place was so dark, so shadowy. She walked among the pillars, treading gently on the inscriptions over graves. A shuffling of footsteps and suddenly the loud confident voice of the guide told her that the tourists had found their way down here. She stood a little apart from them. A footstep suddenly sounded behind her. She turned swiftly. There was no one there. Or did someone move behind that far pillar?

*Was someone watching her?*

"Sylvie!" she whispered in sudden entreaty.

The tourists moved on with a clatter of footsteps. All at once she was quite alone. And then panic filled her. She was being watched! She was sure she was! She had innocently come here and it was a trap.

She wanted to run as hard as she could, up the stone steps, down the long aisle, out into the damp, grey afternoon, out to safety.

One didn't run in a cathedral. With desperate self-control she forced herself to climb the stairs sedately, to walk down the aisle with the thoughtful tread of a sightseer. She didn't even look back to see if anyone followed. Nobody, she knew, would follow in a blatant manner.

The old verger approached her. "Did you find your friend, miss?"

"No, I'm afraid I didn't. I can't wait any longer."

"Can I give her a message from you?"

"Oh, that's very kind of you, but I don't even know what she looks like myself."

The old man was puzzled. Emma fumbled in her bag, and dropped a coin in the box at the door. The verger bowed his head in acknowledgement. The great door opened, and she was outside.

She had time to have tea before she met Dudley. That was a good thing, because she was still, foolishly enough, inclined to tremble. She didn't want him to see her in this agitated state. One might think he didn't notice small things, but all too clearly he did. He would wonder at her upset, and instantly connect it with Barnaby. But what could Barnaby possibly have to do with Sylvie's non-appearance, and that curious awful feeling she had of being watched, not inquisitively, but in a sinister, much more deadly fashion.

It was absurd. She had imagined the whole thing. Sylvie had simply lived up to her reputation for unreliability, and failed to turn up. And that was, considering everything, a very good thing. For what could she have to tell but some trivial scandal of which one was better left in ignorance?

By the time Emma had finished her tea she had regained her composure. She was merely annoyed that the whole thing had been such a farce. When she met Dudley at the car she said gaily, "Well, I hope you had a more successful afternoon than I did. I was left to cool my heels in the cathedral alone. My friend didn't turn up."

"Oh, too bad. Are you worried?"

"Not especially. I didn't know her awfully well. Tell me what you have been doing."

Dudley, climbing in the car, proceeded to give her a minute account of his various business transactions. He grumbled about prices, the casualness of shopkeepers, and why the devil one ever indulged in the profession of farming nowadays. Lulled by this completely normal atmosphere, the peculiar half-hour she had spent in the cathedral faded and took on the quality of a dream. She hadn't known she was so sensitive to a history-impregnated atmosphere. That was all it had been.

Back at Courtlands, Louisa was in tears.

"Oh, Mrs. Court, the children have been quite unmanageable. I confess I just can't handle them."

"Where are they now?" Emma asked sharply.

"I'm afraid I've locked them in their room. I'm sorry I had to resort to those extremes, but they would never have stayed there otherwise."

"Where is their father?"

Louisa sniffed and wiped her reddened eyes.

"He went off in his car almost as soon as you had gone. As a matter of fact, I thought he'd changed his mind and gone with you. I wondered what you would do when he walked in and saw you with Sylvie."

Suddenly Emma was thinking quite unreasonably of the sensation she had had in the cathedral of being watched. Had Barnaby known Sylvie was going to be there with important information and waylaid her, then lurked about watching his wife. . . .

"It wouldn't have mattered in the least if he had seen us," Emma said coldly. "In fact it would have been a good thing. It would have shown up that silly little minx and her tricks. Why did she want to get me in there on a wild-goose chase?"

"You mean she didn't turn up!" Louisa exclaimed. "But how extraordinary! Yesterday she sounded so desperate, as if it were a matter of life and death."

"Nonsense," said Emma impatiently. "If she rings again I'll speak to her. Now let me go and see to the children."

There was an ominous silence when Emma went to the door of the children's room. The thought went through her mind that they had escaped from the window by means of knotted sheets, and run off. But when she opened the door she found them sitting quite quietly on the floor occupied with books and pencils and scraps of paper.

True, Maggy flung up a defiant head, but when she saw it was Emma she merely said, "Oh, it's you," and went on with what she was doing. Suddenly, however, a second thought came to her, and she scrambled to her feet and flung herself at Emma.

"Was she there? Did you see her? Is she coming for us?"

Immediately Dina had joined her, and the two pairs of black eyes fixed on her warily, not daring to hope, reduced all her anger to nothing.

"But, darlings, I wasn't going to see your mother. Surely you didn't think that!"

With almost comical similarity their faces closed, became expressionless.

"Miss Pinner said you weren't, but we didn't believe her." Maggy began to stub her toe in the carpet. "You wouldn't believe anything that woman says," she finished derisively. "Me and my dear little doggie!" Maggy made a rude noise, and Dina began to giggle.

Emma said sternly, "Is this the way you have behaved all afternoon? No wonder Miss Pinner was so upset."

"She was only upset over one thing."

"What was that?"

A fiendish look came into Maggy's eyes and she shook her head naughtily. Dina, looking a little frightened, said, "It was only the candle. We stuck a pin in it, and we said——"

"*I* said," Maggy contradicted grandly. "You don't need to get blamed for this."

"Well, what did you say?" Emma was trying to be patient.

"I said that one night she would find the candle burning in her room, and when it had burned down to where the pin was stuck in, at that minute she would die."

"Maggy, what an unkind thing to do! No wonder poor Miss Pinner——"

"It wasn't just an unkind thing," Maggy interrupted fiercely. "It was a *true* thing. It's a spell that comes true."

"Maggy!"

Maggy shrugged her shoulders aloofly. "It's all right. We haven't lit the candle yet. But we will, if she gets any more sick-making."

Dina said timidly, "Perhaps it's Daddy who has gone to see Mummy. He went away in the car."

"O-oo, yes!" Maggy screamed. "He went awfully suddenly, as if he were meeting a train. He'll be bringing her back. And she'll have presents for us. I wonder what she'll bring."

"A white fur muff," said Dina excitedly.

"No, she brought that last time, silly! It will be a gold watch, or diamond earrings, or——"

"Listen!" said Emma, taking both little girls firmly by their shoulders. "You're both making all this up. Why, only two days ago you were telling me your mother was dead."

She hadn't realised it was so cruel of her to take away their hopes and remind them of their fears. Their small strained faces, brought back to sober reality, were now without defence.

"We – we can't help thinking that when she never comes or writes," Maggy muttered. "Sometimes *I* think she's been dead for years."

"I don't!" Dina whispered. "I don't!"

"Oh, you!" said Maggy contemptuously, and then threw up her head to listen to the sound of a car coming down the drive.

"Daddy!" she yelled. "Come quickly! Now we'll see if Mummy is there."

By the time they had all rushed down the stairs the front door had opened, and Barnaby, with the assistance of Willie, was lifting something from the car. A long, heavy, stiff and very still object swathed in white material.

Louisa, who had also come into the hall, followed by Dudley, suddenly gripped Emma's arm.

"A corpse!" she whispered voicelessly.

Emma blindly put out her arms to gather the children to her. She felt their trembling bodies, their silence. . . .

Then Barnaby called cheerfully, "Make way in there! Grandfather has come home from the cleaners!"

It was Dudley's great cracking laugh that broke the tension.

"Ho! Ho! Ho! For a minute we thought you'd found a body, old man."


# I I


THE two marble gentlemen, long-nosed and austere, were too much. The place was like a graveyard.

Emma, watching Barnaby throwing off Grandfather

Court's shroud, said a little hysterically, "Where did you go to get him?"

"To Chatham. There's a man there who's an expert——"

"Chatham!" Emma exclaimed. "But that's farther than Canterbury."

"What about it?"

"But you said you were going to work."

"I know. I found I couldn't. And then this man rang up to say Grandfather was ready——"

"He's done a jolly good job," Dudley said admiringly. "By jove, he's covered up that crack, too. Where shall we stand him?"

"I should think here, beneath the Mons Retreat. After all, that's where he got his wound."

"Shouldn't think he'd want to be constantly reminded of that," Barnaby observed.

Dudley turned to explain seriously, "He eventually died of that wound, years later. Well, unless we disturb Great-grandfather – can't have 'em flanking the doorway like sentinels, and that old place where he stood at the foot of the stairs was dangerous. Give him a bump and he'd crash on your head."

And enjoy it, thought Emma, looking at the stern, humourless face. . . .

Louisa suddenly began to giggle.

"It's so funny, really. Everyone looking guilty, thinking it was a real body—" She stopped abruptly, remembering the children.

"Why the guilt, may I ask?" Rupert asked, strolling in. "Is someone expecting a body?"

As if it were a caller to tea, Emma thought. . . . "For heaven's sake!" she cried. "What sort of a conversation is this? In front of the children, too!"

"It's all right," said Maggy stolidly. "We can take it. We've been doing spells all afternoon. We were expecting something like this to happen."

But for all Maggy's blasé acceptance of morbid happenings, neither she nor Dina could go to sleep that night. They were constantly calling for drinks of water, for the light to be turned on because they were frightened, then to be turned off because it kept them awake, then that they were cold. . . . Emma went up and read to them for half an hour, by which time the harmless childish story had nearly sent her to sleep. But two pairs of restless black eyes still surveyed her sleeplessly from two separate pillows.

"Now I'll put the light out and you'll go to sleep," she said hopefully.

"No, don't leave us, Emma. Please!"

It was the first time Maggy had voluntarily called her by her name. Of course that could be one of her rare blandishments, but Emma didn't think so. In their insecure world, she believed that the children were beginning to cling to her – as a friend. The knowledge was unexpectedly moving.

"Well, now, look here," she said good-humouredly, "I can't sit here all night. There's no reason why you can't go to sleep."

"We're frightened," said Dina.

"You're not frightened at all. I don't believe anything would frighten you. If you can stick pins in candles hoping someone will die——"

"But we didn't *light* the candle," Dina protested.

"I wish we had," Maggy muttered. "Miss Pinner's *awful*. She's got to go away from here before she wants to stay for ever."

"For ever!" Emma echoed.

"She keeps saying how happy her dear little doggie would be here. That means she plans to stay – if she can. I'd poison her dear little doggie!"

"Emma!" That was Barnaby's impatient voice calling from downstairs. "Leave those spoiled brats and come down."

Both children shot up in bed. "Don't go! Emma, don't go!"

Emma smiled reluctantly. "The other day you hated me."

"We didn't really," Dina said.

"You're better than Miss Pinner," Maggy pronounced grudgingly.

"*Emma!*"

Emma went to the head of the stairs.

"Oh, Barnaby! The children are upset tonight."

"Seems to me they're always upset – or pretending to be."

Suddenly his careless refusal to understand made Emma

95

angry. She cried heatedly, "And wouldn't you be if you constantly expected your – someone you loved to come, and she never did. Wouldn't you make things pretty difficult for other people?"

"Oh, Lord, this myth about their mother!" Barnaby checked an impatient exclamation and came up the stairs. "I'll fix them."

Was he going to be harsh? Emma held her breath. But presently from the children's room there came outbursts of giggles, and then, for a long time, Barnaby's voice talking quietly. When at last he came out there was silence. Barnaby's face was gentle, rueful, even a little sad.

"Darling," said Emma softly.

"I've made a mess of things for them, haven't I? I didn't realise how much they missed their mother."

"Barnaby, it seems so extraordinary that she should be in South America so long, or even that she should go there at all."

"I know. But that's Josephine. Unpredictable. One wonders how good she is for the children if she does come back."

"She isn't good for them at all," Emma said soberly. "They get plunged in excitement, travel, sophisticated presents, all sorts of spoiling, and then there follows a state like this. I think she's becoming a kind of star to them, shining and unattainable. It might be better for them if she didn't come back at all!" The last words seemed to come of their own accord. How much had she said them for the children, and how much for herself who was already made constantly uneasy by the presence of this dark, beautiful, laughing, light-hearted ghost?

"But she must come!" she said definitely, and this time she knew she spoke more for herself than the children. One could not fight a ghost, but a real person, even one full of charm and glitter. . . . That was a different matter. Emma straightened her shoulders. "You must find her, Barnaby."

"Yes, I'll try." He kissed her. "Thank you," he said.

And she knew then that he understood her feelings, as much as he did the children's. She loved him dearly, and it was not only absurd, it was wicked to suspect even for a moment that as well as going to Chatham so unexpectedly this afternoon he had also followed her to Canterbury and waylaid Sylvie in the cathedral.

It was quite impossible to suggest to him that he might have done so base a thing. . . .

Barnaby did not, however, make any further attempt to trace Josephine the next day. There was no opportunity, perhaps no longer any incentive. . . .

But first came the disturbance in the night.

Emma was awakened by a soft but urgent knocking at her door. She stirred sleepily.

"Who's that?"

"It's me, Louisa. Oh, Mrs. Court, I'm frightened."

Emma sat up abruptly and switched on the light. And found that she was alone in the big bed. There was the indentation in the opposite pillow where Barnaby's head had been, and the blankets thrown carefully back. At some stage, while she slept, he had got up and left her.

"What is it, Louisa?" she called sharply. "What's frightened you?"

"Something tapping at my window, Mrs. Court. A sort of muffled sound, like gloved fingers."

The door opened timidly, and Louisa, wrapped in a cotton dressing-gown of an unfortunate orange colour, stood huddled and trembling on the threshold.

"It woke me," she said. "At first I thought it was one of the children at my door. I – I called 'Come in'." Her casual invitation to some unknown bogy seemed now to overcome her. "Just i-imagine if it had."

"What's 'it'?" Emma demanded. "A branch tapping in the wind, I haven't the least doubt. You've been listening to the children too much. Haven't you realised how naughty they are about making up things?" She had got out of bed and was pulling on her dressing-gown. Where was Barnaby? "I'll come with you and have a look."

"There are no trees as close to the house as that," Louisa pointed out. But she quite willingly led the way back to her room, hurrying ahead of Emma with little quick steps, wrapped in her hideous orange-coloured wrap, like an untidy Oriental.

In her room the curtains were drawn back, indicating how she had taken a quick nervous look out. Emma was not content with merely peering through the glass. She threw the window open and looked out boldly. The cold damp wind struck her in the face. It was very dark, although a full moon was struggling through the clouds. As Louisa had said, there was no tree near enough for its branches to touch the window-pane. But a luxuriant creeper, leafless now, grew up the side of the house, and tendrils of that reached across the window.

It did not seem likely that they could make a tapping noise. Emma experimented with a twig, and the resulting sound was so muffled as to be almost inaudible.

"It wasn't that," Louisa said, with some contempt. "It was this sort of noise." She pulled her voluminous sleeve over one hand and rapped on a table. "Gloved fingers," she said, with certainty.

"Then they were not knocking at the window," Emma said, with equal certainty. "For one thing, whoever performed such a trick would need a ladder. And anyway, it is really too improbable. I think you've either been dreaming or the sound came from somewhere else in the house."

"It didn't, I'm sure."

"Then it must have been a ghost." Emma was a little impatient. She was very tired, and Louisa at the moment, open-mouthed and a little pop-eyed, was not an inspiring sight. "Mrs. Faithfull walks about in the night, and my husband isn't in bed either. It was probably one of them you heard."

"But what doing?" Lousia demanded.

"That I really couldn't say. But do go back to bed and forget it. Nothing's going to hurt you."

"I suppose not," Louisa responded uneasily. "But the children did say someone tapped on the windows."

"Another of their tricks." Emma dismissed that, although uncomfortably remembering Dina's fear in the kitchen the other evening, when she had so carefully drawn the curtains. Of course, Maggy could have frightened Dina with her wicked stories.

But there was, too, the night when Louisa herself had tapped on the window and they had all been so curiously, somehow expectantly, startled. As if that sort of thing had happened before. . . .

98

"I'll take a quick look at the children, and then go back to bed myself," she said. "And do go to sleep, Louisa. After all, who in this house is going to hurt you?"

"Of course. That's what I say." Louisa gave the wide, eager smile that exposed her prominent teeth, and began obediently preparing for bed.

Emma, still impatient but obscurely uneasy, tiptoed along to the children's room. The moon had come out from behind a cloud, and by its light she could see quite clearly the children sleeping soundly. She listened a moment to their peaceful breathing, then quietly closed the door. And at the same moment Louisa screamed.

Even then, although it was the high-pitched scream of extreme fear, it was muffled, as if Louisa had remembered to clap her hand to her mouth to avoid waking the children.

When she reached Louisa's room Louisa was cowering in the bed, her nightgown slipping off one thin shoulder, her eyes protruding with terror.

"A face!" she gasped. "At the window!"

Emma swiftly crossed the room and once more threw open the window.

"Oh, don't! Don't, Mrs. Court!" Louisa begged.

But Emma, not allowing herself to hesitate, thrust her head out and again felt the cold wintry wind on her face. And again found that there was nothing to see but the dark trees, the still garden, the empty lawns. No one was peering from behind a tree or unimaginably flying through the air to look in at a first-floor window.

She drew back and turned to survey the white and trembling girl in the bed.

"There was someone there," Louisa insisted feebly. "It had a very white face, like a clown. Yes, it was just like a clown, black eyes and a big nose, and all this white. As if it had been dipped in flour." Louisa began to giggle hysterically.

Emma indicated the moon, free of cloud, sailing round and silver, high in the sky.

"I think you're moonstruck. Look! That's what you saw."

Louisa pointed a shaking finger.

"It was down there, at that corner. And it was laughing. The mouth was a big black hole." She covered her face

99

with her hands. "Oh, it was no moon, it was no moon."

A door opened. Rupert, looking sleepy and ruffled, poked his head out of his room.

"You girls are doing a lot of talking. Is there something wrong?"

His voice, which it had not occurred to him to lower, aroused the rest of the house, for in a moment Dudley came shuffling along the passage, and Barnaby, leaping up the stairs, was calling. "What's all the row about? Has something happened to Miss Pinner?"

Before Emma could answer, another little figure, white-haired and blinking, joined them.

"Is there some trouble?" Mrs. Faithfull asked in her high, inquisitive voice.

"It's nothing, really," Emma said quickly. "Miss Pinner thinks she saw someone looking in her window. But I've been telling her it was the moon."

Louisa had scrambled back into her orange-coloured monstrosity of a wrap, and was at the door protesting in a wild whisper, "It wasn't the moon, Mrs. Court. Whenever did anyone see the moon *laugh*?"

"I say, what did you have for supper?" Barnaby asked. "Courtlands is noted for some things, but not yet for a laughing moon."

Dudley said in some distress, "The girl has had a fright. Don't joke about it."

Barnaby strode over to the window, threw it open, and leaned out.

"Absolutely nothing," he said.

"Whoever it was – has had time to – go away by now." Louisa's voice was almost inaudible. She seemed ashamed to be making accusations in the presence of the men, but on the other hand she did not want to look a fool. Besides this, she really had had a fright. Her face was still pinched and pale, her eyes dilated. "The children," she said hesitantly, "told me the other one – I mean Sylvie – used to be frightened in the night, too."

"Nonsense!" That was Mrs. Faithfull's voice, high-pitched and querulous. "That girl never had a fright in her life. It's a pity she hadn't. Might have made her think less of herself and more of other people." Mrs. Faithfull's eyes were narrowed with dislike. "All this hanky-panky, all this fuss – looking for attention, that's all it is. You'd better all go back to bed. Miss——" Mrs. Faithfull deliberately pretended to be ignorant of Louisa's name. " – this young lady probably saw a white owl fly by. There is one sometimes. Usually only I see it. Dudley, why haven't you got something on your feet?"

Dudley looked at his large, pale, naked feet in embarrassment.

"I came in a hurry, I'm afraid. You know, Louisa, Mrs. Faithfull is probably right. It was the white owl. Or the moon."

Emma held Barnaby's hand. "I woke up and found you weren't with me."

"I couldn't sleep. I was in my study working." His voice was absent, as if he had scarcely listened to her.

Emma dropped her eyes to hide her hurt.

Lousia was saying meekly, "Perhaps you're all right, and there was no one. But I'm not going to sleep in this room again. I'm really not." Her voice began to rise hysterically.

Barnaby, in a sudden movement, took both her hands in his. He gave her his warm reassuring smile. "Of course you're not, my dear. Why, you're as cold as a frog, Emma, I'm going to work for hours. Take Louisa back to our room."

Louisa Pinner, this scared-rabbit, sly creature, to share their bed! Emma looked at Barnaby with acute resentment. Didn't it occur to him that she might have very decided feelings about their privacy, or even the memory of their privacy, being intruded on? But men, apparently, were not sentimental in that way. It might even have suited Barnaby to forget that once Josephine – no, he spoke the truth when he said he had not been at Courtlands at the time of Josephine's visit. One had to believe one's husband, or where did one get to?

"You go and sleep," Emma said to Louisa frigidly. "But I'm afraid, like my husband, I'm no longer tired. I intend to sit by the fire."

In the morning the whole thing should have been nothing but a foolish nightmare that had disturbed their sleep. But Emma, stiff and tired from dozing in the armchair by the fire while Louisa snored faintly in the bed, and Barnaby worked downstairs, felt as if the nightmare still lingered. It didn't help that Barnaby was in a gay and jovial mood, having, by his night-long work, got over the difficulty in his book, and made very satisfactory progress. When he came upstairs saying, with Rupert's heartiness, "How are my two girls this morning?" and Louisa, putting her head coyly on one side, said, "Isn't he sweet! I do think your husband is sweet!" Emma could cheerfully have slapped both their faces. She had waited all night for Barnaby to come up and now was not feeling sympathetic either about his work or his sudden good temper and blandishments.

It was raining again, and the day seemed to stretch ahead interminably. There would be the children's noisiness and naughtiness to cope with, Louisa to convince that her room was perfectly safe, unless she cared to move up to one of the attics, the moony look in Dudley's eyes as he observed Louisa to endure (how after remaining impervious to women for so long, could he fall for so silly and colourless a person as Louisa?), Rupert's heartiness, and Mrs. Faithfull's mutterered complaints to listen to. How, in face of all this, could she care in the least about a handful of imaginary characters that Barnaby was putting in a book?

But it was only that she was tired, and that the rain running like never-ending tears down the window-panes was so dreary. No one else shared her gloom. Even Louisa, whom Dudley fussed over quite nauseatingly, was feeling something of a heroine, though heaven knew how she merited that definition. And Angelina, who burst through the house with her heavy shuffling tread and her cheerful face like a gale of wind and sun, was full of garrulous conversation.

Emma heard her upstairs telling some long fanciful story to the children, and then suddenly she burst into her rich chuckles.

"Ho! Ho! Ho! Who has been playing tricks up here? What were you up to, you little devils. Bats, indeed! That's rich!"

The children came rushing downstairs full of the importance of their news.

"Angelina has found a bat in Miss Pinner's room! Ugh, we hate bats! They're bad luck."

Angelina came waddling plumply after them, her broad

face wreathed in smiles. In one hand, as if she didn't at all mind the feel of it, she carried a dead bat, its small hands curved clawlike in death.

"I found this on the floor in your room, miss," she said, looking at Louisa. "Has someone been playing a trick on you, or do you collect birds?"

At this sally the children giggled wildly. Louisa, who went rather white, said, "Oh, how horrible! The other night it was a dead mouse." She wrung her hands and looked appealingly at Emma.

Emma, momentarily, had nothing to say. A little eddy of fear had gone over her, like a cold wind touching her flesh, making it contract. Angelina carried things in her capacious pockets, she had been told; things like dead spiders, perhaps mice, perhaps bats. . . . But Angelina looked so jolly and full of fun, as if these witchlike practices could not belong to her.

Barnaby, who had just come in, had the plausible explanation.

"Why, there you are, Louisa. That's the tapping you heard. The poor thing was probably flapping about the room before it died. Didn't you see it?"

"No-no!" said Louisa shudderingly, beginning to cry. "Oh, no! I couldn't have borne that!"

Angelina looked at her with bright-eyed contempt. "It's quite harmless, miss. Poor little creature. I'll have Willie stuff it. It'll make a nice exhibit. You ought to come and see my collection one day, miss. I've got moths, butterflies, spiders, beetles, a fine speckled owl. . . ."

Barnaby had taken Louisa's hand and was laughing down at her.

"Silly little thing!" he said. "You're not frightened of those things."

Louisa sniffed. "I am. Truly I am." But her eyes grew bright with pleasure at Barnaby's attention.

Angelina went out, and Maggy exclaimed, "Was there really a bat flapping about your room last night, Miss Pinner? O-oh, I'd have screamed!"

"Don't worry. Miss Pinner did," Barnaby said.

Louisa began reluctantly to laugh. "Bats and moons and things, I must be a bit crazy."

"But why," said Emma coldly, "didn't the bat hang up-side down on the ceiling? Why did it die?"

"I suppose it was very old," Barnaby suggested. "Every-thing has to die sometime."

"But one doesn't see dead birds," Emma's voice was a little wild.

"Well, darling, what do you suggest? An autopsy?"

"I don't know what to suggest," she said slowly, and if she hadn't despised Miss Pinner's weapons she would have burst into tears. But Barnaby couldn't have two weeping women on his hands. That would be too absurd.


# 12


It was later in the day that Emma found Barnaby's brogues rather curiously placed behind the statue of Great-grand-father Court. He must have taken them off when he had come in out of the wet and forgotten about them. Emma, picking them up to take them upstairs, noticed that they were still damp, and that there was mud clinging to them. Sud-denly she realised that Barnaby had not been out of doors at all that morning. He had taken one look at the weather and said cosily, "A good sleeping day today, since I worked all night," and, after the bat incident, had retired upstairs.

Of course the shoes could have been there since yester-day. But it had not rained yesterday, and although they could have gathered mud the uppers would not have had that rain-soaked look.

Rather breathlessly Emma ran upstairs and into Louisa's room. It looked quite harmless now, the bed neatly made, the Victorian furniture conveying an atmosphere of respect-ability. But it was not the room Emma was interested in, it was the window-sill and the creeper.

Last night, by moonlight, the creeper had given an ap-pearance of extreme fragility, as if one tug would dislodge all its tendrils and bring it collapsing to the ground. But now Emma observed that the central trunk was thick and tough. It grew past Louisa's window and up to the attics. It would have been quite possible for someone nimble to climb it, and, when the alarm sounded, instead of going down it to go *up*. No one had thought of looking up.

Someone could have been crouched up there, enjoying the macabre joke, while all the fuss went on.

But in that case the horrid Peeping Tom, if indeed there had been one, must have been someone from outside, because the three men had been in the room.

On the other hand, had they been there instantly? There had been a short interval of time. It was difficult now to remember how long. Barnaby had been the last to appear. He would have had to take off his wet shoes. . . . No, no, no! That was all quite fantastic. She couldn't contemplate such a thought. Louisa had got hysterical, imagined things. How could one place faith in anything such a silly, gullible person said?

"Emma! Darling! Where are you?"

That was Barnaby calling from their room.

"Here." Emma went slowly along the passage.

"Darling!" He was lying on the bed, his hair ruffled, his eyes bright with amusement. "Are you angry with me?"

"What for?" she asked aloofly.

"For leaving you with the eager Louisa all night. But I had to. I was working brilliantly, and one can't ignore a patch like that. Anyway, she had got over her hysterics."

"You don't seem to worry over the thing that caused her hysterics."

Barnaby raised himself on his elbow. He looked interested.

"No. I suppose I don't. Does that seem strange to you?"

"I must say it does. After all, I'm not accustomed to women screaming in the night that there are faces at the window."

"One face, darling. The singular tense. You see, you all exaggerate. I'm afraid I got used to it when Sylvie was here. She started this talk about ghosts or something, and the children heard it and of course they've been repeating it to you and Louisa. So naturally she, at least, imagines she sees or hears something. I expect more sense of you."

He held out his arms invitingly.

Emma said, in a cool clear voice, "When did you last wear your brogues?"

"My brogues? Yesterday, I suppose. I haven't been out this morning."

"Then why are they wet? It wasn't raining yesterday."

Barnaby frowned. The amusement left his eyes.

"What you're suggesting isn't particularly funny."

"What am I suggesting?"

"Why, that I went for a midnight ramble, I imagine. And in passing serenaded the irresistible Miss Pinner from the creeper." Barnaby sat up. "Emma, for heaven's sake, will you stop this nonsense! If you think I'm that kind of person – but surely you can't seriously think that!"

"Why are your shoes wet?" Emma persisted.

"Heaven only knows! I suppose I walked through some wet grass yesterday and they haven't dried."

"Then why," Emma was pursuing another track, "did Sylvie say there were ghosts – or something?"

"Sylvie was a scatterbrain. I don't think she had ever been in the country in her life before. She would scream if a sheep bleated in the night, and a bird in the chimney would have made her die of fright. Besides" – Barnaby looked reflective, his eyes involuntarily softening – "she liked attention. She liked the limelight."

"She eventually ran away from it," Emma commented dryly, and wondered again what had prevented Sylvie from meeting her in the cathedral. Or had the whole thing been a hoax?

"Maybe she wasn't successful enough. Had that idea occurred to you? Oh, look here, darling, this is all a lot of fuss about nothing. Come and let me kiss you."

Emma moved towards the door. She didn't want to go out of the room. Her feet were like lead. She was going the opposite way when her whole impulse was to rush into Barnaby's arms and stop the crazy rocking of the world.

"Maybe there's too much kissing goes on in this house," she said distantly.

"You mean with Miss Pinner?" Barnaby gave his hearty roar of laughter. "But she laps it up. It makes her feel a great deal better. Just as it did Sylvie. They know it doesn't mean anything. They weren't born yesterday."

"Miss Pinner was. For that sort of thing, she was."

"Emma, darling, I believe you're telling me you don't trust me."

Emma met his gaze levelly.

"Actually," she said, "I don't think I do."

It was their first quarrel. It was terrible. Downstairs Maggy was calling excitedly, "Emma, come down. Uncle Dudley's going to play and we're all going to sing. Do come down."

It was nice, she told herself, that today the children seemed happy, nice that Dudley was going out of his way to be thoughtful and kind. Nice, too, she supposed, that Barnaby, at least, did not seem unduly concerned about their quarrel, for he came down presently and joined the group round the harmonium, and began to sing heartily with the rest.

"Come now, it isn't Sunday. No hymns today. Something cheerful. What about 'The Farmer in the Dell.' *Heigh ho, the merry-o, the farmer in the dell. . . .*"

And that was what they were singing when Willie began his frantic knocking at the door.

His normally ruddy face was almost colourless, and he could scarcely speak.

"It's a skilliton!" he kept saying. "There's no doubt, sir. I ploughed it up. In the lower field, by the copse. It be all there, skull an' all. Oh, my God, sir, it ain't nice!"

The police had to be sent for, of course. It seemed an interminable time before they came, and also before the men came back from their trip to the lower field to see Willie's pitiful find.

This was no time to harbour grievances against anybody, Louisa or Barnaby. Emma realised that someone among the women in the house had to keep her head, and obviously it must be her, for no support could be looked for from Louisa, or Angelina or old Mrs. Faithfull.

At first her only thought had been for the children. When Willie, stuttering and breathing heavily, had got out his horrible news, Emma had realised with a quick surge of anger that once again unsuitable and terrifying things were being said in the children's hearing. No one ever appeared to think of them or protect them from a succession of shocks.

Now they were like small rigid scarecrows, white-faced, silent. Emma put an arm round each while the excited talk went on. That did not last for long, for already Barnaby and Rupert were in the hall putting on coats, and Dudley, distressed and incoherent, was plunging after them.

Then Maggy said in a contained voice, "I think Dina feels sick."

Emma looked down at Dina's white, taut face, "We'd better go upstairs."

"But she won't be," Maggy added, tailing behind languidly, as if all the energy had gone out of her thin, wiry body.

Dina was, however, and presently Louisa appeared at the bathroom door.

"I think I might be sick, too," she said faintly.

"Well, go on," said Maggy interestedly.

Louisa gave her a feeble glare. "It's so awful," she began.

"Being sick?" Maggy enquired.

"No, finding that b-body, whatever it is."

Emma turned swiftly.

"Miss Pinner, we won't talk about that at all, please. It's a – a misadventure that has nothing to do with the children. I'm going to tell Mrs. Faithfull that we'll have tea upstairs this evening. The children can get undressed and have theirs in bed."

Maggy gave a small jump that failed rather miserably to express joy.

Dina, who had recovered, said with timid pleasure, "I'd like tea in bed." But Maggy was trying hard to regain her old scornful attitude.

"You only want us out of the way downstairs, that's all."

"We're all going to be out of the way," Emma said calmly. "Come along, Louisa. You're perfectly all right. See the children in to their pyjamas while I go and find Mrs. Faithfull."

In the kitchen Angelina was talking in a rapid voice that ceased instantly as Emma entered. There was a small scattering of broken china on the floor, mute evidence that another cup or plate had slipped from Mrs. Faithfull's old trembling hands. It was like fragile broken bones, Emma thought. She said briskly,

"The children are going to have their tea in bed. Miss Pinner and I will have ours with them."

Angelina gasped. "You heard what my Willie found, miss?"

"Yes, I heard. But there's no point in discussing it, is there? It's a matter for the police."

Mrs. Faithfull, whose brown face seemed to have shrunken and grown even more wrinkled, said querulously, "As if it could be a matter for this house. That field is half a mile away, near the high-road. Anybody could trespass. What a very impertinent thing for anybody to do, burying a strange body there."

"But are you sure it's a *strange* body, Mrs. Faithfull?" Angelina demanded, her brown eyes enormous.

Mrs. Faithfull turned on her with all the haughtiness of her small upright body.

"What do you mean, Angelina?"

"I was thinking – that girl last Christmas – the one that disappeared. . . ."

"Sylvie!" Emma exclaimed involuntarily.

Mrs. Faithfull, instead of being shocked, burst into a little high cackle of laughter.

"What things you will imagine! Sylvie, indeed. It might be what the little flibbertigibbet deserves, but I don't suppose it will ever happen to her. Angelina, put the kettle on. You heard Mrs. Court's orders about tea."

Mrs. Faithfull's own small crooked hands were getting out bread and butter and jam. She seemed quite intent on her task, quite unperturbed.

But there was the broken china on the floor, evidence of carelessness – or a sudden shock.

The children sat up in their respective beds, very clean, very quiet.

"I've been reading them a story," said Louisa. The book in her hands trembled. She gave Emma an anguished glance. It was obviously a great effort to her to sit still, and a still greater one not to talk volubly and hysterically about

Willie's discovery. Whose was the body? How could it have got there? Would it have anything to do with anyone at Courtlands? The questions were in her dilated eyes as plainly as if they had been written there.

Emma set the tea-tray down, and said brightly, "Hot milk and bread and jam, and then an aspirin each to make you sleep. Any protests?"

"I don't feel very hungry," Dina whispered.

"I do. I could eat a thousand pieces of bread." Maggy's bravado showed an order of courage that made Emma suddenly admire the child more than she would have thought possible. Especially since it was so obviously bravado. For she stuck at the first mouthful, and suddenly she shouted passionately, "It isn't Mummy, is it? I know it isn't. It couldn't be. I've always said she was dead, but I never really meant it. It isn't her. Is it, Emma? Is it? Is it?"

Louisa had clapped her hand over her mouth. But even then she didn't suppress her silly shocked scream.

"Maggy!" she gasped. "How *awful*!"

Emma gently took the tray away from Maggy's bed, and sat down to put her arms round the thin, shaking body.

"Maggy, darling, of course it isn't your mother. Of course it isn't. Why, only today Daddy was speaking to her solicitor and he promised to send a letter on to your mother. So any day now she'll be coming."

Maggy's hand was round her waist in a limpet-like grip.

"Is that true? Really true?"

"Of course it's true, my pet." (And heaven forgive me for lying. But somehow one has to get them through this awful night.)

Dina began to smile tremulously.

"Might we be going to Venice after all?"

"Well . . ." said Emma.

"Bags me the first ride in a gondola!" Maggy shouted.

"No, me! Me!"

"Gondolas are big enough to take you both at once," Emma explained. "More to the point, who is going to swallow their aspirin first?"

"Me! Me!" came both the voices at once. "And without milk. We can swallow pills without milk."

The crisis seemed to be over. Presently, the curtains

drawn and the children quiet, Emma left the room. Louisa waited for her on the landing.

"I must say you were wonderful, Mrs. Court, but how about when they know you were lying?"

Emma looked at her without speaking.

"Well, weren't you?" Louisa said uncertainly. "I mean, you did think yourself that – that body might be Jo – I mean, the first Mrs. Court. Didn't you?"

Emma went very white. Her voice shook so that she could scarcely speak.

"What a perfectly terrible thing to say!"

"Don't be angry. I thought——" Louisa's face was tear-streaked, scared, piteous. "Well, what is one to think I mean, she's never turned up, has she? People don't just forget their children exist. I mean, normal people——"

"Do you realise," Emma said, speaking very slowly and coldly, "that this is absolutely none of your business. I'd be very glad if you would at least keep these fantastic theories to yourself."

"I'm sorry, Mrs. Court. I didn't mean anything – anything bad." Louisa was plucking at her arm. "It's just that I got a shock."

With a great effort Emma controlled her almost over-powering desire to snatch her arm away.

"All right. We all got a shock. I shouldn't have spoken to you like that. I think we had better go down and have a drink. The men will be back any time."

The men came back just after dark.

"Police are there," Barnaby said briskly. "Everything's now under control. Lord, I could do with a drink. What about you girls?"

He seemed perfectly cheerful. That was the strange thing. As if he had been reassured about something. Rupert was whistling carelessly, and Dudley, who had got back his look of ruddy health, was stamping his boots and saying that it was a damn wet night to unearth anything, and that he didn't know what Willie had been about trying to plough in that weather.

"You – have no idea who the – the victim is?" Emma tried, rather unsuccessfully, to make her voice casual.

"Not a clue," said Barnaby. "About five feet four inches

and a lot of dark hair. And it's unlikely, the sergeant said, that the cause of death will be ascertained after all this time." He spoke almost regretfully. One would have thought his interest was quite academic, as if that poor little body had never been animated with life at all.

"I'm sorry if I sounded morbid," he added, "but it interests me. Might be a jolly good plot. Pity we can't get the cause of death. I say, don't look so shocked, you girls. All this is absolutely nothing to do with us."

Rupert gave his hearty laugh.

"Good Lord, they didn't think it had anything to do with Courtlands, did they? We haven't a Bluebeard here. At least I don't think so. The police, of course, will make a damn nuisance of themselves for a day or two."

"Yes, you'd better be on hand for that, Dudley, old man," Barnaby said. "After all, you've been around the place more than Rupert and I."

"If this happened eighteen months or two years ago any one of us might have been here," Dudley said.

"As long ago as that?" Emma said involuntarily. (Then it wasn't Sylvie. Angelina would be relieved about that.)

"They're only guessing, until they get the pathologist's report. Actually, I think the sergeant has hit on the explanation. There used to be an army camp about four miles from here. I should think some soldier has lured his girl friend to a nice quiet copse – unfortunately the copse being on our property. The thing is whether they'll ever be able to identify the girl."

# 13

In the night Barnaby said, "Can't you sleep?"

His voice, coming out of the darkness, should have been immeasurably comforting. Instead, Emma lay rigid.

"No," she answered politely.

His arm came across her. "Can I make you a cup of tea or get you anything?"

"No, thank you. I'm all right." She wasn't, of course. The tears were slipping down her cheeks, but in the darkness, thank goodness, Barnaby could not see them. What right had he to be tender to her now? she asked herself furiously. He knew it would get under her guard and make her weakly forgiving.

"Darling, you were marvellous this afternoon. I was proud of you. Louisa tells me you handled the children wonderfully."

"Only by lying to them," Emma said bleakly.

She was aware of his unspoken question.

"They thought it was their mother who had been found," she said into the darkness.

"Josephine!" His voice was incredulous. "But surely — oh, my God, surely——" He could not bring himself to put the shocking accusation into words. His incredulity and horror sounded completely sincere.

"Well, that didn't involve your lying to them," he said presently, very quietly.

"I had to tell them you had been speaking to the solicitor and would presently be in touch with Josephine. But you hadn't had you?"

"No. I hadn't. I'm sorry. I didn't think there was much use in ringing old Quantrill. He promised to let me know if he heard anything." His hand sought hers. His fingers curled into her unresisting ones. "But I promise you to-morrow I'll check again."

"Isn't tomorrow too late?" The words were out before Emma could stop them. She lay rigidly, aghast at the terrible thing she had implied. But at the same time she knew it had to be said sometime. That poor little body in the rain-soaked ground, with the mass of dark hair, and nothing else that was in any way identifiable.

Once — it seemed so long ago now — Barnaby had given her his mother's cameo, saying that as his wife she should have the single piece of jewellery that his mother had valued. But Barnaby had once had another adored wife who should have been the natural recipient of such a gift. . . .

Barnaby had moved away from her in the wide bed. She could feel that he was leaning on his elbow. His face, she thought, would look like the face of Great-grandfather Court, haughty and unsympathetic and made of marble.

"This evening," he said, "the police questioned not only Dudley and Rupert and myself, but Mrs. Faithfull, Angelina and Willie. They were interested to know whether there had at any stage in the last two years been a girl here aged about eighteen to twenty-five years. But we were all quite sure that there hadn't. Mrs. Faithfull looked after the house entirely alone during the war years and up until last year, when it became too much for her, and Angelina and Willie came. Dudley, as you know, is anti-women, especially the young and pretty ones who throw him into a complete dither. Which is probably why he has taken kindly to our Miss Pinner, who certainly has no pretensions to beauty."

"So the only one who might have been here," said Emma, as if she were working out a quite impersonal problem, "would have been Josephine."

"The police," Barnaby went on, as if he had not been interrupted, "are pretty certain their first conjecture is the correct one. The girl has been somebody's pick-up, probably when the soldiers were in camp not far away, and the poor little wretch has come to a tragic end. They are going to work on the theory of murder, but it isn't going to be easy until they have identified the body. And that isn't going to be easy, either. So Marlene or Shirley, or whoever she was, may go into another unnamed grave. There wasn't even any jewellery that might have helped identification. Teeth, of course. The pathologist will work on that." Barnaby was getting out of bed.

"Where are you going?"

He switched on the bedside light and stood looking down at her.

"It so happens I can't sleep either."

The dim light scored his face into lines. He suddenly looked much older, graver, care-worn. As perhaps once he had looked when Josephine—— Emma, unable to finish her thought, longed to put out her arms and draw him down to her.

114

But now it was too late. That terrible accusation stood forever between them. She hadn't meant it. She knew that now. Nothing would ever make her believe it, no matter how black the evidence looked.

But the thing had been said. And Barnaby had gone away from her.

"There's too much you won't tell me!" she cried out defensively. "Sylvie at Christmas time, the face Miss Pinner saw at the window, all the other things——"

"My dear, you should have been the writer, not I. It doesn't matter so much in fiction if one can't separate fantasy from reality."

But the body of the unknown girl was not fantasy, Emma told herself bleakly, as she lay alone in the darkness. Poor little creature, unwept, unmourned. The lines of Catullus, that long-ago gentleman of Verona, to his lost love, came into her head, *the long, unbroken, lonely and interminable sleeping* and *night must be endured*. . . . Poor little dead girl without a name, enduring her long night. . . .

Louisa, in the morning, announced that she hadn't slept a wink, not because anything strange had happened in her room, to which she had bravely returned in spite of her fright the previous night, but because she had been so shocked and grieved about that poor kid who had come to such an untimely end. She toyed with her breakfast, and when Maggy and Dina, as a reaction from their own shock the previous night, were more noisy and irrepressible than ever and seemed to be full of some unholy glee, tears filled her eyes and she said helplessly, "I can't cope. Really I can't."

Barnaby gave her an impatient look, but said in his most persuasive way, "Oh, come, Louisa, my dear, you can cope beautifully if you try. Think up one of your clever excursions."

Much gratified, not only by the endearment, but by the implied praise, Louisa smiled wanly. "Well – perhaps an outing would do my head good."

It was Dudley who interposed reproachfully, "Really, Barnaby, all this has been a frightful shock for these girls. I think they ought to take things quietly. If it comes to that,

I'll be responsible for the children this morning. They can come to the village with me." Then he shyly sought Louisa's eyes. "Of course, if you would like to come for the outing, you would be more than welcome."

Louisa brightened instantly. Much pleased with the tender and thoughtful treatment she was getting, she became in her own mind something of a heroine again, as if it was only natural that a person of her sensibility would feel yesterday's shock much more keenly than anyone else.

"That is *so* kind and thoughtful of you," she said, her eyes as eager as a terrier's promised a walk. "I'd love to come."

"We might even have lunch at the pub," Dudley suggested.

"Good idea," said Rupert. "They do one very well there. I'd join you, but I think I'll hang around and try to clear this business up. I'll have to break the news to Jean, too. Convince her I'm not a Bluebeard, eh? You'd better watch Dudley on the Guinnesses, Louisa. He's inclined to get out of hand."

Louisa giggled. "Oh, Mr. Court!"

"Come off it, old man," Dudley muttered in embarrassment. "I'm only trying to help."

When they had gone Barnaby said conversationally, "That's the first time I've known Dudley voluntarily take a girl anywhere. Our Louisa must have something."

"I think he's very kind and sweet," Emma said. "And Louisa isn't too beautiful to frighten him."

"You mean as Sylvie did?"

"And Josephine."

Barnaby gave her a quick sharp look. Then he said casually, "That reminds me, I have to do some telephoning."

Emma went towards him. "Barnaby, last night – I didn't mean – what you thought I meant."

"I should hope not." His voice was cold. "But nevertheless we'll do what we can to provide indisputable proof."

So he had gone away from her. And now she most desperately wanted to tell him that it didn't matter how many mysterious and unexplained things there were, nor how peculiarly stubborn he was about taking her into his confidence, she still loved and trusted him.

It was during the morning that Willie began hacking at the creeper that grew so strongly up the wall and past Louisa's window. Looking out in surprise, Emma saw that he was methodically cutting off any of the slim strong branches that might have provided a foothold.

"Willie, why are you doing that?" she asked involuntarily.

Willie lifted his head. He looked like an early Saxon, with his fair hair cut pudding-basin style, his red face and his pale blue eyes. There was no great intelligence shown in his face, but there was a shifty quality that may have been caused by bashfulness. Although how a man married to the garrulous and lively Angelina could remain bashful was difficult to understand.

"Master's orders, ma'am," he said in a surly voice.

Emma went downstairs.

"Barnaby, did you tell Willie to cut down the creeper?"

Barnaby looked startled. "No, I didn't."

"Well, he's cutting it down."

"Then Dudley has told him to. I wonder——" Emma watched the reflective glint come into Barnaby's eye. She finished the sentence he had hesitated on.

"Dudley must think it possible somebody climbed it the other night, to play a horrid Peeping Tom."

"Could be. Dudley is sometimes overcautious."

Emma said slowly, "Dudley didn't cut down the creeper for Sylvie's safety. He didn't care what happened to her, but with Louisa he does care. So he'll be able to do the kissing this time. . . ."

Barnaby shrugged. "You relieve my mind."

"I hate it all!" Emma cried violently. "Nobody is telling me the complete truth. You're all being evasive. Yes, even you. It's left to the children to hint at things – Sylvie was frightened, Sylvie cried, Sylvie suddenly disappeared. But what happened? You must know. You or Dudley or Rupert. Or even Willie. Why do you all pretend it is such a mystery? Which one of you has a guilty conscience?"

"My darling Emma, you're being melodramatic."

"Was it melodrama that made Sylvie ring here the other day to ask to see me – secretly and urgently?"

Now she had his startled attention.

"When was this?"

"You didn't know?" She was thinking of his unexpected trip to Chatham.

"How should I know?" His voice was impatient. "When did this happen?"

"The day we were in London. Sylvie spoke to Louisa. She said it was important that no one else should be told. She made an assignment with me in Canterbury Cathedral at three o'clock to tell me something important."

"And what?" His voice was hard and urgent, as if he could not wait to hear what had happened.

Emma shrugged her shoulders. "She didn't turn up. It was another myth – or I suppose you will tell me so. Or a stupid practical joke like the dead things in Louisa's bedroom. I think the police ought to be told all these things."

"You're suggesting they're connected with that discovery of Willie's yesterday? But that's fantastic. An unknown girl dead two years."

"Well?" said Emma in a hostile voice.

"You don't really care about these curious things that have happened to Louisa, and to Sylvie too, for that matter. You're only trying to tell me that you think that body is Josephine's. Aren't you?"

The bleakness of his gaze was frightening. Emma felt sick, she tried to shake her head, but failed. She heard herself saying in a cold remote voice, "You must prove to me that it isn't."

It seemed as if Dudley and Louisa and the children would never come home. It seemed even stranger that she should be eagerly looking forward to their company.

But after Barnaby had briefly reported that all his endeavours to discover Josephine's whereabouts were abortive – she still, according to her solicitor, had not returned from her South American expedition, nor sent any news – he had gone into his study and Emma was left alone until the others returned. This was not until it was growing dusk.

The children bounced in first, waving sticks of peppermint rock.

"We've eaten absolutely tons of things," Maggy said nonchalantly. "I expect Dina will be sick."

"Well, never mind," said Emma soothingly. "Did you have fun?"

"Not much. Uncle Dudley only wanted Miss Pinner. Dina and me were in the way, actually." Maggy had her most adult and blasé look. "My God, it will be awful if Uncle Dudley *marries* her!"

"You mean with a veil and things," Dina said.

Maggy darted into the dining-room, snatched the cloth off the table, and draping it over her head solemnly paraded up the hall chanting,

> "Here comes Miss Pinner
> To cook Dudley's dinner. . . ."

Inevitably Dina began to giggle, and Emma, biting her own lips, but inwardly suddenly loving Maggy for her sense of the ridiculous, said firmly, "Maggy, you're being absurd. Put that cloth back on the table at once. How can Mrs. Faithfull get the tea?"

"We couldn't possibly eat any tea." All at once Maggy was drooping. "We were given sweets and things in the parlour while Uncle Dudley and Miss Pinner went in to the bar. They said they wanted to talk. I don't know what they said. But Miss Pinner was crying again. She's always crying. And we heard people talking about the body."

"What about it?" Emma asked involuntarily.

"Oh, just that the police thought it was some girl from London. Miss Pinner's from London. We wish it had been her."

"What were you saying about me, Maggy dear?" came Miss Pinner's arch voice from the front doorway.

"Nothing," said Maggy airily. "Except I did tell Emma that you and Uncle Dudley seemed awfully friendly."

A wave of colour went over Lousia's face. Her lips quivered, showing her prominent teeth. A lock of her straight hair fell in an abandoned way over one eye. Really, thought Emma, Dudley does have the oddest tastes, poor darling, and waited for Louisa's eager revelation.

It came at once.

"Oh, Mrs. Court, we've had the nicest time. Dudley has been – well, I can't tell you just now how sweet he has been. Little pitchers, you know. But he's done me so much good, I can't tell you."

At that moment Dudley, too, appeared and put a hand briefly but possessively on Lousia's shoulder.

"Well, I've looked after the girls," he said, beaming.

"I think you've both been drinking." Emma's voice was tolerant, but inwardly she found it hard to bear their smugness. If they were in love, this hardly seemed a suitable time to show it. But how could they be in love – Louisa, beneath her fluttering Victorian ways, would have a hard mercenary little heart that had summed up all the advantages of being the mistress of Courtlands, and Dudley, who was pathologically shy of women, could hardly have been more stupid then to allow someone like Louisa Pinner to break down his prejudices.

"To be quite truthful, we have had one or two drinks," Dudley admitted. "Louisa needed them to buck her up. But she's fine now. Aren't you, my dear?"

Louisa fluttered her eyelashes and giggled.

"Any news, Mrs. Court?"

"News?"

"About the corpse?"

Emma turned on her angrily.

"Really, Louisa! In front of the children."

"Oh, I'm sorry. I didn't think——"

"Of course there's no news!" Dudley boomed. "May take weeks or months. Personally, I think Scotland Yard won't be able to crack this particular nut. If the girl was a Londoner it would take years even to trace her dentist. Where's Barnaby?"

"Working."

"Naturally. This is right up his street. The case of the unidentified—— Oh, sorry, Emma. Anyway, it's time you youngsters were in bed. You've had a good day, lots of things to eat."

"Yes, come along, children," Louisa said briskly. "Upstairs."

The children went obediently enough. Emma felt a cowardly relief that they had not asked whether anything had been discovered about their mother. A little later she heard Dina crying, but Louisa, with her new-found confidence, was able to cope with that situation, and when she came downstairs she reported that both little girls were practically asleep.

"The poor pets are worn out," she said hypocritically. "Actually, I believe I am, too. I shall have an early night."

But she did not look tired. Her eyes, full of excitement, kept darting from Dudley to Barnaby to Rupert, and every now and then the tip of her tongue moved delicately over her lips. Emma waited for the expected announcement that during the day she and Dudley had become engaged. Nothing was said, however, and presently Louisa did get up to have her early night.

"It's been a heavenly day," she said. "I suppose it's mean of me to be able to enjoy things when – oh, you know what I mean. But we can't all suffer for other people's follies, can we? And I expect that girl got what was coming to her."

"My dear Louisa, from someone with your tender heart, that sounds very callous." Rupert was making his usual hearty attempt at a joke.

"That's the sensible way to look at it, isn't it?" Dudley demanded belligerently.

Barnaby interposed, "Shall we say that as a topic of conversation this has become a little boring." When Louisa had gone out he added, "By the way, was it you who told Willie to cut down the creeper, Dudley?"

"Yes, I did." Dudley's large, good-natured face was unexpectedly stern. "I didn't tell Louisa because there's no need for her to think we took that episode seriously."

"Then you do think there was something?" Rupert asked interestedly. "I say, old boy, that's most intriguing. Which one of us is masquerading under an appearance of innocence?"

"There's no point in taking chances. It's a nasty thing to happen to a sensitive girl." Dudley was not quite meeting Barnaby's eyes. "Actually, I've never quite trusted Willie. He and Angelina – those dead bats and things – or just Willie himself. . . ." He was mumbling a little incoherently, seeking about for reasons why Willie and Angelina should be in league against any newcomer to Courtlands, so that he did not have to admit who else the culprit may have been.

In their room, Emma wanted to tell Barnaby that it seemed inevitable he was to acquire a sister-in-law shortly. But Barnaby did not come to bed until midnight, and by then her spontaneity had gone. She pretended to be asleep. The firelight fluttered in red uneasy shadows behind her not quite closed eyelids. She listened to Barnaby quietly moving about. She knew his habits now. He was untidy with his clothes, dropping them casually on chairs or even on the floor. He was also very quick and silent, at one moment being fully dressed and the next in his pyjamas. When he got into bed it was usually as if a great wind had lifted all the coverings and then settled them warmly on her again.

But tonight there was no wind, no cold draught and then the ensuing warmth. He lay quietly on his side of the bed and was farther away from her than if he had stayed downstairs in his study.

It was Great-grandfather Court beside her, cold, silent, arrogant, full of his own secret affairs which naturally he would not wish to share with his wife.

The rain patted whisperingly on the long windows, and the dying fire gave out small sounds of ash settling. An owl, perhaps Mrs. Faithfull's rare white one, called twice, and was silent. In seven hours it would be daylight. "Count the hours," Great-grandmother Court had worked into her sampler. Had they been these kind of hours, a rigid lying awake beside her frightening and unapproachable husband?

Emma moved slightly, and knew, by the cessation of Barnaby's even breathing, that he, too, was awake. Suddenly she had a crazy desire to say, "Darling, I know you didn't kill Josephine. But you know how her body got in the field. Don't you?"

The words, however, did not come. The silence between them remained unbroken.

# 14

SOMEWHERE in the night Emma came to the decision that, distasteful as it was to have to do that kind of thing, she must begin some enquiries of her own. She could not go on like this, her head in the sand, telling herself that nothing was really wrong, that all the vague happenings, even the pitiful little body in the field, were moonshine. Tomorrow she would go up to London and see Josephine's solicitor. She knew his name, an unusual one, Mr. Quantrill, because she had heard Barnaby mention it on the telephone the previous day. She had looked up the telephone book, and found him listed; A. M. Quantrill, Bedford Square.

If he could tell her nothing other than the story of the South American expedition (so unlikely for a woman like Josephine, delicate, pampered, luxury-loving), there would be nothing more she could do. But at least, unpleasant as it was to do so, she would have checked on Barnaby's story.

The day began badly when she woke, headachy and unrefreshed, with a vague memory that at some time in the night she had heard a puppy crying, to find Barnaby gone, and the children rapping impatiently at her door.

The fire lay in cold grey ashes in the grate, the room was dark and wintry, the diamond shine of rain sparkled on the window-panes.

"Emma! Emma, can we come in?"

At least, Emma thought wearily, the children seemed to have overcome their hostility towards her, but that may have been only because she was the better of a poor alternative. Before she could answer, however, they had both come bursting in, still in their pyjamas, Maggy's hair hanging round her face in rats' tails, Dina's tousled and untidy.

"Why aren't you dressed?" she demanded.

"Because we can't find Miss Pinner, and we don't know what to put on." Maggy, as usual, was the spokesman. Her black eyes were glittering with excitement. "We wanted to come and tell you ages ago, but Daddy said we weren't to wake you."

Emma felt a pang of gratitude for that small thoughtfulness of Barnaby's, and thought helplessly how impossible it was to stop loving him and, in consequence, being hurt by him. Being in love made one so pathetically vulnerable.

"Miss Pinner has *gone*!" Dina now burst out in suppressed excitement.

"Don't be absurd!" Emma exclaimed sharply. "How could she be gone?"

"She has. Her bag's gone, too. Daddy says she must have got up and caught the early train. He's furious!"

Emma leapt out of bed and caught up her wrap.

"I don't believe a word of this," she said.

"It's true, it's true!" squealed the little girls. "She's left a note to say."

Emma swept along the passage to Louisa's room. She didn't know what she expected to see, certainly not the complete normality of the room, the neatly made bed with its white tasselled spread, the tidy dressing-table, the absence of any sign of occupation.

This was all in character. Louisa Pinner was a neat, methodical person. Before her departure from any room she would always see that it was left spick and span. As the next person would like to find it, would be her motto.

But that was assuming her departure was normal. This had not been a normal departure. She had apparently crept secretly out of the house before daylight, planning to walk to the station. It was hard to believe that under such circumstances she would take pains to tidy her room first.

Unless she had not slept in it last night. . . .

Emma flung open the wardrobe and saw it dark and empty of the unobtrusive colourless clothes Louisa had used to wear. She went to the dressing-table and pulled open drawers. All empty, mute evidence of Louisa's methodical packing.

But why? Why? Yesterday she had been so happy and excited, obviously having great trouble in suppressing the news that Dudley had asked her to marry him. She *wouldn't* run away on the verge of such a splendid thing happening to her.

"Where are the men?" Emma demanded of the little girls who were pleasurably gaping at her back.

"Downstairs. They said we weren't to wake you. Daddy said he didn't believe the letter."

"*What* letter?" Emma was full of exasperated bewilderment.

"The one Miss Pinner left, of course. It was for Daddy. He wouldn't let us see it. I expect it was all love and kisses or something like that."

"Maggy!"

Maggy, unabashed, began dancing round the room chanting,

> "Poor Miss Pinner
> Will get a lot thinner
> If she misses her dinner . . ."

and the gale of giggles swept the little girls again.

Emma said firmly, "I expect Miss Pinner has simply gone back to London to get her dog. Uncle Dudley has probably told her she can have it here. Run along and get dressed while I go downstairs and——"

"It isn't that, madam," came Mrs. Faithfull's voice from the doorway. "She's gone. Like the other one."

There was satisfaction in the old lady's face. Her eyes snapped with unaccustomed brilliance. She nodded her little head and said, "Good riddance to her! She was up to no good. As you would have found out before long, if I may say so. A schemer. Like the other one. I wouldn't fret about her. Let her go."

It sounded as if Mrs. Faithfull had been expressing her obvious satisfaction in this monotonous chant all the morning. It would not be surprising to discover that she had used some mysterious and sly means of persuasion to get Louisa out of the house. But just then Emma had no time for Mrs. Faithfull and her fancies. She hurried downstairs in search of Barnaby.

He was in the dining-room. Breakfast was still on the table. Emma, hesitating at the door, noticed that Barnaby was eating, but that Dudley had obviously made no attempt either to sit down or to eat. He was pacing up and down, his face flushed with distress, his plump hands clenching and unclenching. His hair was disordered and he had not yet shaved. He looked, too, as if he had been weeping.

Barnaby was not similarly distressed. He was trying, Emma saw at once, to keep his patience and be sympathetic with his brother's obvious suffering.

"But I tell you, I've never even looked at her twice, much less given her any reason to think that I cared about her. I simply don't understand that letter and all I can say is that she is a silly, hysterical and unbalanced female."

"Expressed very succinctly," murmured Rupert from behind his paper. "I'll leave you two to fight this out. Louisa was not mine. The straight and narrow for me, even had I been enticed, which I was not." He strolled out with his jaunty air, glad to escape, Emma thought, for he looked at her rather guiltily as he passed.

Dudley noticed neither his departure nor Emma at the door.

"What about Sylvie?" he flung out accusingly.

"Sylvie was a charming little flirt and knew all the rules of the game. I still don't know why she left us so abruptly, but my own hunch is that she had other more interesting fish to fry. Anyway, Sylvie is nothing to do with Miss Pinner."

Here Emma decided that it was politic to make her presence known, and calmly entered the room.

"My belief," she said, as if she had been a participant in the conversation, "is that it's this house that's hostile to women. We all feel it in varying degrees, and gradually one by one we reach breaking point. Josephine, Louisa, me next?" Then she laughed, lightly dismissing her theory, which privately was not an idle one. "Well, what's all this about Louisa walking out on us? I thought, apart from certain unexplained incidents, she was happy here."

"So did I," Dudley declared. "Why yesterday——" He swallowed convulsively. His protruding accusing eyes were on Barnaby again.

"The children," said Emma, "tell me she left a letter."

"She did." Barnaby's answer was brief.

"Then can't I see it?"

Barnaby shrugged his shoulders.

"If it weren't in her handwriting, I'd believe it was a fake. As it is, she's copied it from Elinor Glyn or Ouida, or some other melodramatic female fiction writer." He tossed the piece of notepaper over to Emma. His blue eyes were mocking.

Emma read the words inscribed in the prim tidy handwriting.

"Dear Barnaby,

I love you too much, so the only fair thing to do is to go away. I cannot tell you how much it grieves me to leave the children and a job half done, but this must be the better of two evils.

I am catching the early train this morning. I am too unhappy to write more.

Your
Louisa."

"It comes out of a cheap novelette," Emma said slowly.

"True. On the other hand, it is essentially our Louisa."

Dudley found Barnaby's light scathing tone intolerable, for he turned on him angrily.

"What right have you to talk like that? Our Louisa! She wasn't yours. She was mine."

"I'm all for that theory," Barnaby said mildly. "But the lady obviously thinks otherwise."

"Why?" Emma demanded perplexedly. "She was with Dudley all day yesterday. She seemed so happy when she came home."

"Dudley," she went on, "yesterday did you ask Louisa to marry you?"

Dudley had his back to her. His broad shoulders were shaking.

"More or less." His voice was scarcely audible.

Emma could imagine his embarrassed approach to such a momentous subject, and her sympathy for him grew.

"She understood what you meant?"

"Oh, yes. She said something about not being in too much of a hurry – after all, we had only known each other a week. But I took it as encouragement. So that this letter this morning, and her going away——"

"Better have a brandy, old man," Barnaby suggested. "Women are the very devil. I thought you knew that."

Dudley gave him one look of perplexed hatred and suddenly plunged out of the room. His heavy footsteps echoed across the hall. The front door banged after him. He had gone hatless and coatless into the rain. His exit was almost as dramatic as Louisa's and just as foolish. But it had not meant to be either thing. He was running away to hide his sorrow and his sudden hatred of his brother.

Poor Dudley. But at least his enemy was a visible one. All Emma's were elusive; the dark mysterious Josephine, the blonde Sylvie, the eager-eyed, rabbit-toothed Louisa — oh, no, surely Louisa was too much. Verging on absurdity, indeed.

Emma, with Maggy's welcome sense of the ridiculous, almost began to laugh.

"What's amusing you?" Barnaby asked.

"You ensnaring Louisa. That couldn't have been much fun. She'd be so boringly susceptible. I'm sure you didn't do it deliberately."

"Don't talk such damned nonsense! You know very well I did nothing of the kind. Good grief!" He obviously dwelt a moment on the thought of Louisa in his arms. He sighed in bewilderment.

Emma said, "Well, willy nilly, she's been ensnared. You underestimate your fatal charm. And it's entirely too bad about Dudley. We'll have to cheer him up."

"I can't help the wretched girl's stupidity," Barnaby said in exasperation. "One can only say thank goodness she's had the sense to go. Anyway, it's partly your fault as far as Dudley is concerned. You encouraged him to come out of his shell, and look what you found."

Emma had a vision of a soft, defenceless, amiable, turtle-like creature boldly discarding its shell and beginning its hopeful journey. The mock turtle, she thought ridiculously who wept and wept. . . .

"And aren't you going to have some breakfast?" she heard Barnaby saying. "Anyway, I thought I gave orders that you weren't to be disturbed."

Warmth stirred foolishly in Emma's heart. She was like Dudley herself, hopefully seizing on straws. But at least, in spite of everything, Barnaby had thought about her and was being kind. In spite of those unforgivable things she had said.

"We seem to be speaking again," she said casually, going to the sideboard to pour coffee.

"We never stopped speaking. Oh, I admit some of our utterances were – tactless – to say the least." He was looking at her, his eyes not merry, but grave, bright. . . .

"I agree," she said humbly. "Tactless and foolish. I knew all the time they were. I wanted to tell you they were non-sensical things——"

His arms were about her. Again the world was ceasing to rock.

"Do you always talk so much?" he said impatiently.

But that interlude, although it made her feel immeasurably happier, failed to solve anything. And now she could not keep to her plan to go to London to see Josephine's solicitor, because there was no one to look after the children. All at once it didn't seem so terribly urgent about Josephine. It was more important to stay here and occupy the children, and try to cheer up Dudley who had chosen such an unfortunate time to so wholeheartedly discard his prejudices.

Besides, the sky was actually clearing and for the first time in a week the sun was shining palely. Let them forget Miss Pinner who was so determinedly being a martyr (the insolence of her to fall in love with Barnaby!) and decide that her departure had been a good thing. Maggy and Dina were very willing indeed to do just this, and Emma wholeheartedly encouraged them. Until she found the candle. . . .

It was on top of the wardrobe in Louisa's room, almost out of sight. It was stuck in a china candlestick ornamented with roses – the one the children had had in their bedroom the other day. It had burnt down past the place where the pin had been stuck in, for the pin had fallen out in a little runnel of congealed grease. After that someone had blown the candle out.

Emma ran to call the children.

"Maggy! Dina! Come here at once."

The children came reluctantly, cast down by the tone of her voice. What temperamental little creatures they were, standing glowering at her, fatalistically expecting that the fun was over.

"What made you do such a naughty thing? Lighting this candle, scaring poor Miss Pinner to death. After all, you had told her what it was supposed to mean, hadn't you – that she would die when the pin fell out. Of course, it's all absolute nonsense, but she was such a silly scary creature——"

"Someone's *lit* the candle!" Maggy was exclaiming in a hushed voice full of awe.

Dina had shrunk against Emma, clinging to her skirt.

"Does that mean Miss Pinner is really dead?" she whispered.

"No, of course it doesn't. She's very much alive." But was she? Who knew? The small cold doubt began to stir in Emma's mind. "But what made you play that trick with the candle? When did you light it? And who put it up on the wardrobe when it was blown out?"

For the first time Maggy had lost both her blasé confidence and her defiance. She was a little girl, indignant, frightened, crying, "We didn't! Honestly we didn't!"

"We'd have been too scared to," Dina added. "Even though last night——" She stopped nervously, looking at her sister for help.

"What about last night?" Emma persisted.

"Oh, she just means Miss Pinner was saying if we didn't behave ourselves and go to sleep quietly she would go to the police and tell them how long it was since – since——" Maggy's voice trembled childishly, her face puckered with incipient tears. "Since we'd heard from Mummy," she finished in a despairing wail.

Emma remembered then the brief sound of Dina's crying after the children had gone to bed the previous night. She remembered too how some time in the night she had thought she had heard a puppy whimpering. Or had she dreamed that? Suddenly she wanted very much to have dreamed it.

"Truly we don't know anything about the candle, Emma." Maggy said earnestly. "I expect it was Angelina who put it there. She told us about the trick. And she didn't like Miss Pinner. She used to do this" – Maggy stuck out her front teeth comically – "behind her back."

Dina tugged at her skirt.

"Emma, is she dead? Is she?"

> "Miss Pinner didn't go to bed
> Because she was quite dead . . ."

Maggy chanted, with rather quivering bravado.

"Look," said Emma, "Miss Pinner is just as much alive as you and me. So will you stop that nonsense and go and tell Mrs. Faithfull and Angelina that I want to see them. Tell them to come up here."

Mrs. Faithfull had said good riddance to Louisa, Angelina had made fun of her behind her back. Neither of them, apparently, had liked her, but that did not mean they would make these strange efforts to get rid of her. The dead mouse, the dead bat, the face at the window. . . . Had these all been crude attempts to show her she was not welcome? But why do that to a perfectly harmless woman whose chief offence was her silliness?

Or was the thing that had brought Louisa to the panicky state of running away the result of someone having overheard her conversation with the children last night – the sly cruel threat that she would go to the police and tell them the mystery of Josephine's absence . . . ?

When the children had gone downstairs Emma stood alone in the room trying calmly to reconstruct what must have happened last night.

Louisa, after bidding her usual goodnight to them downstairs, would have come up here perhaps a little nervously, because of the strange things that had happened, but determined not to be a coward, determined to show the men that she was a calm, contained and unhysterical person.

Then, on her dressing-table, or wherever it had been put, she would have seen the candle, lighted, and burning down inexorably to the place where the pin was stuck in the side.

It was a silly and quite harmless trick. She must have known it was harmless, and that there could be nothing sinister about a pin which presently would tip downwards in a little runnel of hot wax.

But she knew the meaning of it. Maggy had explained it to her in deliberate cruel and callous tones the other day.

It had upset her enough for Emma to find her in tears when she had come home. And last night she would have interpreted it as a warning.

So she had hurriedly packed her bag and run away. The note to Barnaby had been a ruse to cover the real reason for her leaving.

The real reason one did not know, but it must have been something that had frightened her badly, more than the dead things in her room and the imagined face at her window. More too, than the burning candle, though that was perhaps the final incentive. . . .

Sylvie, too, had been frightened by something and run away. . . .

And last night Emma had thought she had heard a puppy crying. It was funny how that forlorn sound kept coming back into her mind.

Absently, still seeking for a clue, she turned back the blankets of the neatly made bed. And then she saw the nightgown under the pillow. Louisa's simple inexpensive cotton nightgown folded neatly in readiness for another night.

Of course she could have forgotten to pack it. Anyone could have overlooked various articles when packing. But Louisa was not the kind to overlook things. She was too prim and methodical. The forgotten nightgown mutely proved two things – that she had made no attempt to go to bed the previous night, and that she had packed in a hurry, probably in something of a panic. . . .

And after she had gone someone had come in, blown out the candle, and put it out of sight on top of the wardrobe. Someone who had expected her to go. . . .

There was a clatter of footsteps without and the children arrived, followed by Angelina, panting loudly, and Mrs. Faithfull, neat, small, unhurried.

Emma picked up the candlestick and said quietly, "Who put this in here last night?"

Angelina gave a loud gasp. Her dark, gipsy-like face was suddenly full of fear and dismay.

"The death candle!" she whispered. "It's been lit!"

That was what Maggy had said, too, in tones of great awe. "Someone has lit it!"

Mrs. Faithfull blinked and muttered querulously. "What's all the fuss about? The death candle, indeed – stuff and nonsense! Is that all that made that silly girl run away?"

"What I want to know," Emma insisted patiently, "is who lit the candle and put it in here?"

Angelina turned vociferously on Maggy. "You naughty one! When I told you that spell, didn't I say never to do it? Never, never to do it!"

Maggy shrank back, her face white and pinched.

"I didn't!" she screamed. "I didn't, I didn't. Emma knows I didn't."

"Tut, tut!" said Mrs. Faithfull. "Such a noise for a small girl." She turned her small wrinkled face to Emma. "Madam, I thought it was something important you wanted to see us about. Not just a child's game. If you will excuse me, I have the lunch to see to."

"Wait a minute," Emma demanded. "Did any of you hear anything strange last night. A – a sort of whimpering, or anything like that."

Angelina backed towards the door. Her eyes expressed terror and excitement.

"Willie and me don't sleep in this house, thank heaven. We wouldn't hear anything."

"Owls," said Mrs. Faithfull briefly. "If it were anything at all I've lived here forty years and I've never heard anything but owls. And the wind." Her pale, contemptuous gaze rested on Emma, including her now in her contempt for foolish and nervous females. "Lot of fuss about that new girl. Let her go. Silly creature."

It was no use, Emma could see. If either of these women knew anything about the candle, they were not admitting to it. She had got nowhere at all – except in her conviction that Louisa had not run away because of unrequited love, but from fear.

But when she went down to tell Barnaby what had happened she found that the police had come back. Someone had sent them an anonymous letter, Dudley said, telling them about Josephine's unexplained absence for so long. They were questioning Barnaby now.

The sender of the letter would be Louisa, of course. But Emma could not tell Dudley that just now, for he was in such a bad state of nerves. He kept saying, "Everything is too much! Everything!" And Emma knew he wasn't referring to Barnaby's cross-examination about Josephine, or to the unidentified body, pathetic and unmourned, but to Louisa's absence which was such a mortal blow to his pride.

Emma, however, could think of nothing but what the police were saying to Barnaby, and what he was answering. Suddenly she was as nervous as Dudley, forgetting about the death candle, which now seemed nothing more than a childish prank, and not even caring why Louisa had left and where she had gone.

But when the police left, Barnaby, it seemed, was angry only at whoever had given the malicious information anonymously.

"They seemed to think it suspicious that I couldn't give them the name of Josephine's dentist," he said indignantly. "It was quite useless for me to assure them that Josephine had not been to the dentist all the time I had known her. She hadn't needed to. Her teeth were perfect. Now they seem to think I'm hiding something."

"Bad luck the height is about right," Rupert observed.

Barnaby turned on him. "What the devil are you insinuating?"

"Nothing, old man. It just makes it more difficult for you, I should think. After all, these fellows have to produce some kind of report, and their file of missing persons doesn't seem to suggest anything."

"Oh, keep your theories to yourself," Barnaby snapped. "God, and I'm supposed to be writing a book! Emma, what are we going to do with the children now? Risk another woman in this apparently bewitched household?"

In the moment before answering Emma saw Dudley's eyes flicker with distaste or pain. Then she heard herself saying smoothly, "As a matter of fact I'm taking them up to London to spend the day with Aunt Deb. There are some things I want to do, and the change will do them good. These last two days have been more than any child should be expected to go through."

Then she had forgotten Dudley's expression of aversion to a new woman in the house in her awareness that Barnaby was suddenly apprehensive and disturbed.

What about, she wondered. What she might discover in London, or because he feared she was leaving forever.

"We'll be back this evening," she said lightly. "It will be a treat for Aunt Deb, too. She'll enjoy the children. I wouldn't be surprised if she isn't even a match for Maggy."

Barnaby suddenly took her hand in his. "What train will you return on?"

"I'm not sure. Probably the nine-thirty."

"Make it definite and I'll meet you."

She realised he was tying her to a promise because he knew she would keep it. Of course she meant to come back. It had never entered her head to do anything else – unless she discovered some very startling information. . . .

"All right. The nine-thirty," she promised.

# 15

JUST before leaving however, Emma said casually to Dudley, "While I'm in London I'll call on Louisa and find out what she meant by leaving so theatrically. Can I give her a message for you?"

Dudley flapped his large hands in panic.

"No, no. Don't mention me, please."

"But, Dudley, I believe she did like you a lot. I think we'll find there was another reason altogether for her leaving."

Dudley, however, refused to enter into a discussion.

"I don't want to see her or hear from her. I know now she was just playing with me."

"Oh, Dudley——"

"Leave it! Leave it! Not another word."

He had gone back into his shell, and it seemed improbable that he would ever venture out for another woman. That Louisa, silly, shallow, scheming, had been able to do this to him seemed extraordinary. Her very plainness and naïveté had been his downfall. He had thought that such a woman would not interest Barnaby, Rupert was absorbed in his new fiancée, so he had an open field. Consequently his failure was doubly bitter.

Emma meant to tell Louisa about this when she saw her. But she did not see her.

Mrs. Peach, the landlady of the Fulham Road house, said bewilderedly, "But Miss Pinner isn't here, miss. She's in the country at a nice governess job. I'm looking after her dog for her. What made you think she was in London?"

"Because she left Courtlands early this morning presumably to come back here," Emma said patiently. "Where would she go if she didn't come here?"

"Why, that I couldn't tell you, miss. She hadn't anywhere else, as far as I know. That's why she asked me to keep the dog. Might I ask if she was in trouble, miss?"

The vague witchcrafty things – could one call them trouble?

"Not with anyone at Courtlands. On the contrary, she was getting on very well indeed."

"Well, now, isn't that a queer thing?" Mrs. Peach, who was plump with kind but inquisitive eyes, was deeply interested. "She told you she was coming back here?"

"Not exactly. She left a note. Does she enjoy doing things in a theatrical way?"

"I don't know exactly what you mean, miss, but I do know she was a nice quiet girl, living there in my top room for three years now, and with no friends in particular but the dog. She fair doted on the dog. I haven't much time for dogs myself, but I must say Humble is always as nicely behaved as her mistress. Fetches the paper in the morning, clever as paint, really. If she's left her job in the country she'll be back here to see Humble, you can count on that."

Emma hesitated on the doorstep, bewildered.

"It's only two o'clock, miss. She'll probably turn up later. I'm on the telephone. Why don't you ring and see? By the way, if she does come, who shall I say was asking for her?"

"Mrs. Court."

"Mrs. – but it was a Mrs. Court she was working for."

"Yes," said Emma, smiling pleasantly. "That's why it's so odd, isn't it?"

Just as she turned to go the dog came running out, a

mongrel of the terrier type, square-jawed and rough-haired. Her eyes were bright and eager, her stump of tail wagged in a friendly fashion. She was nondescript and full of trust. It was curiously like looking at another version of Louisa. It accentuated Emma's uneasiness in such a strange way that she had to stop herself from breaking into a run as she left the house.

The children had settled down very well with Aunt Deb. Maggy, after relating a confused tale of corpses, death candles, mysterious disappearances and so on, with deliberately invented lurid details, and seeing Aunt Deb, as cosy as a very white woolly sheep in her shawls, nodding gently and quite unperturbed, calmed down and became almost normally quiet and well-behaved. Dina seemed fascinated by Aunt Deb's plump cosiness, and followed her about, occasionally rather timidly rubbing her cheek on the trailing end of one of the lacy shawls.

"They're like little lost lambs," she said to Emma. "There's nothing wrong with them that a little mothering won't cure. We've got to find this mother of theirs and have things out with her."

"Yes," Emma agreed rather limply.

"Now don't shirk things, dear. It won't be easy, but——"

"Oh, Aunt Deb, if only we could have things out with her! If only we could find her!"

So then everything came out – the discovery of the dead girl, small and unknown, Louisa's disappearance, the police's visit this morning to cross-examine Barnaby about his first wife, all the other small, apparently pointless but disturbing things. . . . Aunt Deb was eagerly absorbed in the story.

"My dear, how fascinating!" she kept saying. "I thought Maggy was making all of this up. I must say this is much more entertaining than a film. Do go on."

"Aunt Deb, I'm not telling you this for your entertainment," Emma said sharply.

"No, dear. But you can't deny it is entertaining. Didn't I tell you not to trust Barnaby? Oh dear, and my married life, much as I adored your uncle, was quite uneventful."

Emma smiled reluctantly.

"I want advice, not envy."

"You shall have both, my dear. Now, first, this Louisa.

You must ring and see if she has turned up yet. If she hasn't you must go to the police."

It was only then that Emma admitted that her uneasiness about Louisa's departure was fear, a treacherously growing fear that was becoming heavier and heavier inside her.

"Oh, no, Aunt Deb. If anyone goes to the police it must be Dudley or Barnaby. After all, Sylvie did this, and there was nothing extraordinary about it. She was perfectly all right, because she rang up that day."

"Are you sure she rang up? Or was that message something Louisa invented?"

"I wonder," said Emma slowly, "if I've just been a dupe."

"No sign of her, miss," Mrs. Peach's puzzled voice came over the telephone in answer to Emma's ring. "It all seems very queer to me. If I was you I would go to the police."

"Oh no," said Emma involuntarily.

Aunt Deb, watching her, said cheerfully, "Still trying to protect him, dear? I know he's handsome and irresistible, but he could be a scoundrel. You really ought to find out."

Emma turned heavily away. "I have to go to see the solicitor now. I made an appointment. After that——" Suddenly she covered her face with her hands.

"Now, now, darling, Barnaby's all right. There might be something queer he won't talk about, but you'll find it isn't his fault."

"It's all so horrible," Emma whispered. "I didn't realise before how horrible it was."


Mr. Quantrill, a small neat man, faintly brown, as if he were kept in some kind of preservative, said courteously, "I'm afraid I can't tell you anything more than your husband knows already, Mrs. Court. The first Mrs. Court left this country about three years ago. She was on the Italian Riviera, and then in Venice for some time – that was the last time she had the children, I believe. After that I had a letter from her telling me that she was going on this expedition up the Amazon, and if I heard no more news for some time not to be alarmed."

"She didn't come back to England in the interval?" Emma hated herself for the question.

"She could have done so without notifying me. That I wouldn't know."

"Didn't you think it a strange thing that a woman like her should go on such an expedition? It wouldn't be easy."

Mr. Quantrill smiled faintly. There was a trace of admiration in his eyes.

"That kind of woman is unpredictable. And frequently, I believe, much tougher than she seems to be. I'm sorry I can't help you more about this. As a matter of fact I'm expecting——" He hesitated, as if he had committed an indiscretion. Then he went on, " – a visit from Scotland Yard. I heard you've had some trouble down at Courtlands." He met Emma's anguished eyes. "I shall tell them exactly what I have told you," he said.

"Of course," Emma agreed lamely.

Mr. Quantrill stood up. "Might I say, Mrs. Court, that I have the greatest respect for your husband."

"Thank you, Mr. Quantrill."

"Not at all. The police have to put up a show, you know. Sometimes they do what seems to be unnecessary things." He held out his hand. "If I can be of any service to you at any time, do let me know."

"Thank you," Emma said again. "You're very kind."

She wanted to apologise at once to Barnaby for doubting him. Josephine really was in South America, strange as it seemed. Unless, at any time, she had come back to England without letting Mr. Quantrill know. . . .

When Aunt Deb, worried by her strained and weary look, urged her to stay in London for a few days, Emma said unhesitantly, "I can't. I promised Barnaby I would be on the nine-thirty."

"Surely you can tell him you have changed your mind?"

"No. I promised."

Aunt Deb shook her head. But her shrewd old eyes expressed approval.

"Then leave the children here. Hannah and I can take care of them very nicely and, really Courtlands doesn't sound quite the place for them at present."

That offer was not only typical of Aunt Deb's kindness and generosity but it also seemed a very sensible idea. The surprise came when the children utterly refused to stay.

Maggy gave Emma a wounded look as if she had been betrayed. Then she went upstairs, put on her hat and coat and came down to say to Aunt Deb with icy politeness, "Thank you very much for your invitation, but we don't care to accept it."

"Oh, Maggy, it would be nice for you here," Emma protested. "Aunt Deb really wants you."

"Nobody," said Maggy aloofly, "really wants us. But don't let that worry you. We don't care, actually."

Dina's lips began to tremble. "D-Daddy might w-want us."

"Him!" said Maggy, stalking to the door. "Not now he's got her."

"Maggy!" Emma exclaimed. "Come back here at once. At least if you don't want to stay with Aunt Deb you can be polite about it. And the suggestion wasn't made because you were in the way at Courtlands. It was simply because we thought it might be fun for you."

"We'd go to the zoo," Aunt Deb said winningly. "It seems like a thousand years since I had children to take to the zoo."

Maggy's black eyes sparkled with hostility.

"Dina, if you don't want to miss the train you'd better get your coat. Or if you'd rather let them push you around——"

"Maggy! Maggy!" Emma implored. "Where do you get such ideas?"

"Miss Treadgold at school said it was a pity the way we were pushed around," Dina said breathlessly. "I'll get my coat. Wait for me, Maggy."

Maggy, Emma fully believed, was capable of stepping out at Aunt Deb's front door and hailing a taxi and getting on to the train at Victoria all by herself. She found herself smiling reluctantly.

"Don't be in such a hurry, darling. We've half an hour yet. Of course you can come back to Courtlands if you want to. Did you think I was deserting you?"

Maggy's eyes flickered. But she was not going to admit to any childish hurt or sentimentality.

She said gruffly, "Miss Pinner is probably dead, isn't she? Why should Dina and me miss the fun?"

"Good gracious!" Aunt Deb murmured in disbelief.

"Oh, our Maggy's tough," Emma said lightly.

Maggy snorted. Her small face remained bleak, hostile, unapproachable. The barriers, which had been almost down, were up more impregnably than ever. Emma was furious with herself for letting the child think, even for one moment, that she was not wanted. But now the damage had been done. Maggy, and consequently her faithful slave Dina, were once more enemies.

The intolerable thing was to know that she had almost won the prickly little heart. It was astonishing how much it mattered that now she had lost it.

Maggy and Dina – small pieces of Barnaby – suddenly it mattered very much indeed that they should love her.

In the train Maggy said suddenly, "Mummy might be there when we get home," and instantly the light sprang into Dina's face.

They were playing their game of make-believe again, and Emma was shut out. She hadn't realised until this moment that for two days they hadn't played it, because the need to escape from reality had not been so vital. She herself had partially removed that need.

But now, by one false step, she had destroyed their fragile and precarious security.

If only, she thought longingly, Josephine were there when they got home. Perhaps with the humming-bird in a cage. Or a small expensive monkey, or quantities of bizarre jewellery, or an exotically feathered turban. But alive. Surrounded with her exciting and compelling aura of elegance and vivacity and unpredictability. But safely alive. . . .

There was no one but themselves in the compartment. Maggy and Dina sat on the seat opposite Emma. Dina was struggling with sleep. Her head nodded on to Maggy's insecure shoulder, only to be impatiently rejected. Maggy herself kept her eyes wide open in an unblinking stare, like a small basilisk.

The wheels of the train made a rhythm that rendered even Emma drowsy. Maggy's black stare turned into the bewildered gaze of Mrs. Peach who could not think why Louisa Pinner would not have come home to her dog . . .

The kind but withdrawn look of Mr. Quantrill who said that the police had to do their duty and explore every avenue, no matter how unlikely. . . . The bitter hurt and dislike in Dudley's accusing eyes. . . . The soberness of Barnaby's blue gaze turned to tenderness. . . .

Barnaby – as unpredictable in his own way as Josephine had ever been, as secret and as exasperating. And yet holding one inescapably in one's love for him.

Love him but don't trust him. . . . Love him . . . trust him . . . love him . . . I love you too much so I am going away . . . so I am going away. . . .

No, that was not how it went. Emma shook her drowsy head impatiently. It went, I love you too much so the only fair thing to do is to go away. . . .

But someone else, not Louisa, had said the other thing. I love you too much so I am going away. . . .

The sentence was firmly in her head. Where had she read it or heard it? There had been voices chanting, "I love you too much so. . . ." Suddenly she remembered. The children. Maggy and Dina in their bath one night. Where had they come by that odd sentence, so similar to the one Louisa had written? So curiously, significantly similar. . . .

"Maggy!" Emma exclaimed urgently. "Where did you hear those words you and Dina were saying the other night? 'I love you too much so I am going away.' You kept saying them."

Maggy gave her basilisk stare.

"I don't know any words like that."

"But you kept saying them. As if you'd read them. Or heard someone saying them. Do think, please. It's important. You couldn't have made them up. But you did say them."

"I wouldn't say anything so wet," Maggy said definitely. "Nor would Dina." She clamped her lips together and closed her eyes.

Dina was already asleep.

Barnaby was waiting at the station. He helped the stumbling, sleep-drunk children into the car, and turned to Emma with the familiar lift of his brows.

"Some trouble?"

"Not really. Aunt Deb wanted them to stay, but it seemed to hurt their feelings. They'll be all right. We stayed in town too long."

"Yes," said Barnaby. "You did."

There was nothing more than that, his simple agreement, his hand on her elbow, but suddenly she was caught again in one moment of illogical happiness, one perfect fragment of time.

They didn't even talk as they drove through the chill damp night, a spatter of raindrops on the windscreen, the headlamps piercing the quiet countryside.

Then Emma said, "Anything new?"

"Nothing."

By that brief answer she knew that the police had not come back, and that so far their "routine enquiries" regarding Josephine had yielded nothing, that the slim handful of bones was still no real person, still nothing but a strange nightmare. *I love you too much so I am going away. . . .* But where to? Into that "long unbroken, lonely and interminable sleeping. . . ."


Mrs. Faithfull had waited up with hot drinks for them. She clucked over Maggy and Dina, saying that it was too long a day for children and she would put them to bed herself. She was almost motherly, a strange little brown hen fussing over her chickens. It was a glimpse of what she had once been with the boys. It made Emma feel more friendly towards her, and grateful for her help.

She drank her hot cocoa and laughed to see Barnaby grimacing over his.

"It's good for you," she said. "Did you have a dull day?"

"Very dull."

"Mine wasn't. I called on Louisa's landlady."

Here, Dudley, who had been sitting crouched over the fire, a large disconsolate shape, turned.

"What happened?" he asked tensely.

"Curiously enough, nothing. Louisa had not arrived back."

"She wasn't bound to go directly there," Barnaby observed.

"No, but it's strange she didn't. There's her dog, you

know. Mrs. Peach thought it was strange too." Emma hesitated, and then said slowly, "Mrs. Peach thinks we ought to tell the police about this. Actually, I rather agree with her."

"In the face of that mid-Victorian letter?" Barnaby queried.

"In face of several things."

"Well, I don't know." Barnaby appeared to consider. "We seem to have had more than enough unpleasantness already, with Willie's discovery."

"I'll say we have," Rupert said emphatically. "If we make a thing of Louisa, too, what's my Jean going to think – or, more to the point, what will her old man think?"

"What do you say, Dudley?" Barnaby asked.

Dudley put his hand over his eyes.

"For my part, I don't want to see her again. But if the girl should happen to be in trouble, God knows how or why, I suppose it's our duty——" He smiled rather pathetically, his plump cheeks unusually pale, his eyes strained and tired. "I'm afraid I've behaved rather badly today. It's the shock. I'm not very – worldly is the word, I imagine. You must despise me, Emma."

"I do nothing of the kind," Emma said warmly.

"No? Thank you for that, my dear. Then what about the police? Shall we sleep on that proposition?"

"Oh, lord, yes," said Barnaby. "We're not having another series of examination questions set by Sergeant Bloodhound tonight. I really don't think I would pass."

Emma planned to soak away some of her tiredness and strain in a hot bath, and to take a sleeping pill. Otherwise, all night the problems of the next day would worry her – the police again, trying now to tie up Louisa's disappearance with the unsolved mystery of the body in the field, when of course the two things had no connection, Dudley's silent unhappiness, the children's renewed hostility, and Barnaby's jauntiness that was put on to conceal something else, something he did not mean to tell. . . .

She took the pill before her bath, because it said on the bottle that one should be taken fifteen minutes before retiring. But in her bath, her intention to relax in the warm water was thwarted. For she suddenly remembered that the day the children had been chanting those significant words, "I love you too much so I am going away," had been the day they had played the dressing-up game and had come downstairs in those extraordinary clothes.

Obviously the clothes were the clue. The children had found something in the attic, perhaps an old letter, received long ago. Its melodrama had appealed to Louisa so much that she had copied it, or the words had remained subconsciously in her mind.

Whatever it was, the letter must still be there – somehow associated with those faded flamboyant clothes. Perhaps tucked in a pocket, yellowed with age, telling a story that had happened in this house to Grandmother or even Great-grandmother Court. Or to some woman who had stayed here and fallen in love with one of the two marble gentlemen in the hall. Great-grandfather Court with the haughty arrogant nose, had he had a secret love? Or was it more likely to have been Grandfather Court, or even, later still, the boys' father?

Emma could not wait to investigate. She hastily dried herself, pulled on her warm dressing-gown, and left the bathroom to go quietly up to the attics. She remembered to take matches to light the candles, and when she had groped on the window ledges for them and lit them the attics sprang into flickering life.

The trunks, with the mysterious collection of garments, were still there, the little wooden cradle also. It was the cradle that had held the most modern of the assortment of clothes, and it was in there that Emma proposed to look first.

But when she opened it, lifting the wooden lid that made a false bottom, it was empty.

The children, then, must have put the clothes in the trunks. It would take a long time to sort all of those things. Hesitating, Emma heard steps on the stairs. She remembered how the last time she had been up here the candles had mysteriously blown out, and her heart began to beat violently. But there was no secrecy about these approaching steps. They came slowly and solidly across the uncarpeted floor into the attic.

It was Dudley who stood in the doorway.

He said, "I thought I heard a noise up here. Whatever are you doing?"

Emma began to laugh shakily.

"You gave me a fright. It's rather eerie in the candlelight."

"But what are you doing?" Dudley asked again. He also was ready for bed, and in his thick plaid dressing-gown looked enormous, filling the doorway almost as if he were meaning to block her escape.

Emma gave another breathless laugh.

"I realise that what I came to do is going to take far too long. I will have to come up tomorrow. Anyway, all these old clothes should be sorted out and got rid of. Some of them might do for a jumble sale. Mostly I think they should be burnt."

"I agree. It should have been done long ago. But one doesn't sort clothes at midnight, Emma, my dear."

"Actually I was looking for a letter or a scrap of paper or anything where the children might have got those curious words from. It just suddenly seemed to me so odd that Louisa's letter to Barnaby was almost exactly similar to some words the children were chanting the other day. Do you understand what I'm talking about?"

She added this question anxiously, because all at once the sleeping pill she had taken was beginning to have effect, and the room seemed to be turning quite slowly, with Dudley's enormous shadow across the ceiling turning, too, very ponderously, as if it might be preparing to spring.

"I don't understand at all," came Dudley's slow deep voice. "Some words, a letter?"

"An *old* letter," said Emma earnestly. "Such as some woman might have written perhaps to your great-grandfather. Does this all sound fantastic?"

"Quite fantastic," Dudley said, in his kind, serious way. "Emma, my dear, I don't think you are well. Which is not to be wondered at, after all this strain. Anyway, whatever you think you are looking for can very well wait until the morning. Let me help you downstairs."

The attic with the leaping shadows and the too frail candlelight was part of a nightmare, and as unexplainable as a nightmare. Emma pressed her hands to her eyes, and thought that if only her head were clear there would be something that would make itself clear to her, some very obvious thing. But it was no use. She was tired.

"Yes, let's go," she said. Her voice seemed to come from a long way off. "What a good thing – you found me here. Otherwise I would have slept – among the old clothes. Who – did they – belong to, Dudley?"

Dudley had her arm firmly, and was guiding her down the stairs.

"The crimson velvet – the turban——"

They had reached the first floor, and there was only the long carpeted passage to her bedroom. The light dazzled her. She put up her hand to her eyes again, and the rest of the crumpled velvet in the old trunks seemed to flash before them.

"Who?" she persisted.

Dudley answered something then, but she thought she must have heard wrongly. She thought he said, "A whore," and that surely could not have been his answer.

Barnaby had not yet come to bed. Emma noticed the bed stretched wide and empty before her. She made a last desperate effort to stay awake. How idiotic of her to have taken that pill – when it was not safe to sleep. Why did she suddenly think it was not safe to sleep? The half-formed nightmarish thought vanished as she fumbled her way beneath the blankets, lay her head on the pillow and slept.

In the morning her plan to search the attics and get to the bottom of the mystery about the letter could not be carried out, because the telegram came from Sylvie.

# 16

IT was Mrs. Faithfull who brought the telegram in. She said a boy had just delivered it, and thinking it might be something important she had come straight up with it.

Emma didn't notice at first that the old lady lingered as she tore open the envelope and read the printed message:

SORRY COULDN'T KEEP APPOINTMENT OTHER DAY SAME PLACE ELEVEN A.M. TODAY URGENT DON'T TELL SYLVIE

Emma drew in her breath sharply, and saw Mrs. Faithfull watching her with a curiously intense look, as if her faded eyes were striving to see more than their vision permitted.

"Something's come up," she said casually. "I'll have to go out for two or three hours. Do you think you and Angelina could manage the children for that time, Mrs. Faithfull?"

She didn't wait for the old woman's reply. This was no time to ask favours. She was giving orders now, and the woman could like it or not as she pleased.

"Must you——"

"Yes, I'm afraid I must. Send the children to me, please."

It was only after Mrs. Faithfull had left the room that Emma realised her half-spoken protest may not have been because of the work involved for herself and Angelina, but because she was frightened of something.

It came to her in a clear cold moment of intuition that Mrs. Faithfull, in her secretive way, had been trying to conceal fear and apprehension.

But there was no time to worry about that now. If she was to keep the appointment with Sylvie in Canterbury at eleven she had to catch the ten o'clock bus, and it was already nearly half-past nine. She *had* to keep this appointment. It was vitally important, as if what Sylvie had to tell her would not only clear up the mystery of Louisa and the face at the window and the body in the field but also the reason for Josephine's long-delayed return.

She began to dress quickly, pausing only when the children came.

They were dressed in their jeans and jerseys. Their hair was unbrushed and their general appearance that of street waifs.

There was no time, however, to worry about this either.

"Listen darlings," she said, "I have to go out this morning. I'll be back directly after lunch. In the meantime will you be quiet and good and do as Mrs. Faithfull and Angelina tell you?"

Dina nodded, but Maggy said belligerently, "We don't care if you never come back. We hate you."

"Sometimes," said Emma calmly, "I'm not awfully fond of you either. Run along 'now, and if anyone asks, tell them I'll be back after lunch."

"If you come back, we'll put spiders in your bed. Won't we, Dina?"

Dina gave a half-hearted and nervous giggle.

"Or bats, or mice, or toads. We'll get them from Angelina. She doesn't like you, either."

So that, no doubt, had been the source of the unpleasant vermin in Louisa's room. Angelina, at the instigation of Maggy who had disliked Louisa on sight. Maggy, it seemed, was budding witch material.

"We might even light the death candle," Maggy declared. But that last threat seemed to frighten even her, and her small taut face was suddenly full of uncertainty.

Emma put down the hairbrush and picked up her coat.

"Really, Maggy, all this is rather boring. And rather baby-ish, too, don't you think. When I come back we'll think of some much more interesting games."

Dina's eyes gleamed with sudden hope, but Maggy, refusing to be placated or outwitted, tossed her witch-locks and stalked out of the room.

It was so difficult to know how to deal with Maggy. Hurt, Dina was content to be pathetic, but Maggy fought back with the same weapons. She would go down fighting, bless her tough, courageous little heart.

One had to win her, when all these sinister obstacles in one's way were overcome. Perhaps, by this afternoon, when Sylvie had cleared up some at least of the mystery. . . .

It was awful to go without telling Barnaby, but this time she was taking no risks. She would slip out of the back door and walk across the fields to the bus stop. She might even be back before Barnaby had discovered her absence.

What was it that Sylvie had to tell her? Would it be something that she would have preferred not to know?

Angelina saw her go through the kitchen. She called, "You're never going out in all that rain, madam?"

"I have to, Angelina."

Angelina's eyes, like polished black grapes, stared at her. "That's the way Miss Pinner went yesterday."

"Miss Pinner!" Emma was forced to pause. "Did you see her go?"

"No, I didn't see her. Guess she crept out in the dark. But I picked up her handkerchief on the back steps. Got it in my pocket now. See. L. Pinner in the corner."

"She might have dropped it the day before," Emma suggested. Suddenly her heart was beating very fast.

"Couldn't have. Someone would have picked it up, wouldn't they? I was first to come in yesterday morning. I'd say she was up to no good, that lady." Angelina picked up her broom and began sweeping vigorously.

"If you know anything about Miss Pinner, Angelina, you ought to tell Mr. Court."

Angelina grinned slyly. Her eyes gleamed. "Which one, madam?"

"Aren't you being a little impertinent?"

Angelina flourished her broom noisily. "Oh, I don't care. Willie and me are leaving, anyway. This place gets on our nerves. It did even before the body was found, what with women disappearing and Peeping Toms and things.

"Why, they even tried to suggest that Willie might have been the Peeping Tom. My Willie! I'd like to catch him at it, that's all I can say."

Angelina's eyes flashed sudden fire. "And I didn't have nothing to do with lighting that candle, neither!" she finished vehemently. "That was them kids. Give 'em an inch and they take a mile."

So Louisa had left the house quietly, by the back door, so as to disturb nobody. After all, there was nothing extraordinary about that. She was doing the same thing herself. If, by any strange chance, she didn't come back, would Angelina tell anyone that she had seen her go? Or would she remain silent as she had about Louisa's dropped handkerchief?

This was different, however. The children knew she was going out. So did Mrs. Faithfull. And they knew she was not keeping a clandestine appointment with a lover – as Louisa may have been. . . .

What made her think such a stupid thing? For, if Louisa had merely been meeting a lover, she would have come back.

It was raining quite heavily by the time Emma had crossed the fields by the path that led to the main road. The bus stop was under the large oak tree on the corner. One reached it by going through the little copse which had also screened that pathetic grave from the road. Emma had not realised how near she had to pass to the small mound of earth, not quite tidied over since its secret had been discovered. She paused a moment, the rain falling with little thuds on her water-proof hat, and thought how pretty this copse must be in the spring and summer. An idyllic spot for making love. . . . The girl had probably got off the bus and been met by her lover. Or was it he who had alighted, and she who had been loitering there . . . ? The police had worked on that theory, just as they had worked on the one that the couple had come by car or motor-cycle, or even walked from the camp across the downs.

It didn't matter how they had got there, but they had been strangers to Courtlands, trespassers. They *must* have been. . . .

The trees were budding now, in spite of the dreary weather. When at last the warm spring days came it would be beautiful here. The children would go back to school, but she and Barnaby might stay on, because to be in love in springtime in the country was a very memorable thing. . . .

Emma realised that she was clinging rather desperately to normal thoughts, as if normality was going to be a very difficult thing to achieve. With relief, she thought she heard the bus approaching, and began to hurry down the slippery path that led through the copse. The spindly trees cleared, there was a patch of gorse, overgrown and prickly, through which one had to . . .

Emma was conscious of the gorse scratching her badly as she slipped and fell. But had she slipped? It seemed that a branch, moving suddenly, had tripped her. She gave a little whimper of pain as she crept backwards, and at the same moment the dark muffling cloth went over her head, cutting off her breath.

She struggled violently. She was not a small person, not

nearly as small as Louisa Pinner had been, she found herself thinking in a flash of horror – but she knew that she
had been dragged roughly into a car, for she felt herself
fall across a seat, and one of her feet was caught as the door
slammed.

The pain of that, and the suffocation of the thick woollen
stuff over her head, caused her partly to lose consciousness.

She realised dimly that her struggles were weak and futile
as cord was bound round her wrists and pulled agonisingly
tight. She tried to cry out again, but now her breath was
really failing her, the darkness was becoming hot, black,
airless night. . . .

Night . . . she thought from a vague, far-off plane . . .
must be endured. . . .

# 17

IT was Dina who suggested timidly that Emma might not
come back. Maggy turned on her fiercely, "Of course she'll
come back. She didn't write a letter did she?"

"Sylvie didn't, either," Dina pointed out.

"She did so. What about that one we found the other
day? That must have been Sylvie's. *I love you too much,
too much, too much.* . . ." Maggy began the familiar chant,
dancing round the room.

"But those weren't Sylvie's clothes the letter was in.
Why should she put it in that old coat?"

"She was a silly," Maggy said contemptuously. "Why
do people go away if they love other people too much, anyway? You'd think they'd want to stay. Oh, come on, what
shall we play this morning? Something that makes a lot of
noise."

Dina agreed, rather half-heartedly, to the ambush and
ransom game that Maggy liked to play in the passages and
on the staircase. She could not, like her sister, escape from
her fears in a great deal of screaming and shouting. Actually

she wanted to cry. She would go on wanting to do this until Emma came home again. Unless Mummy – but Mummy no longer seemed real, and Emma did. She wished Maggy hadn't said those things about putting dead things in Emma's bed. And the death candle. . . . Unwittingly Dina shrieked in something approaching terror as Maggy sprang on her from behind a curtain.

Barnaby came out of his study downstairs and called, in tones of frayed patience, "Isn't there something a little more quiet you children could play? Where's Emma?"

"She's gone," said Maggy laconically.

"Gone! Where?"

Maggy sighed and went to the head of the stairs.

"We don't know. She didn't tell us."

"How long ago?"

"Oh, just after breakfast." Maggy shrugged with adult boredom as her father came up the stairs. "You don't need to worry, she said she would be back after lunch."

"Where was she going?"

"She didn't tell us. She just said she had to go suddenly. And she didn't leave a letter, so it's all right."

"What do you mean, it's all right because she didn't leave a letter?"

Maggy looked at her father with pained tolerance.

"Don't you know it's only when they leave letters that they don't come back?"

"What ridiculous nonsense!" Barnaby marched off in search of someone who could tell him more about the reason for Emma's absence, and Maggy, feeling curiously deflated, said to Dina, "I suppose we'd better go and look for that letter."

It was Dina's turn to look puzzled. "But you just said Emma didn't write a letter."

"Oh, don't be dumb. The letter we found in that old coat the other day."

Maggy did not go on to explain that ever since she had been so rude to Emma in the train about the letter, which she had pretended hadn't existed, she had had a gnawing feeling of guilt and fear. It was as if, by denying that she knew anything about it, she had caused something dreadful to happen. She didn't know what. She just had that awful feeling that only rushing about and making a lot of noise could dispel.

"Oh, come *on*!" she shouted to Dina, and tore up to the attics.

Even when they had emptied the two large trunks of their hoarded store of clothes, however, there was no sign of the shabby red coat in whose pocket the crumpled letter had been discovered.

Maggy sat back on her heels, looking puzzled.

"Oh, do let's go downstairs," Dina begged. "I'm scared."

"You are a coward," Maggy said contemptuously. "What are you scared of?"

"You know we're not supposed to touch these things."

"That's because someone didn't want us to find the letter. And now it's gone, anyway. I think——"

"What?" Dina faltered, for seeing Maggy uncertain increased her own nervousness.

"We'd better tell Emma when she comes home," Maggy decided.

"Yes," Dina agreed with relief. "Emma will know what to do."

Lunch, without Emma, was a silent meal. Uncle Dudley and Uncle Rupert seemed as surprised and startled as Daddy had been to find Emma away.

"I expect she's chasing up some clue about Louisa," Uncle Dudley said heavily, and all at once his face twisted, as if he might begin to cry.

"Well, I wish she wouldn't without telling anyone," Daddy said shortly. "Apparently she got a telegram this morning, which Mrs. Faithfull says she burnt, so nobody knows what was in it. Then she left by the back door apparently to catch a bus."

"I didn't see her," Uncle Dudley said. "I've been out with Willie since dawn helping with the lambing."

"Women!" Uncle Rupert complained. "Why do we get involved with them? What endless trouble have I let myself in for?" He twirled his moustache jauntily and looked smug.

"I've phoned the police," Daddy said. "They'll be here shortly. I intend to report Louisa's disappearance, and if Emma isn't back by then we'll have her traced, too."

"By the police!" Uncle Dudley said, in a shocked voice.

"For protection," Daddy snapped. "It may be unnecessary, but I'm not taking any risks."

"I say, old boy!" Uncle Rupert murmured in surprise.

Maggy choked suddenly, and Daddy remembered hers and Dina's existence.

"You children," he said, "had better play outdoors this afternoon. It's stopped raining. But keep out of the way if cars come."

Then, by his worried and abstracted look, Maggy knew he had forgotten them again. He was thinking of Emma, who should be home by now. But Emma was all right. She *had* to be all right.

In the garden, with the rain stopped, and the air suddenly clear and mild, Maggy felt full of madness. She tore round the trees, through the rhododendrons where drops of rain shook from the branches and ran coldly down her neck, and then towards the stables. Dina panted behind, calling, "Where are you going? What are we playing?"

"I'm a horse and you have to catch me," Maggy shouted. "Oh, look, there's a scarecrow. Willie must have been making it for the garden. Oh, how silly, he's put its coat on inside out. Let's fix it."

The scarecrow was leaning against the stable wall. Its foolish straw head wore a lop-sided beret, and the coat was dragged crookedly over its stiff wooden arms.

"Poor old scarecrow," said Dina soothingly. "We'll dress you properly."

They unbuttoned the coat and dragged it off unceremoniously. The scarecrow fell in the mud, and while Dina was picking it up carefully and apologetically, she heard Maggy saying in rather a scared voice, "Dina, it's the red coat!"

Dina dropped the scarecrow again. "The one in the attic," she faltered.

"Yes, and the beret, too." For a moment they stared at one another, their eyes round and startled, afraid, and yet not knowing why they should be.

Then Maggy said vigorously, "Well, now we can get the letter for Emma, anyway. She wanted it, I don't know why."

But the letter had gone. The pockets were empty, even the little one stitched in the lining.

Willie came round the corner of the stable and saw them.

"He be for the kitchen garden, to frighten the birds off the peas," he said. "Quite the gentleman, ain't he?"

"He's got a lady's coat on," Maggy said. "And I don't know where you found it, because it should be in the attic, and I expect you'll get into trouble——"

But at that moment Uncle Dudley appeared. He wore a tweed jacket, an old felt hat pushed back on his head, and thigh boots. His face had changed from the way it had looked at lunch and was now quite merry.

"How'd you children like a bonfire?" he asked, indicating a pile of old straw, wooden crates and boxes that was heaped up in the centre of the yard.

"Is it Guy Fawkes Day?" Maggy demanded excitedly.

"No, but I don't see why one shouldn't have bonfires at other times. Willie started building this one this morning."

At that moment Uncle Rupert drove up in his car. He put his head out.

"Is that a bonfire? I say, how splendid! But you mustn't light it until dark. Then a little petrol thrown on at the last minute, like brandy, you know, makes a most impressive blaze."

Maggy began to dance in wild excitement.

"Oh, let's build the bonfire. Come on, Dina, let's help!"

# 18

NIGHT, it seemed, was not always black. Sometimes it was red, a rich dark warm colour that lay heavily on one's aching eyelids, so that it was a major effort to lift them. . . .

Emma did at last get her eyes fully open, although for a few moments the room spun dizzily. She found that she was lying on an old-fashioned couch, covered with shabby red plush. This was in a small, low-ceilinged room, heavy with shadows. It was a room she had never seen before.

As memory came back to her she realised that she must have been brought here in an unconscious state by her unknown assailant. She was sure that this room, which seemed to dissolve before her eyes in a red blur, was not part of the house at Courtlands. It was a strange house, probably a cottage. The low ceiling and the small dark window suggested that. Probably it was an upstairs room in a cottage. But where? How many miles away from Courtlands? Sitting up cautiously, waiting for her head to stop spinning, she surveyed the room.

There was a round table, covered with a red tasselled cloth, in the middle of the room. On it was a tray containing a bottle of brandy three parts empty, a glass and a jug of water. Beside the tray was a sheet of paper with writing on it, also some letter paper, a bottle of ink and a pen.

There appeared to be no electric light, and the small window, which was entirely overgrown with some dark creeper, gave only a dim green light which left the room in perpetual gloom. Emma had to take the sheet of paper and hold it up to the window to read what was written on it.

All it said, cryptically, was, "Please copy the following letter in your own handwriting."

The letter was to Barnaby. It read,

"DEAR BARNABY,

I am sorry that I cannot continue with a marriage that is such a fiasco. It is obvious that you are still in love with Josephine, and as for the other two, Sylvie and Louisa, I do not know what to think. I love you too much to endure this, so I am going away. Do not try to get in touch with me.

YOUR UNHAPPY
EMMA."

The thing was so absurd that Emma would have laughed had she not felt so sick and so afraid.

Her clothes were still wet from her walk in the rain, too. That was why she was shivering. Although there was no use in denying to herself that fear, also, was making her shiver.

For twice before absurd melodramatic letters had been written at Courtlands, and no one had ever been able to explain them. The writers had not appeared again.

Certainly, Louisa's letter was not two days' old. But she had vanished as completely as if it were forever.

Had Louisa, too, first been shut in this small, dark, claustrophobic room that was somewhere in Kent, somewhere not too far from Courtlands because Emma's clothes, wet from the rain, had not yet dried?

But perhaps she was not shut in? Perhaps she was panicking unnecessarily.

Emma hurried to the door and turned the knob.

It was locked, of course. One had known that would be so. And the tiny window, covered with its mat of ivy, was rusted shut. Emma dragged a chair close, and stood on it to struggle with the resisting frame.

It would not move. She could not even brush aside the ivy to look out and see where she was, whether the cottage faced a road, or was in lonely fields or a garden.

But perhaps there was someone downstairs, her jailer who would come if she made enough noise. Still in the grip of panic, Emma began to knock on the door, to call out, and then, when there was no response, and no sound at all from downstairs, to stamp and to bang on the floor with the one ricketty chair that was all she could find in the room.

In the intervals of her clamour, when she stopped to listen, the silence in the house seemed to grow. Outside a bird twittered in the ivy. Her watch told her that it was only just past noon, although the room seemed full of twilight.

She banged and shouted again, and then her head ached so violently that she thought she would faint. She poured a generous measure of brandy into the glass and drank it. Gradually her panic subsided.

She must remain calm, she told herself. This was an absurd situation, but it must solve itself. No one could keep her a prisoner indefinitely. Why should they? It was so outside the bounds of reason. The children would tell Barnaby that she had promised to return after lunch. When she did not arrive he would instantly get in touch with the police. He would not hesitate as he had done about Louisa.

Or indeed about Sylvie. But one did not instantly run to the police when girls walked out of their jobs, whereas one did if it were one's wife who mysteriously disappeared. Especially if there were no reason. And there would be no reason because that letter, at least, would remain unwritten.

The letter planned by the plotter with the taste for melodrama. I love you too much so I am going away. . . . I love you too much so the only fair thing to do is to go away. . . . I love you too much to endure this, so I am going away. . . .

Going away, going away. . . . That was the theme. The letters written by the victims, so that their disappearance was voluntary. . . .

Victims?

Emma resolutely thrust that thought out of her mind, and began calmly to work out again what would happen.

When Barnaby discovered her absence he would question everybody. Mrs. Faithfull would tell him about the telegram (which one realised now was a trap into which she had tumbled with ridiculous ease), Angelina would say she had left by the back door to cross the fields to the bus stop. They would investigate, Barnaby and the police, and the wet ground would show signs of a struggle, there would be car marks. . . .

But there were already car marks and a great deal of trampling in the grass where that mysterious grave had been investigated. Would the ones made today show?

Was the girl from that small and lonely grave the one who had written the first letter *I love you too much so I am going away.* . . . ? How had the letter begun? Darling? My dear one? Dear one?

And who was the dear one? Barnaby? For one could at no stage imagine that Rupert, with his jaunty fooling, or Dudley, repressed, shy, awkward, could inspire that kind of love.

Sylvie. The pretty blonde girl whom the children said had been frightened. Where was she?

She had not appeared in the cathedral that day. Had the telegram this morning not been from her at all, but from someone who had deliberately planned a trap?

No, no, Emma thought, pressing her hands to her temples. The body in the grave had not been that of Sylvie, because it was only three months since Sylvie had disappeared. The pathologist had said eighteen months, two years. . . .

Josephine, who had told everyone she was going on an expedition to South America . . . Such an unlikely thing for a delicate and luxury-loving girl to do. . . . Had someone made her write a letter to that effect?

Suddenly Emma ran to the window and banged madly on it with clenched fists. There must be someone outside within hearing. It was impossible that she was in an isolated cottage miles from help.

One of the small panes of glass shattered, cutting her hand. Ignoring the injury, she thrust her arm out and began dragging at the thick strands of ivy. But they were too tough and too thick. It was the growth of a whole thicket successfully concealing the window from sight. Peering through she could vaguely catch a glimpse of elm trees, and beyond them the chimneys of a house? Or was that wishful thinking?

Her hand was bleeding severely and she had to get off the chair to tie her handkerchief round it. When that failed to stanch the flow of blood she looked desperately round the room for something to serve as a bandage. There was a dresser along the wall with drawers that, surprisingly, held worn table linen. There was also a little cheap cutlery, and, in the cupboards beneath some plates and cups and saucers.

It was like the meagre equipment given by a landlady in a furnished room, Emma thought. The couch could have been a bed. . . .

What *was* this place she had been brought to, and who had brought her here?

Emma tore a strip off a worn tablecloth and bandaged her injured hand. It was a pity she had been so impulsive about banging on the window. If she had stopped to think she could have done the same thing with the chair leg, and not injured her hand which she would require, presently, to start pulling away the ivy, branch by branch, until she had manufactured a hole through which to look, and call.

The table knives in the drawer would provide weapons with which to saw. It was a pity they looked so blunt, and ivy was so tough.

Her last thought was dismissed abruptly by a sound without.

Someone coming!

Emma's heart began to beat violently as slow, stealthy footsteps climbing what was evidently a steep staircase came nearer.

She stood motionless as the doorknob rattled gently. Then a hoarse whispering voice came through the keyhole.

"Are you awake in there?"

It was impossible to tell whether the voice were a man's or a woman's, it was so disguised and distorted.

Emma flew to the door. "Open the door at once, whoever you are, and let me out."

There was a faint breathy chuckle. Then the voice whispered, "Not so fast, my dear. Have you written the letter?"

"Of course I haven't written the letter. It's a foul lie, apart from anything else. Open the door at once and let me out."

She realised at once that she had made a mistake. She should have said that she had written the letter, anything, so that the door would be opened and she would catch a glimpse of her jailer.

For now the voice came regretfully, "My instructions are that the letter must be written first. But take your time. There's all the time in the world. Some husbands have imprisoned their wives for as much as ten years, for unfaithfulness. No one knew. The pretty things just pined away in lonely houses. No one to hear them calling. . . ."

"Whoever you are, you're mad!"

The faint chuckle came again. Then the footsteps began to recede.

Emma banged desperately on the door.

"Please! Please don't go! Open the door. Let me talk to you."

The footsteps paused.

"The letter first, my dear. Conversation afterwards."

"Then I'll write the letter now, if you'll wait."

"I'm afraid I haven't time to wait at the moment."

Emma cried after the stealthy receding steps, "Where's Louisa? Where's Sylvie?"

There was no answer.

"Barnaby will have told the police by now," she called wildly. "They'll be searching for all three of us."

But the only answer to that was another chuckle, more audible, ever so slightly like Barnaby's own.

That was what defeated her. If by any monstrous chance it were Barnaby outside, mocking her, behaving in this cruel mad way, she would like to die. Even shut up here and starving she would rather die before she was found. . . .

The footsteps had gone and the silence had come down. Silence in the almost dark, stuffy and claustrophobic room. In utter despair Emma stumbled towards the couch. She misjudged the distance, and her half-fall moved the couch backwards. Her foot touched something underneath.

For one moment unreasoning horror, like a suffocating wave, swept over her.

Then she cautiously put her hand down and pulled out the object. It was only a shoe. Quite a new one, too. New and fashionable. A little tan court thing, with a bow. The sort of shoes Louisa Pinner wore.

Actually—one realised—it *was* Louisa's shoe. . . .

# 19

MISS JAMES at the employment agency couldn't understand what had gone wrong at that place of Barnaby Court's in the country. Why should two perfectly reliable girls walk out of their jobs? Though one had to admit that Louisa Pinner had not been the type who struck one as entirely reliable. Miss James had known at the time that she might not have been sending the right person, though she did think that even had Miss Pinner not wanted to stay she would have had the courtesy to give notice in the usual way.

One didn't know where one was with girls nowadays. Nor with men either, for that matter. For one would have thought Barnaby Court would have been the last person to get into a state over a girl's behaviour. Certainly he had been angry about Sylvie Lester, which was perfectly justifiable, but now, over the telephone, he sounded positively jittery.

"Didn't Miss Pinner give you *any* address beyond that of her rooming house?" he kept demanding. "Can't you think of anywhere else she would have been likely to go?"

Much as she admired Barnaby Court, Miss James became slightly impatient.

"We're an employment, not a detective agency, Mr. Court," she pointed out.

"Yes, yes, I'm not suggesting you check up on your girls. But this is all rather strange. You say you can't give me Sylvie Lester's address either?"

"Oh, Miss Lester was a bird of passage, I'm afraid. Not the sort we have on our books, usually. Too restless, and hard to please. Wait a minute, I think she did give an address of her grandmother in Bournemouth."

"Can you give me that?"

"Certainly. But I hardly think she'll go back to you, Mr. Court, after all this time, and leaving the way she did."

"I'm not asking her to come back, I merely want to see her. And if Miss Pinner should call on you, let me know instantly."

Miss James's smooth exterior was ruffled.

"Mr. Court, she wasn't dishonest, I hope?"

"No, nothing like that. But I particularly want to see her."

"Yes, of course." Kept tabs on his female employees, didn't he? "I expect she'll be back in London any time. Wasn't there something about a dog she had?"

But Mr. Court had hung up. He hadn't even asked for Miss Pinner to be replaced. Which, on the whole, was a relief, because one hesitated to send a girl down there now. There must be something odd going on. Hadn't Sylvie said something about wolves?

Silly little fool. Miss James patted her waved tinted hair and sighed. Didn't she realise they made life more interesting?

The bonfire was going to be immense. On top of the pile of straw Uncle Dudley had thrown packing-cases and dead branches of trees, and on top of that again the contents of the trunks in the attic. Maggy hadn't realised he was going to burn those old, strange-smelling, but colourful and exciting clothes. She was regretful about it, although they would make a wonderful blaze, and Uncle Dudley said they should have been burnt years ago.

"Who used to wear them?" Maggy kept asking, imagining some splendid beautiful creature sweeping down the stairs in the crimson velvet or the emerald satin.

At first Uncle Dudley was too busy to listen to her. But at last he said impatiently, "No one you ever knew," and Maggy was also a little regretful that apparently even her grandmother had not worn the clothes.

It was fun getting the bonfire ready, because it used up the afternoon, and one stopped wondering about why Emma had not come home. When Dina, every now and then, said, "She said she wouldn't be this late. Why is she this late?" Maggy answered loftily, "How should I know? Anyway, Daddy knows. He's seeing about it."

It had been impossible to talk to Daddy because ever since lunch-time he had been speaking on the telephone. Also, he had looked particularly angry and unapproachable. Maggy, on her occasional trips inside, had heard him talking about Sylvie, and Miss Pinner, and Emma and Mummy. He had talked about Mummy a great deal to someone. All those ladies, Maggy had thought. Why was he so interested in them?

Then he had had Mrs. Faithfull and Angelina and even Willie in the drawing-room asking them questions. Angelina had been crying afterwards, but when Maggy had asked her what was wrong she had snuffled noisily and said something about forgetting to put her lucky potato in her pocket that morning.

Then two policemen had arrived in a fast black car, and a little later Daddy had gone off with them. That had frightened Dina a great deal, and secretly Maggy, too, although she scorned to show fear.

"Are they taking Daddy to prison?" she asked Uncle Dudley.

Uncle Dudley, for a moment, had seemed a little afraid himself. His face had been quite pale.

But he had said, "Of course not. They would have had to

have a warrant for that. And handcuffs, too. Like this." He gripped Maggy's thin wrists tightly in his large hands, and suddenly it was a game. She wriggled free, shrieking with laughter, and Uncle Dudley, shouting "Ho! Ho! Ho!", said jovially, "What a perfectly splendid time to finish building our bonfire while everyone is away. Let's have it all ready to light when they come home."

So they had toiled tirelessly again, gathering sticks and dead leaves, tidying up the large rambling garden in their eager efforts.

Just before dark the police car came back. Daddy got out alone, and the policeman drove away.

Maggy and Dina darted towards him.

"Did you find Emma? When is she coming home?"

Daddy said in a very slow, tired voice, "I don't know where she is. I just don't know." And his face looked awful, old and lined and sad.

Maggy suddenly had to bite her lips hard to stop from bursting into sobs.

"It's my fault," she whispered. "I was awful to her. I said I would light the death candle. But I didn't, Daddy. Truly, I didn't!"

Uncle Rupert came over.

"I say, old boy, are you seriously worried about Emma? But I expect she's gone up to London again. Did you phone her aunt?"

"Good God, did you think I wouldn't have done that hours ago? She hasn't been to any of the places one would expect. Neither has Louisa Pinner. Can two women just disappear off the face of the earth?"

"Aren't you being a bit melodramatic?" But Uncle Rupert frowned, biting his moustache. "This isn't being awfully amusing, is it? I mean, people talk. We're getting quite a reputation. Just as I set out on the straight and narrow, too."

Uncle Dudley called across the yard, "I expect the girls have met somewhere and not bothered to let us know. Thoughtlessness. Another of women's faults. Have nothing to do with 'em. That's what I say."

He pondered a moment, biting his full lower lip moodily, then with one of his abrupt changes of mood he swung round and cried in his loud voice, "Let's strike the first match. Let's set this magnificent edifice alight."

"What are you burning?" Daddy asked uninterestedly.

"Those dreadful old clothes in the attics." Uncle Dudley's voice was low, as if he were telling a secret. "We should have got rid of them long ago."

"I quite agree," Daddy said, and turned away.

But suddenly Maggy didn't want him to go. Suddenly, in the gathering dusk, he represented security. She was going to be afraid of the leaping flames. Intolerably excited and afraid.

She clung with a cold hand to his large warm one, and he looked down with a faint ghost of his kind and tolerant smile.

"I think I'm scared," she admitted, with unusual honesty.

"You and not Dina?"

But Dina was, too. For, just as Uncle Dudley stooped to strike a match, she began to shriek,

"Oh, no! No, no, no!"

Uncle Dudley looked up, a little irritably. "What's wrong now? I thought you wanted this fire?"

"Not the scarecrow! Someone's put the scarecrow on top! Maggy, the scarecrow's on the fire!"

Surely enough it was. Maggy could see its stiff arms, still clad in the shabby red coat, sticking out appealingly. She thought of the stupid lolling straw head, and the helplessness of the wooden creature, and suddenly she was as distressed as Dina.

"Uncle Dudley, take the scarecrow off! We don't want him burnt. We like him."

Uncle Dudley straightened slowly. His face was red, as if already heated by flames.

"Why, who put him up there? Never mind. We're getting rid of all rubbish, didn't I tell you."

Dina burst into sobs, and Maggy leaped about in a fever of distress.

"He isn't rubbish. Daddy, make Uncle Dudley take the scarecrow off. He's got the coat on that the letter was in. He's too nice to burn. It would be like burning a person!"

"The letter," said Daddy, very slowly.

"One of the 'I love you' letters," Maggy said impatiently.

166

"Oh, quick, Daddy, Uncle Dudley is going to strike the match."

The match was not struck, however, for in a flash Daddy had reached up to the top of the bonfire and dragged down the silly, lolling-headed scarecrow. Uncle Dudley stood watching him, his arms hanging loosely. A little further back Willie stood also, and beside him Angelina huddled and shivered.

There was complete silence as Daddy, helped now by Uncle Dudley, stripped the coat off the wooden arms and searched it, feeling in all the pockets, even tearing at the lining. Uncle Rupert watched without saying anything.

Maggy wanted to say that it was no use now, because the letter had gone already, but all at once she couldn't speak. The moon, which had hung pale and unnoticed in the sky all day, had suddenly brightened, and shone down as cold as ice. There were no warm flames from the bonfire, so everyone was shivering, herself most of all. She clung to Dina, because once again there was no one else to cling to, and together they trembled like frozen puppies.

Then Daddy straightened. He dropped the old coat. His hands were empty.

"You'd better all go inside," he said. His voice was quiet and strange. He added, almost as if he were speaking to himself, "Emma said because I put things like this in books I didn't believe they happened in real life. Perhaps they do, after all."

Dina whimpered, with cold and fear. Everyone was turning to go. There was to be no bonfire after all. Or perhaps Uncle Dudley would light it later. He was making no attempt to do so now. The yard suddenly seemed very forlorn. As they went, Maggy thought she heard a bird cry, thin and wild. She gasped, and turned to see who she could run to for comfort. But there was no one.

# 20

THE feet were on the stairs again. Emma heard their slow deliberate approach, and for all her determined self-control she began to tremble.

It was quite dark in the little room now. She didn't really mind that, because it shut out the red walls and the couch and the table-cloth, all that hot dark colour that gave her such a suffocating feeling. Her attempts at clearing the ivy from the window had not been successful. It grew too deeply and she could not reach the outer strands, so that even when the inner leaves were torn away there was still a veil across the daylight. It was possible to see only a white glimmer of the moon that grew shinier and colder as the dusk increased.

She had called at intervals until she could call no longer. There had been faint voices in the distance which proved that wherever this place was it was not too isolated. But the voices had been too far-off for their owners to hear her cries, and later she had thought that perhaps she had imagined them and they were no more than birds twittering.

Her cut hand had bled a good deal so that with loss of blood and the way her head ached her senses were blurred, and she had an overwhelming desire to lie down and sleep. It didn't seem to matter any more about calling for help.

But when the steps sounded again she was jerked back into life.

She heard the stealthy tap at the door and then the hoarse distorted whisper.

"Have you written the letter yet?"

"Yes," she lied, then gripped her hands together as she waited for the door to open.

"Push it under the door to me," came the instructions.

Emma looked round frantically. What could she do? Push a folded but empty sheet of paper under the door?

No, her trick would be discovered at once. This adversary was too wily for that.

"I—I began it, but it's too dark to see," she improvised wildly. "Come in and give me a light."

Come in. . . . Whom was she inviting into this small dark room where she would be defenceless, where some time yesterday or in the early hours of the morning Louisa had lost a shoe, and had not come back for it . . . ?

There was a "Tch-tching" of disapproval outside the door. Then the voice whispered, "You would be quite safe if the letter were written, my dear. If it isn't, then – who can say? I will give you one more hour. And you don't need a light. No one in that room has needed a light."

Emma tried to ignore the sinister quality of that remark.

"Was Louisa safe after she wrote the letter?"

"Perfectly safe."

"Then why is her shoe here? Where did she go with only one shoe?"

For a moment there was no sound from the other side of the door. Then the distorted voice, impossible to identify, said with a kind of grotesque reassurance, "You will see for yourself – when the letter is written."

It was no use to bang on the door and demand to be released. For already the stealthy footsteps were disappearing. The wooden stairway creaked. Somewhere a door shut softly. Then again there was silence. . . .

A little later the room was filled with a queer flickering light that penetrated even the veil of ivy. It was like lightning flickering in a cloudy sky. There was a smell of smoke, and for an aghast moment she thought the cottage in which she was imprisoned – like a Victorian wife with a sadistic husband – had been set on fire.

But then the voices began, clearer now. They sounded like children's. She strained her ears, thinking she could identify Maggy's and Dina's shrill excited squeals. Then, louder, men's voices, in alarm and protest. What was burning? The flickering light gave no warmth, reassuring her that this cottage was not on fire. But the blaze must be enormous, as if Courtlands itself were ablaze. Was she near to Courtlands after all, and had someone set the old house on fire?

Unaware that she did so, Emma sank on her knees, whispering desperately, "Maggy and Dina! You'll be all right. Really you will. No one hurts little girls!"

# 21

NEITHER of the little girls could explain why they felt so affectionately towards the scarecrow. He had seemed to become a person to them, stupid, witless, with his lolling straw head, and his neck tied with twine, but in some strange way full of friendliness and good nature.

It was the person who had dressed him in the red coat who had made a mistake. Because hadn't Daddy and Uncle Dudley been cross the other day when they had dressed up? Now it wasn't even allowed that the poor scarecrow should be dressed in those borrowed clothes.

But it wasn't the clothes Daddy questioned them about. It was the letter. He kept urging them to remember exactly what had been written in it, just as, in the train, Emma had urged them.

But neither of them could remember the letter in its entirety. Maggy thought it had begun "Dearest" and then giggled, because it seemed so soppy. But Dina said it had been dear somebody, but the name had been rubbed out. They didn't think there had been a date on it, and they were sure there had been no signature. The letter just hadn't been finished. It was as if someone had been practising.

Now it had disappeared, so no one could see what was in it. And anyway, it was just a silly old letter. Surely it wasn't important.

"Daddy," said Maggy timidly, "do you think Emma will be home soon now? She said after lunch and it's nearly dark."

Daddy's face looked strange. He seemed to speak with an effort.

"Yes, of course she will. Any time now."

"Daddy, you said that about Mummy, too, and she hasn't come."

"Mummy is in another country. Emma is——" Daddy stopped, all at once. His face was all lines, frightening. "Run along to Mrs. Faithfull. She'll give you your supper and put you to bed. In the morning Emma will be here."

Maggy flung herself at him.

"Promise!" she demanded.

Daddy gave her a quick hard hug. Then he did the same to Dina. He said, "Run along, now." But he didn't promise. Maggy, noticing that, felt a lump in her breast that wouldn't even allow her to cry.

Anyway, she never cried. She shouted and tore about the house instead, and refused wickedly to obey anybody. It was easy enough to do that with Mrs. Faithfull, almost as easy as it had been with silly old Miss Pinner, but somehow tonight the noise and the rushing about had lost their zest. Because Mrs. Faithfull didn't take any notice of them. It was almost as if she didn't even know that Maggy, and inevitably Dina, were being naughty. She had brought up a tray with bread and butter and jam and milk, but when she poured the milk into the cups she slopped it on to the tray and some of it ran on to the floor.

"Dear, dear," she muttered. But she didn't attempt to mop it up. Her hands, Maggy noticed with detached curiosity, were shaking all the time, as if she were cold, and some of the pins had come out of her thin grey hair, allowing it to tumble on her thin shoulders so that she looked like a quaint, wrinkled, little girl.

Maggy suddenly lost her desire to be naughty, and said politely, "Your hair's coming down, Mrs. Faithfull."

The old lady put a trembling hand to her head.

"Dear, dear," she murmured again. "Now drink your milk like good little boys."

"Boys!" Maggy shouted derisively.

Dina giggled into her cup. "It's because we've got our jeans on."

Mrs. Faithfull nodded and smiled, but her pale blue eyes, as faded as withering hyacinths, didn't really see them.

171

They kept looking out of the window into the dark night. Then, when the children had finished their supper she picked up the tray and carried it out, every dish clinking and trembling.

Maggy suddenly wanted to be in bed, with the blankets pulled warmly up to her eyebrows. When Dina said hesitantly, "Can I come in your bed, Maggy?" she didn't make scornful remarks about people who were cowards, but said off-handedly, "I suppose so. If you want to."

It was nice to have Dina curled tightly against her when, a little later, there were loud angry voices downstairs, as if the men were quarrelling. Then the telephone rang, and Maggy, straining her ears, heard Daddy saying sharply,

"Canterbury! She was meeting Sylvie! The other day? Then you think she might have gone there again today? Thank you, Aunt Deb. I'll check on that. And don't worry. Yes, I promise to let you know the moment there's any news. No, of course I'm not seriously worried."

Maggy ducked her head under the blankets, because she knew that Daddy was telling a lie. He was very worried indeed. Because Sylvie and Miss Pinner had both gone away and never come back, and now he was afraid Emma had done the same. And Mummy, too, a much longer time ago.

It was funny that it was hard to remember Mummy now. Emma's face was so much clearer. It had been nice. One wished one hadn't said those awful things. . . .

Maggy's thoughts broke off as a curious flickering light played through the window. In a few seconds it had grown much brighter, until the whole room was almost as light as day.

Maggy shot up in bed, followed by Dina, who exclaimed, "O-oo! Someone's lit the bonfire!"

In a flash Maggy, full of the most intolerable excitement and apprehension, was out of bed and tearing down the stairs.

"Daddy! Daddy! Someone's lit the bonfire. Look! It's blazing!"

Daddy spun round. He said into the telephone, "I've got to go now, Aunt Deb," and, hanging up, went to fling open the front door.

From there the reflections of the leaping flames could clearly be seen. Maggy was going to rush outdoors to dance madly in the light of the flames, when she saw Uncle Dudley coming from the drawing-room. He wore carpet slippers and carried the evening paper. He looked flushed and perplexed.

"I say, Barnaby, I can smell burning. Oh, good Lord, look at that!" His prominent blue eyes gazed aghast at the rosily lit tree trunks and pink sky. "Someone's lit the fire."

"Where's Rupert?" Daddy said curtly.

"It couldn't be Rupert, old man. It's probably Willie. He's a bit child-like, you know. He was longing to set the bonfire ablaze. Well, it's done now, I must say. Come along, you girls, want to see the fun?"

Maggy gripped Dina's hand.

"Anyway, the scarecrow isn't burning," she said comfortingly. "Daddy took him off." Then the mad excitement overcame her, and she flew outdoors to watch in fearful joy the leaping flames that blazed higher than the house.

In a few minutes everyone was there, even Mrs. Faithfull, shrinking into the shadows, looking like a relation of the scarecrow herself, thin, flat and with dishevelled hair. Angelina had found the little girls, and holding their hands cried in alternate exultation and fear, "That's a real witch's bonfire. Look at those flames! But I thought Mr. Court said it wasn't to be lit. Who lit it, I'd like to know."

"Willie! Willie!" Maggie said, hopping madly.

Angelina turned on her, dark eyes blazing.

"That he did not. My Willie's been blamed for enough that goes on round here. I suppose next they'll be saying he kidnapped the new Mrs. Court, and that skinny Pinner woman, too."

"D-did he?" Dina asked fearfully.

Angelina burst into hysterical laughter.

"You think I'd let my husband run off with another woman! Not me. My, look at that fire. It's going to catch the old stables, I believe. Listen, can you hear the telephone ringing? Oh, let it ring. This is too exciting to miss."

Afterwards Maggy wondered if it had been Emma ringing, and getting no answer. She thought she should have told Daddy, but Daddy, all at once, was talking to some

173

policeman who seemed to have appeared from nowhere. As the flames died down they began, strangely enough, to pour buckets of water on them. Angelina stared agape for a few moments, then seemed all at once to realise that Maggy and Dina were in their pyjamas and shivering violently. She hustled them inside and upstairs, muttering, "The two of you will have pneumonia next! This house has a hoodoo on it. To say nothing of what they think they're going to find in that fire. I'm leaving, the same as Sylvie and the Pinner woman did. Well, don't you kids worry. Get into bed and go to sleep."

Dina looked at Maggy. Her face crumpled.

"Don't you dare to cry!" Maggy said fiercely. "Don't you dare! It's no use anyway." Her voice trailed away forlornly. "There's no one to come."

"W-what will they find on the fi-fire?" Dina whispered.

"Who cares? Silly old fire. It wasn't any fun, really."

"E-Emma?" Dina's voice was almost inaudible. It seemed she feared that by saying the name it really did involve Emma in such a terrible disaster.

Maggy flung around, ready to protest violently. But before she had time someone shrieked. Three loud shrieks. Then as abruptly there was silence.

The flames outside had quite died down. It was dark, except for the flat, cold white moon. By this light Maggy, on tiptoe at the window, could see the dim forms of the men in the yard. They seemed to be lifting something very carefully.

She thought for a moment she was going to be sick. But it was only Dina who got sick, not her. By a tremendous effort of will she overcame the spasm, and turning to where Dina cowered on the bed she said flatly, "That was Angelina screaming. For someone who thinks witches are fun she's an awful coward."

Dina could not say anything. She just stared with her enormous eyes, black and glittering, like cat's eyes in the dark.

Maggy looked out of the window again. The men were talking. There seemed to be several policemen now. It was hard to tell which was Daddy and Uncle Dudley and Uncle Rupert, and which the strangers. But all at once she heard

Daddy saying quite clearly, in a hard urgent voice, "How long before you can get a report?"

One of the men made an inaudible answer.

"Then you understand the search must go on urgently? Because this may not be——" The rest of his words died away. Maggy saw him putting his hands to his face. Abruptly she sank on to the floor, out of sight of the window, and began to sob noiselessly, her small body as taut as a tightly drawn thread.

# 22

EMMA thought, for a moment, that she had imagined the footsteps on the stairs this time. They hadn't been a real sound at all, but a whispering, a scuttering, scarcely more noise than a mouse would make. She waited tensely for the distorted unidentifiable voice. It didn't come. Instead, very stealthily, the key turned in the door.

This, then, was the moment. This was what Louisa had faced when, by some accident, her shoe had come off and been left forgotten—because, apparently, she wasn't going to be walking anywhere. . . .

But the door didn't open. There was a slight stealthy sound again, and then silence. The door remained closed.

Or perhaps in the darkness she couldn't see it opening.

Emma said sharply, "Who is there?" and stared into the gloom until her eyes ached intolerably.

There were no more sounds.

Slowly the thought sank into her consciousness that someone had unlocked the door and she was no longer a prisoner – unless it were a trap.

Trap or not, anything was better than being shut in this stuffy dark room slowly going mad. Emma fumbled her way to the door and turned the knob. It opened. Dimly she could see a narrow wooden flight of stairs that seemed to lead into a barn. Moonlight through the opening where there were no doors showed what looked like an old carriage. Why, she was in the loft over the disused stables at Courtlands! It had been Maggy and Dina she had heard a little while ago. She was so near and had not known.

But the flames? What had they meant?

And now, without doubt, someone at Courtlands was a kidnapper, perhaps a murderer. . . .

Perhaps he stood concealed in the dark, waiting to strike as she came down the rickety stairs.

The door, so stealthily unlocked, must have been a trick. . . .

It was difficult to walk quickly because she was so stupidly weak and dizzy, her head still aching, her injured hand a difficulty.

How strange it must be to be lurking in the shadow of the old carriage watching one's victim approach. . . .

Emma completed the descent of the stairs and momentarily held her breath. Nothing moved in the darkness. The doorway remained open and the moonlight invited.

Quite incomprehensibly, she was free. The whole thing had been a monstrous joke. . . . All except Louisa's shoe, left untidily. . . .

There was a track through the shrubbery that led to the house. She avoided crossing the yard because there seemed to be men lurking about the remains of a fire. So that had been the cause of the glow she had seen, simply some sort of innocent bonfire.

Everything, reduced to real-life scale, now seemed slightly bizarre and absurd. She didn't want to be seen in her dishevelled state by strangers. She must get into the house, find Barnaby, tell him about the one clue there was to Louisa's disappearance, the carelessly abandoned shoe, then have a hot bath, a drink, and realise that she had come out of that long dreadful nightmare.

Would Barnaby believe her when she told her extraordinary experience? She had her injured hand, the painful bump on her temple and her bruised wrists as proof. Barnaby would have to believe her and get all this sinister business solved at last.

The case of the disappearing women. The pretty ones.

Josephine, Sylvie, Louisa, Emma. . . . But Emma had escaped. . . .

And one small unknown body had been found. . . .

The short walk from the stables to the house seemed extraordinarily long and exhausting. There were cars parked near the front door, but no one about. A limping ghost, she was able to cross the gravel drive and go through the open door into the hall unnoticed.

There, however, she stopped. For there was a birdcage standing on the floor and in it was an emerald-green parrot, with a red beak, swinging upside down.

Emma blinked, thinking she must be having an hallucination. But the bird was real enough, for when she put her finger in the cage the parrot swung sideways to nibble at it. There was perfume in the air, too, a subtle expensive smell, and furs flung over a chair. Then Emma heard, from the drawing-room, a light metallic jingling, followed almost at once by a woman's voice.

"Darling, I didn't really mean to surprise you at this hour of night. Such a bore. But you wouldn't answer your telephone. And then when I came there were all these police milling around. What *is* going on?"

"At least, thank heaven you're here!" Emma heard the gratitude and pleasure in Barnaby's voice, and was rigid.

"Darling, I can't tell you how dreadfully sorry I am about missing the children's holidays. But we were lost on the upper reaches of the Amazon for months. I couldn't even send a cable. Harry kept saying not to worry, and it was all so ghastly and uncomfortable that I couldn't think about anything except mosquitoes and snakes and other horrors. Barnaby, you're not listening. Aren't you pleased to see me? What *is* going on here?"

"Emma is missing."

"You must forgive me for not knowing who Emma is. But if she's young and attractive, did you look in that hidey hole where once one of your brothers lured me? Ugh! Not for me, that kind of love nest. Apparently your mother was once found there making love to the groom."

"*Mother!*" exclaimed Rupert, and burst into roars of laughter. "Oh, come now, Josephine, you haven't forgotten how to romance."

Barnaby said swiftly, "Where is this place?"

Emma came slowly into the room. She didn't know how she looked, but she felt as ghostly as the expressions on the men's faces told her she was.

"I suppose the groom used to live there," she said, as if she had been taking part in the conversation. "There was a sort of bed and a tasselled tablecloth on the table. I know everything in that room by now. There's only one thing that doesn't belong. The shoe. That wasn't your mother's, I'm afraid."

Reality had left her again. She knew she was in the drawing-room at Courtlands, with the battle scenes on the walls and Great-grandfather Court's arrogant nose poking round the door. She knew they were all staring at her, the three men, Barnaby, Rupert, and Dudley, and the dark, slim, beautiful woman who was Josephine and who was, blessedly, alive; so that even if Barnaby loved her still, it was better than the other thing she had once fantastically imagined. But it seemed a dream. Even when Barnaby exclaimed in a great voice, "Emma!" and sprang to take her in his arms, it was still a dream. She had wanted it so much to happen that it couldn't be true.

"Well, I say, we'd almost decided you were dead," she heard Rupert saying in his hearty voice. "This is certainly the return of the wanderers. Barnaby, you old devil, two wives, and here's me and Dudley——"

The rest of his sentence was lost as Barnaby demanded, "Emma, can you tell me what happened?"

"Hey, there, I was lost for months and she's only been lost for a few hours, apparently," Josephine protested. "But I can tell you for her what happened. One of you boys took her to the love nest to make love to her, and when she wouldn't play locked her in. I know. You tried it with me once, didn't you?" Her brilliant dark eyes lifted and began to pass significantly towards——

"Look out!" shouted Barnaby. "Stop him!"

But it was too late. Dudley had crossed the room in a lumbering run and was in the hall.

"Whores!" he cried in a voice full of hate.

"*Dudley*" whispered Emma.

"Dudley!" came another voice, high and thin and

full of despair. Momentarily this voice caused Dudley to pause. Rupert, coming to life, plunged after him. Dudley changed his direction and started for the stairs, but clumsily his foot slipped on the polished parquet. He grabbed wildly for support. His arm went round the cold heavy bust of Great-grandfather Court. Great-grandfather toppled slowly sideways, and with all the weight of his life-size marble head and shoulders crashed with heavy dignity on to Dudley's sprawling form.

The last thing Emma remembered was the emerald parrot from South America squawking raucously. Then, at last, the darkness overwhelmed her.

"Of course there was a row at Customs," Josephine was saying in her light, gay voice. "But I told them the bird was for my twin daughters' birthday, and if they wouldn't let me bring it with me immediately it was no use and they would have to keep it. So as long as I promised to keep it away from domestic fowls – am I boring you? But one must keep sane, mustn't one? I find talking a great deal does the trick. I think Maggy takes after me in that respect. Oh, look, Barnaby, Emma's coming round. Who is she, anyway?"

Emma realised that she was lying on the couch and Barnaby was holding both her hands. She saw the sudden proud tilt of his head as he said, "My wife," and, once more, and this time, surely, for always, the world steadied.

"Congratulations," said Josephine, without rancour. "Actually, I was getting round to telling you that Harry and I were married in Rio a week ago. He wanted me still, even after that ghastly eighteen months in the jungle. We'll have to break the news to the children. I *am* talking too much, aren't I?"

"I like it," Emma murmured, and smiled at this woman whom she had once stupidly imagined to be her enemy, who was endlessly talkative, who wore too much jingling jewellery, but who had a kind of indestructible gaiety and friendliness that was compelling.

"Darling, are you all right now?" Barnaby asked.

Emma sat up. "Perfectly, thank you. Sorry to be so feeble. It's been quite a day."

179

"It certainly has. Josephine, get Emma a drink, and have one yourself. I must do some other things."

Involuntarily Emma looked towards the hall. But the door was closed. She gripped Barnaby's hand.

"Barnaby, it will come right."

He nodded.

"For everyone, except, I fear, Miss Pinner. Josephine, look after her."

"Indeed I will. She's charming. I've wanted that colour hair ever since I was fifteen. What will you drink, Emma? Whisky, I think, don't you? Neat."

"Louisa is dead." Emma was not asking a question but stating a fact.

"They seem to have found something on that macabre bonfire. Such a clumsy method of disposal. One was bound to be found out. Not that Dudley was ever clever. Diabolical, but not clever. He got away with his simplicity, didn't he? He almost did with me the only time I ever came down here, after Barnaby and I had separated. I thought he was being sympathetic, but I soon knew better. I thought I was doing the decent thing, keeping quiet about it. One's brother-in-law, after all. But I realise now I should have told the story."

"But why – murder?" Emma said, shivering, but not at present daring to think of Louisa. Silly, gullible Louisa with her eager smile and her mercenary little heart.

"Heaven knows. Some twist. I chose a queer time for my homecoming, didn't I? Here, where are you going?"

"The children. They must be scared to death."

"They're all right. I looked. Maggy was asleep on the floor. Collapsed from exhaustion, by the look of it. She didn't even wake when we put her into bed. She always wore herself to a standstill. Personally, I never could cope. Have your drink and relax."

"I think you'd be good in the jungle," Emma said, with admiration.

"Oh, I always live in the moment. This particular moment is ten minutes' peace before the fuss and bother starts." She gave her brilliant smile. Her thin dark face was alive. "You're just right for Barnaby, I can see. Not restless and dissatisfied like me. You'll make him happy."

180

"Thank you," Emma murmured, blinking back her tears.

It was, as Josephine had said, only ten minutes' peace. After that a doctor and an ambulance arrived. Dudley, unconscious with a possible fractured skull, was taken to hospital. There was a detective at his side. But unless he recovered consciousness no story would be told. It seemed as if, after all, certain things were to remain shrouded in mystery.

The body in the field. . . . Sylvie. . . . No one seemed to know the answer to those problems.

Strangest of all was the fact that life went on. People got hungry, cold, tired. Barnaby built enormous fires, as if their warmth and cheer would take away the eerie feeling the house now possessed. In the kitchen Angelina and Willie cut sandwiches and made pots of tea. Angelina was temporarily bereft of words, but her eyes, huge and bright, gave hint of endless garrulity to come.

Mrs. Faithfull, after her one stricken cry to Dudley, had not appeared again. Rupert said, "Poor old thing, better leave her alone for a while. She idolised Dudley, you know. I believe she still thought he was a small boy. Actually, we all did that a bit, didn't we? I wonder how he got this thing about women, both loving and hating them. Rather nasty actually. That Peeping Tom business. He must have been up the creeper that night, and got in through his window quickly when the alarm was raised. Then he shrewdly had the creeper cut down to make suspicion fall on someone else. Willie, I rather think, although he did plant Barnaby's wet shoes one day. But Willie was a more likely suspect. He had to build the bonfire, too – once Dudley had laid its grim base, of course."

"We still have to trace Sylvie," Barnaby said.

"And get that body identified." Rupert looked at the two girls apologetically. "Sorry for this morgue-like conversation."

Emma said thoughtfully. "I believe it was only the girls who had no family and no one to raise awkward questions about their disappearance who died. Louisa had only that pathetic dog, and – the other one – probably she had no one either. Dudley must have imagined the farewell letter as a gambit was tremendously clever and effective. He probably hadn't realised when the first girl died that she had practised the letter he had forced her to write, and one version had been put in her pocket. The original one, I imagine, had never needed to be produced, as no one can have queried her disappearance. And that, too, would make Dudley careless about getting rid of her clothes. He just left them hidden in the old cradle."

"I say," Rupert exclaimed, "did you have to write a letter, too?"

Emma was trying to forget the horror of that long dark afternoon. The words of the letter, unwritten, yet seemed burnt into her brain. Was it because she had Barnaby, Aunt Deb, and others to enquire about her disappearance that she still lived?

But Dudley must have known that to set her free would be disastrous. She had already known too much when she had realised the significance of the letters.

"I wonder why he did come and unlock the door," she said.

"Just before you came in?" Barnaby asked.

"Yes."

"But Dudley was with us all the time. The police had asked none of us to leave the drawing-room. He hadn't stirred. Actually, we had tried to buck him up. We thought he had had a most ghastly shock. About Louisa, you know."

"It was I who unlocked the door."

No one, at first, realised where the words had come from. They all turned abruptly to see Mrs. Faithfull, so small and shrunken that her stature seemed that of a little girl, in the doorway.

She said in her high expressionless voice, "Heaven knows, I may have fostered Dudley's dislike for women, but I didn't know he murdered them. I couldn't have him doing that, could I? The naughty boy." Her voice had become playful, loving and tolerant. She smiled, as if she were chiding a disobedient child. Her little nut-like face was curiously vacant.

The awareness came back to it, and she said tiredly,

"I have always loved Dudley very much. When his mother left him he became mine, whatever your father or your mother may have decided to the contrary."

"His mother!" Rupert said. "Do you mean we didn't

have the same mother? There was another one who had fun and games in the stable loft?"

"My God!" Barnaby murmured. "The clothes in the trunks. And I thought they must have belonged to some mistress Father had had. I wasn't criticising him but I didn't particularly care to see my children wearing them."

"This," said Josephine, "is *so* intriguing. Do go on, Mrs. Faithfull."

The old lady shot her a look of pure hate. It seemed as if Dudley's prejudices had not been unshared.

But she continued to talk in an unemotional sensible way, as if the events of the night had shocked her back into complete sanity.

"Your father was twice married. His first marriage was a failure. His wife was a slut." She made no apology for the expression, but went on, "Dudley was her son by a previous marriage. He was two years old when your father married her. Your father was very fond of Dudley, which wasn't surprising, as he was a charming child. He adored his mother. He was seven years old when he discovered her visiting the groom in his room above the stables. Naturally he was too young to understand the situation, but he did know that later she deserted both your father and himself. Your father was a very fair and generous man. He legally adopted Dudley, and when he married again your mother genuinely believed that Dudley was his son by his first marriage. When you two boys were born you were never told that the three of you didn't share the same mother, and when your father died Dudley was treated in his will as his own son. He was a very fair man."

Barnaby stood over Mrs. Faithfull. His face was stern and angry.

"*You* have done this to Dudley! You have made him hate women. He was too young at seven to know his mother had behaved so badly. You must have worked on his mind while he was growing up. Mrs. Faithfull! You have made him as he is."

The old lady shrank back, her mouth a tight line.

"I loved him, I told you. I protected him. His new mother didn't love him, really. She only pretended to, and later she had you and Rupert. I was all Dudley had."

"And you were afraid some day some young woman would take him away from you. So you made him hate and distrust all women. You tried to frighten them away from the house. Don't deny that it has been you playing those cheap childish tricks with dead mice and other things."

"I kept the secret," the old lady cried. "Dudley even came to believe himself that your mother was his. Don't you remember how he used to talk about her? Singing hymns on Sundays, taking you all on picnics. He was perfectly all right until that girl came."

"*Which girl?*"

"The first one, of course." Mrs. Faithfull was mumbling now, the vacant look returning to her face. "That Norah. After she went I said I'd never have another single maid in the house. I'd have married ones or none at all."

Barnaby spoke very quietly, "When was Norah here?"

"Oh, about two years ago. You weren't here. You and Rupert were both away most of that summer. Dudley was bored, I suppose. But at last the little hussy left. I suppose she realised Dudley didn't mean to marry her, so she found other fish to fry. That kind always does."

"And where did Norah come from?" Barnaby asked in the same quiet voice.

"The labour people sent her. I think she was an orphan. Oh, she was pretty enough. But Dudley isn't the marrying kind, I could have told her. After that things were all right until you got that silly chit, Sylvie. But I got rid of her."

"Rid of her?"

The old lady gave a macabre chuckle.

"She frightened easier than the Pinner one. A toad in her bed – what a little coward she was. But the Pinner woman——" Now Mrs. Faithfull's eyes were full of a lifeless misery. Her voice lost its firmness and she said inarticulately, "I unlocked the door for – your wife. I guessed she would be there when I found – what Dudley had done. Yes, I expect you are right. I did spoil him. I did want to keep him myself. You see, I had just lost my own little boy – when I came here to work. . . ."

# 23

DUDLEY recovered consciousness just before midnight. He confessed quite simply to the murders of the maid, Norah, and Louisa Pinner. Norah, he said, had been pregnant and intended to make a fuss. He hadn't meant to kill her, but he had been angry, and somehow, under his hands, she had died. Louisa, he had genuinely begun to care for, but she had, quite accidentally, through something he had said on their last evening, suspected him of knowing more than he admitted about the body in the field. So, as she had already written anonymously to the police about Josephine's long absence, he could not trust her. He had lured her out of the house easily enough that night, and afterwards had come back and packed her bag.

Emma, who had begun to understand the significance of the letters, had become dangerous, so he had made an early trip to Canterbury and sent her the telegram purporting to be from Sylvie. Then it had been easy enough to kidnap her. He had simply appeared to be bringing home motherless lambs in the car.

But Sylvie he denied all knowledge of, and he swore that he had seen her, alive and well, in the cathedral the day Emma had gone to meet her.

From exhaustion, Emma did sleep a little that night, held tightly in Barnaby's arms. When she awoke the sun was shining, and downstairs Josephine's parrot was squawking with all the energy of a dozen birds.

Emma sat up in agitation.

"That parrot will wake the children. They'll wonder whatever it is."

"Let them find out," Barnaby murmured. "Their mother has come for them, and we can go to Spain. Do you realise that, my darling? Will a month of sun and wine and all the spoiling a devoted husband can give you make up for all you've been through?"

"Y-es," Emma said slowly.

"You don't sound very sure. Do you mean to say you're still listening to your ridiculous aunt, and not trusting me?"

"No-o." Emma's voice was still uncertain.

"Then what are you hesitating about? Surely——"

But the children had been awakened and were scampering along the passage. Emma was listening to their voices, suppressed, but with excitement escaping in occasional high notes.

"Dina, I can see a bird cage. Truly! Look, down there!"

"The humming-birds!"

"Humming-birds don't make a noise like that. It's – oh, it's a parrot. Come and let's see!"

"Mummy's home! Mummy's home!"

Now all caution vanished, and the feet flew down the stairs, the voices, as shrill as birds themselves, drifting up in company with the parrot's raucous squawks.

Emma said slowly, "One cannot forget everything all at once. Louisa, that poor little Norah. . . ."

"Of course one can't." Barnaby's voice was brisk, reassuring, resolved not to dwell on horrors. "Get your gown on and let's go down and see the fun."

The sun was shining in a long slant across the hall, and the parrot, swinging by its beak, was obviously showing off to the two spellbound children. As Maggy stooped to put a tentative finger into the cage Josephine appeared and went flying down the stairs, her arms held out, her pale blue négligée floating in a cloud about her.

"Darlings!" she cried. "Darlings, the parrot's for you. Isn't he a handsome old gentleman? And I've loads of other things. Aren't you pleased to see Mummy again?"

Dina lifted a happy face to be kissed and held within the embrace of the blue perfumed cloud. Maggy, after an instinctive movement forward, suddenly stiffened and stood back a little way, withdrawn and unfriendly.

"That's my pet," murmured Josephine to Dina. "Maggy darling, come and kiss me."

Maggy said aloofly, "You were an awfully long time coming for us. We thought you were dead."

"I didn't," Dina declared loyally.

"Oh, you did so. You're telling lies."

Josephine raised her slender brows.

"Maggy, that almost sounds as if you hoped I was dead."

Maggy's eyes fell. She looked thin, plain, a little gawky. Her hair stuck out in its witch locks. Her pyjama trousers were slipping dangerously.

She didn't answer her mother's question, but asked instead, "Are we going to Venice?"

"If you want to, darling. Anywhere you say. I've some exciting news for you, too. Darling, what's the matter? Don't you want to go to Venice?"

"It will be all right," said Maggy non-committally.

"Maggy, darling——"

"She's worrying about Emma," Dina said shrewdly. "You see, yesterday she was rude to her, and Emma went away, and – and——" All the excitement of their mother's return had not removed yesterday's shadow. Dina's lip began to tremble and Maggy shouted in her belligerent voice, "I won't go to Venice without saying good-bye to Emma! So we'll have to wait until she comes home."

Emma leaned over the banisters.

"Hi!" she said softly.

Maggy's head shot up like a startled bird's. Dina's automatically followed, and two pairs of brilliant black eyes surveyed Emma speechlessly.

"How'd you like to trade that ticket to Venice for one to Madrid?" Emma suggested. She watched, wonderingly, the incredulous joy coming into Maggy's face. Maggy, the tough one, whom nobody could manage, Maggy with the undefeatable courage and the loyal heart. Dina, with a lingering look at her mother, whispered, "Would we, Maggy?"

"Yes," shouted Maggy. "Yes, yes, yes."

Josephine, with a half-sad, half-humorous look in her lovely face, yet with something of relief, too, said, "I suppose I deserved that. I just don't seem to be a natural parent."

Barnaby's arm tightened round Emma's waist.

"Do you realise you've got yourself quite a family?" he asked with some anxiety.

Emma nodded firmly.

The telephone rang. Barnaby sighed, and went down the stairs to answer it.

He said in a startled voice, "Who? Miss James? You're a little early in the morning, aren't you? Yes? What is this urgent message. . . ." He listened intently, making brief comments, then at last he said, "Thanks a lot, Miss James. You don't know how relieved I am."

He hung up and turned.

"Miss James has had a message from Sylvie," he said.

"Sylvie! A real message! I mean, not a faked one?" Emma was incredulous. She had begun to think that Sylvie had never existed.

"A real one. Miss James says Sylvie didn't stay to meet you in the cathedral that day because you were followed, according to her, by the wolf."

"Dudley!" Emma whispered.

"I expect so. Apparently Sylvie wanted to give you and Louisa the warning never to be persuaded to go with Dudley to his private retreat." Barnaby twisted his mouth wryly. "His love nest. She had had quite a fright there, which was why she left so suddenly. Dudley had threatened her with rather dire things if she ever told. She had a boyfriend in the village who kept her informed of what went on at Courtlands. When she learned of your arrival she knew you ought to be warned but she got scared when she saw Dudley follow you into the cathedral. So she didn't stay. But her conscience got the better of her, and she rang Miss James last night, asking her to pass on the message. Miss James, I might say, is most intrigued."

"Oh, thank heaven she's——" Emma stopped abruptly, seeing the children's watching eyes. It was going to take quite a time to allay their suspicions and turn them into normal happy little girls. But it would be done. And she was going to have the privilege of doing it.

"Seems as if I'm superfluous," Josephine commented. Then, in her unexpected way, her face became alight and she exclaimed in excited rapture, "Now Harry and I can go right ahead with our next expedition. We're planning to go to Tibet. It should be madly amusing." Her gaze flickered over the children uncertainly. "I'll send you a postcard, my pets."

"We'll keep the parrot, if you like," Maggy said magnanimously, "May we, Emma?"

Emma sought Barnaby's eyes. She saw them tender, loving, amused.

"Yes, you may. But not to take to Spain."

The telephone rang again. Emma, nearest to it, picked up the receiver.

"Aunt Deb! But, darling, of course I'm all right. . . . There's nothing at all to worry about any more. I'll tell you about it some time. . . . Just now I can assure you I am very well indeed. Barnaby and I and the children are planning to go to Spain." She caught a glimpse of the children's radiant faces, and listened with only half an ear.

"What's that, Aunt Deb? But how ridiculous! Of course I trust my husband. I always have!"

Sales of Dorothy Eden books have recently risen very sharply, and it is good to know that this very fine storyteller is moving into the best seller lists with each new book.

These are the other Dorothy Eden books at present in print with Hodder Paperbacks, some historical, some eerily atmospheric, all eminently readable:

| | |
|---|---|
| NEVER CALL IT LOVING | 5/- |
| NIGHT OF THE LETTER | 3/6 |
| WINTERWOOD | 5/- |
| SLEEP IN THE WOODS | 5/- |
| WHISTLE FOR THE CROWS | 5/- |
| THE BIRD IN THE CHIMNEY | 5/- |
| SAMANTHA | 5/- |
| SIEGE IN THE SUN | 5/- |
| THE DEADLY TRAVELLERS | 5/- |
| LISTEN TO DANGER | 5/- |
| AFTERNOON FOR LIZARDS | 5/- |
| THE SLEEPING BRIDE | 5/- |
| LAMB TO THE SLAUGHTER | 5/- |

'Dorothy Eden is a mistress of the macabre.'—GUARDIAN